Son of a Mujeriego

Abel Veloz

*It's a tragedy that young boys don't aspire to be
more like the exemplary women in their lives.*

*Because generations of learning to be a "man",
exclusively from other "men",
has led to an overpopulation
of shitty people.*

Abel Veloz

CHAPTER ONE

"A man without two girlfriends is not a man." My father's favorite Dominican idiom rings in my head. I flex my wrists. I wonder what he'd say about a man in handcuffs.

I glance over at Esmeralda. He'd probably say that hiring my bougie ass half-sister was my first mistake. "Women don't argue, they nag." Another one of his favorites. Yeah, I don't think he'd approve of a female lawyer. But, I mean, what else was I to do? She kinda just showed up. And at free-ninety-nine, she's the only lawyer I can afford.

"Listen, Mr. Estrella." She lets those three words linger for a sec, making sure I acknowledge our distant relationship and her professional approach to the matter. Or recognizing my recent eighteenth birthday (which she didn't congratulate me on). The latter is a long shot, though. 'Cause yep, she still hates me.

"You keep repeating you don't remember and that you must be innocent. I get it. But…" Esmeralda tilts her head towards the guilty side of the scale.

"But nothing. Don't you dare say it. Guilty or not, that's not what you're here for," I say.

"You're right. I'm not here to pass judgment. But let's talk about what you do remember. How about that? Start with the party." She crosses her legs.

I lean back to look under the table. "I *see*. So *that's* where the fish smell was coming from." I hold tight onto my laugh, but her riled-up expression causes me to bust out in laughter.

"DANNY."

"Okay, okay."

She is so uptight. This is all a mistake. I was nowhere near Hawk Union High School last night…yet I'm here. Same way me and Esmeralda were nowhere near each other for most of our lives…yet *we're* here. Two half-siblings in a tiny interrogation slash visitation room in Hawk Union's police station.

"So, as you may or may not know, I was dating this mami chula with the finest ass for about three years." I attempt to shape out an hourglass figure, but the cuffs don't let me round out the booty. "Top three at Hawk Union. No debate. Type of girl that is worth all the time in the world. Type of girl that—"

Esmeralda slaps her forehead, then slowly massages exactly where her horns used to be. "Can you act serious for once? Look around. This could be your new home."

What is she talkin' 'bout? Did she not hear me earlier? I was nowhere near Hawk Union High School last night. So, I'm… wait. Is that a tear squeezing out of her stern, glass-half-empty eyes?

She crosses her arms and looks away towards the double mirror.

Wow, that's crazy. She really going for an Oscar nomination. I didn't even know she cared. Last year at our father's funeral—the last time we spoke—she said she resented me for popping into her life and ruining her perfect family. As if I chose to be the bastard son of a top-class mujeriego. As if *I* had a say in his romantic entanglements. Makes no difference, though. She still blames me for her parents' divorce. When it happened, we had just met. She was sixteen, and I was eight. It also didn't help that, as the only son, I received everything in our father's will.

I'd leap across the table to hug her and tell her she's the sister I've always wanted…had. Have? I've missed annoying her, which is why I can't help the jokes. It was the only thing I remember from our brief siblinghood that ended when she went off to college. But we've never done that before. Show affection, that is. To annoy is to love, right?

I correct my nonchalant posture. "I'm sorry. You need to realize that this is how I tell stories, so bear with me."

As she continues to face the double mirror, she takes a deep breath and nods.

"So, I was dating this girl for three years, but then we broke up. And after two months without social media and repeated one-sided conversations with Drake, Romeo Santos, and Ana Gabriel, I decided it was time to go out. You know, be single. So I hit up one of my boys, who is always throwing open-cribs and basement parties."

"Wait, before you continue," she takes hold of her tablet and stylus, "what's his name? The party guy."

"Eldon. Jamaican dude. Throws all the bangers in Hawk Union." I peek to ensure her spelling is correct. "So yeah, I'm on the way to this party…"

The Uber driver honked and vroomed through traffic. He was rooting for me, like he knew I was going to bag some shorties. And that was the goal.

"Ayo primo, let me see that AUX cable," I said. I pressed play on Bad Bunny's "Soy Peor".

The driver started dancing; he was doing the most. He thought I had tip money, and I didn't blame him because my outfit was on point: all white everything, so the ladies knew I came in peace. But I needed him to slow down. Because it wasn't just the streetlights that blurred with each additional pound of pressure exerted on the gas pedal, it was my anxieties too. Was there going to be a fight? Was the condom in my wallet still good? Was I ready to be single? Was my ex going to be there? To think, I'd still get nervous before a party like I hadn't been to dozens of hooky parties, telly bashes, and basement bangers. I even spent half the day grinding with the Swiffer and shadowboxing in front of the mirror to prepare for this party. It all felt new, even the car ride.

"Papo, this the address?" the driver said.

With the window down and one arm hanging out, he stared at two girls young enough to be his daughters. Licking his lips, his stalker-gaze confirmed that he indeed was rooting for me. Perhaps he wished he were me. Young and well-positioned to pick on the ripest of fruits—unlike the bruised and rotting one he avoids at home. I do it for old men like him. Like our trifling father and cheating uncles, it's in my blood.

I pounded my chest twice, then kissed a peace sign to the ceiling. "Sammy Sosa all day, baby," I said to myself. My way of pumping myself up. My way of digging into the batter's box.

We were in front of the address. As I got ready to get out, I fumbled my phone and wrestled with the seatbelt. The driver observed me through the rear-view mirror and scoffed at my clumsiness. Probably thought I was a palomo, but that's far from the truth. Nervous, that's all. But still, I tripped out of the car like the non-suave Fresh Prince of Nowhere.

The car peeled off. I swiped five stars but left no tip 'cause he was low-key hating on me. I applied ChapStick, bit into a fresh stick of gum, brushed my patchy beard with a bristle brush, and adjusted my white bucket hat.

The two mami chulas that captivated the Uber driver sat on the stoop smoking cigarettes. A dead turn off, but as I approached, one of them glanced at my crotch. She didn't even try to hide it. But who cares? As long as she found what she was looking for without squinting, I take no offense.

Standing in front of them, Birdman-rubbing my hands together, I said, "Y'all names must be Bella and Linda, 'cause y'all look it."

Sadly, that couldn't be further from the truth. By the time I got close enough to accurately assess them, I was too committed to spitting game—being near-sighted is the worst. Plus, those the girls you hook up with after all other options are exhausted.

One of them giggled, while the other said, "Well, thank you." She looked me up and down. "What are you supposed to be…a saint?"

"I can be." I licked my lips. "But something tells me you rather me be a sinner."

Smooth shit, right? My uncle-cousin, Martín, taught me that line.

Anywho, the cigarette-ugly…I mean cigarette-fea—sounds better in Spanglish—replied, "Mmm, I like that." She bit the side of her bottom lip, which was impressive considering she managed to balance the cigarette on the other side.

"Well then, I hope to see y'all ladies inside," I said. But of course, I didn't. If I noticed them inside, it meant I struck out for the night. But they could at least help me reach the quota. When Pops would say his "a man without two girlfriends" quote, he never mentioned they had to be bombshells. The quality is in the numbers.

Aight, so then I proceeded towards the basement entrance. Looked at my spiked Gatorade bottle, two gulps for confidence. When I opened the door, an escaping tornado of trapped heat, clearance-rack fragrances, and weave smacked me off balance. My guess was the party remained at a standstill because if people were dancing, a hint of booty-sweat would have slapped me too. And I was right!

But man, before I strode down them stairs, I got nervous again. Should I have come? Was it too soon? Was my ex downstairs? It was a local party, so she surely got an invite.

It was the point of no return.

Inside, the lights were off, but nobody was dancing. And the odor situation was worse than I thought—the basement was damper than the middle of a dryer-cycle. Though from the hair lengths and heights of the dark outlines, I estimated an even male-to-female ratio—a rarity for a party of this sort. Mainly because parents were stricter on their daughters.

"Oh. Who. Is. THAT?" a prospective rebound whispered in the darkness.

Dressed in all white, I must have looked like the mystery-flavor Airhead. Too bad I couldn't locate her, as my eyes gradually adjusted.

"YER."

"Yer."

"YEEEERR."

A bunch of yers came from all directions. The music was low, so those indoor yers reverberated like every New Yorker's dream yer. The exaggerated welcome added to my zamn-zaddy appeal. But it also added to my who-the-heck-is-this-bozo factor; a few male-haters jocking the walls looked unimpressed. My friends—correction, my party-acquaintances and best friend, Rubio—rushed to greet me.

"It's about time!" Rubio hugged me. "Missed you, bro." By the embrace, I knew he meant it.

Can you believe Rubio was the only person to hit me up when I was depressed, karaoke-ing Usher all summer? All the wingman-ing I've done for them clowns, and I couldn't even get a text. I heard one of them dared to holla at my ex, too. But, whatever…in the case of friends, it's quality over numbers.

"Missed you too, Rubio." I scrambled his blond, corn silk hair that was easy to reset with a few touches. Everyone else got a distant hand wave 'cause I wasn't about to forget their fakeness. But that didn't stop them from being fake.

Encircled, they pulled, pushed, and shoulder-massaged me forward towards the table with all the liq. And I don't know why, and I don't know how, but a creepy roach feeling came over me when I saw it was Rubio behind me. The hug, cool. But the direct path and distance from my butt and his penis…yikes.

He has a secret that he's never told me. Early summer, the day after I broke up with my ex, there was this feeling of freedom that came over me. Like a burden had been lifted. So I holla'd at some shortie. Some sophomore that I heard had a thing for me. During our first (and last) chill sesh, she confessed that one of her friends, who had class with Rubio, saw him using an app called Grindr. It's basically Uber but for a different type of ride. Now, I'm not homophobic per se, at least I think I'm not, but it's weird to know I can hit him with sexual harassment when he touches me. Honestly, with all these new gender classifications, he should just come out already. Gay sounds as normal as straight.

Shit. Am I a fake friend too? Is it my fault I can't shake off the cringe? It's not like I hate him or anything. Again, he's my best, and likely, only friend. But I had to do something to shake off the roach.

"*Ayo*, get y'all dirty hands off the white." I jumped forward, loosening their grips—more specifically Rubio's grips.

The bottles at the table were lower than what my older cousins called bottom-shelf. Bunch of vodkas in plastic bottles mixed into Tampico and Minute Maid juices. Several MD 20/20s and Four Lokos. Nothing appealing enough to commemorate my first party back. So I poured myself anything that would do the job.

"Tonight, we drink to a new man. Me," I declared.

And I felt like a new man. For the first time in three years, nobody asked me, "Did your girl invite any cute friends?" For the first time in three years, I could ask an annoying, "Where the bitches at?" Although only cornballs would ask such a question. And one did.

"Ayo, Danny-boy. Where the bitches at, though?" one of my fake friends said as he hung an arm over my shoulder. He was pressed up in my ear. Hot breath and everything.

"At your mom's place. Now get out of my face." I shrugged him off with my shoulder.

"Wow. You've changed, Danny."

Yeah, yeah, whatever. None of those goons were gonna ruin my night.

For the first time in three years, my girlfriend—now ex-girlfriend—was not around; at least I didn't see her at the moment. I scanned the basement for her presence, but confirming her absence didn't bring me the comfort I expected. 'Cause low key, I was there to win her back. But I couldn't count on that. So leaving with two new shorties was still the primary goal. I was playing for the consolation prize, not the first-place trophy.

So we took the shot. I winced as the liq burned its way past my mending heart and down to my empty stomach. Oh, and I drew a crown on my red Solo cup; a king stays king, even without a queen.

The fellas then dragged me to the beer pong table. It was clear they volunteered to chaperone my whole night—not because they actually cared, though. Now that I was single, they knew I was out for fresh blood. And they all wanted to be a part of the hunt.

'Cause that's what fake friends do: they show up for the good times, never the bad. "Don't worry, we going to let you win," one of them whispered. Another pointed at the next-to-play list with his lips. "We gotchu."

On the list, two female names were up next. I missed my first five shots thinking about how pathetic this was. Accepting charity from fake friends was not like me. Neither was scheming for girls. Yeah, I chase skirts, but I never sucker them. I always make sure they come to me on their own volition. I'm a man, not a savage. Unfortunately, my partner carried us to victory before it became obvious that the opposition was throwing the game. So I had to play along with the desperate scheme.

Now, two potential cuties stood across the wet fold-up table as our new opponents. And I say potential because I held off on looking at their faces; if they matched their jeans, I knew I'd fall in love. One of them had Colombian jeans accentuating her wide hips. The other had Fashion Nova hugging her culazo. I knew the brands because that's where my ex shopped. I licked my lips. Something about tight jeans sitting on hourglass hips and plump derrières that resurface animal instincts.

"Let me know if you need backup. I'll take the one you don't choose," a member of the losing team said as he brushed past me. Making me want to give up. Too much scheming, too much scheming, too much scheming. Women are to be enamored, not duped. And again, no more wingman-ing for fake friends.

The party remained in a nervous stage, but I couldn't front. My first night back was setting up real nice. We continued to play pong, and I continued to play coy. I also plotted a less predatory scheme: if I won, I could approach them later with a, "How about we get a rematch on the dance floor?" If I lost, I'd say the same thing. We lost.

Relegated to the sidelines, the ideas kept flowing. Nobody was dancing, but it looked like everyone had caught the eye of someone. Only the atmosphere wasn't right.

That's when I found an unattended Jose Cuervo bottle on the liquor table. And if it's on the table, unclaimed, it's fair game. I poured out a dozen shots, and passed them out in a discriminatory fashion, ignoring the majority of male hands reaching out for one.

"Yo! What about me?" one of my fake boys said.

"What? This?" I focused in on the plastic shot cup. "Yeah, you don't need this. What you really need is…" I leaned closer for a whisper. And I'll admit, I was getting a little saucy at this point. I didn't give a fuck. So I leaned in and whispered, "…to get out of my face. Now go fuck yourself."

Good thing it was one of the soccer players. If it had been one of the football heads, I might've gotten stomped out for that. But I'm cool with most of the school. Someone was bound to help out. If not, it would have been me and "Ride or Die" Rubio, back on back, defending ourselves.

After the shots, I connected my phone to the Bluetooth. Bachata was the perfect warm-up to the perreo. Immediately, Fulanas grabbed a Fulana.

One second ago, they were in dull conversations—probably about Fulano, who had not replied to their texts. Now they were roach-stomping bachata moves like their boyfriends cheated on them with another dude, and the floor was their dicks. They even twisted their feet into the tile floor at the pause-step.

I looked around for Rubio. Even if he was sus, he still a kickass dancer and wingman. But he was nowhere to be found. Instead, I located a random sophomore to take under my wing. I elbow-nudged the fellow sucio and pointed at two baddies.

I slow whined forward onto the dance floor, the back corner of the basement. I couldn't control it. She was rocking the boat and working the middle so well, it lured me closer.

I pulled up my shorts right before connecting my swaying pelvis onto her butt. I was an airplane docking at a gate. And I swear her butt sizzled more than a burger patty flung onto a scorching grill.

She looked back at me.

I winked.

She smiled.

Her friend in front of us gave a quick glance of approval.

Score! I was in. And the booty was soft too. Made me wish I had pajama pants on. Matter of fact, someone should have handed me a blue You-Should-Be-Here sign. Pirates yearn for booty like that, and what Sirena wouldn't enjoy lying on my girthy rock?

Just kidding. I'm not that conceited. But…I *did* think it. Perhaps it was the liquid courage.

But as if she heard my inner thoughts, she abruptly turned around, ready to slap me. "Oye fresco, you know this is bachata, not reggaeton?"

She disengaged and danced with her friend again. The end.

Eh. Well, I guess there is more. I'm here, aren't I?

After the failed dance, I wasn't discouraged. I repeatedly tried to grind on something until the next thing I knew, my ex was there with some herb-ass-chump. Boom! The curtains fell. That was the end of the party for me. This morning, I wake up here at Hawk Union Police Station. With a crazy hangover, zero girlfriends, and no idea why I'm here.

CHAPTER TWO

Five minutes have passed since Esmeralda began pacing around the cramped visitation room, but it could've easily been an eternity. With one arm clutching her ribs and the other elbow tucked at her side, hand on chin, every time she passes me, she sighs. It's like she's conducting her own private shaming of me. And it oddly brings me comfort.

For the first time in eight years, we're having an older sister, younger brother moment. Younger sibling does dumb shit, older sibling scolds. Still, five minutes of silence is too long. I always assumed a Harvard-brain worked faster than this. (Another reason I low-key look up to her. My big sis went to Harvard Law!)

"Where do I begin?" Her first words.

"Let's start with getting me out of here."

She sighs. "Don't speak. That wasn't a real question." She clears her throat. "One, do not, I repeat, do not retell that story to anyone else. Your grotesque perversions are alarming. You sound like a rapist in-the-making. Also, quick fact, you are homophobic, narcissistic, and a womanizer. A real triple threat."

"Wha—"

"Shut up," she says. "I'm not done talking."

"But—"

She glues her hands onto my mouth and presses the back of my head onto her surprisingly rock-hard abs.

God dang! That kinda hurt too. Her grip is extra strong. Crack-head strong. Almost manly.

"Zip. Hush. Nada. Don't wanna hear it."

Even if I tried to, I doubt I could get a vowel through. But why would I want to? This is now a full-blown sibling moment!

"Two, your rambling had more ego than anything relevant. At what point did you interact with someone named," she releases her iron-clad hold and walks toward her tablet, "her name is…" She slides through her digital documents. "There it is, Ida Monterey."

Ida?

I gulp my tongue and snap off the exposed end of Cupid's arrow. It had been lodged in my heart since the day I met Ida, the only girl I've ever loved.

"Well, you see…" I nervously play with my ears. Ashamed. Hesitant. "That's my ex-girlfriend."

Esmeralda laughs like she finally understood something so obvious.

"So *that's* what this is all about."

"*Whatchu mean?*" I inch up on my chair. What does Ida have to do with my arrest?

Someone knocks on the door.

Esmeralda scrambles to clear her face full of curly stragglers and checks her teeth at the double mirror.

"How do I look?" She straightens her blazer and dusts off her matching skirt.

"You look—"

"Ah, why am I asking you? You clearly know nothing about women."

O-kaaayyy. That was unnecessary.

She prances to the door, then abruptly stops in front of it for a second or two, recomposing herself.

"Right on time, Detective Handsome," Esmeralda calmly says.

A coconut-white, basketball-player height detective walks into the room. If he were fifteen years younger, we might have beefed over a few girls.

"It's Hanson, not Handsome," he says with a playful chuckle.

"Oh, that's what I said." Esmeralda rubs the nape of her neck in embarrassment.

No it wasn't! This bitch thinks she slick. She smitten as fuck. She is even avoiding eye contact with me. Ooh, she knows I'll expose her for no reason. That's what little brothers are for, right? This is my chance. Muahahaha.

"So Danny, this is Detective Hanson with Hawk Union Police. He has a generous proposal for you."

"Wait. Is it Hanson or Handsome? I didn't quite get it." I wink at Esmeralda, who is now more flustered than ever. Gotchu, big sis! I got years and years of backed-up annoyance to deliver on.

"It's Hanson," he reasserts.

"Yep. Exactly like I said. Pay attention, Danny." Esmeralda jabs a hard glance at me, filling me up with joy.

To annoy, really, is to love.

"Now Danny, I'll be brief. How does school expulsion sound to you?"

What!? That's something nobody says casually.

"School expulsion sounds…wack. At the very least, not fun." Like, what kinda answer does he expect?

If I were to be expelled, my mom would get her WWE on. She would Rock-Bottom me and follow suit with a People's Elbow. After that, she'd irrationally call her church friends to perform a desperate exorcism. I can visualize them there now. Holding hands in a circle, with me sprawled out in the middle. Me chugging holy water, and them chanting, "Alabaré, Alabaré. Alabaré, Alabaré. A-laaa-baré a mi Señor."

It's my senior year too!

"And how does an attempted burglary charge sound to you? And landing on the sex offender list?"

"WHAT!?" My hangover throbs as I attempt to recall how the FUCK I'd be charged for any of that. I can vaguely remember being read my rights when I was arrested.

Detective Hanson doesn't wait for an actual reply, he reads my response from my face: all the charges sound absurdly wild and unpleasant. "Then I got an offer for you. And it can only stay between us three. Understood?"

Esmeralda nods at me. Insisting that whatever the deal is, I ought to take it.

"It concerns Ida," he says. "I'm sure you won't refuse."

CHAPTER THREE

Esmeralda did good by convincing Detective Hanson to drop the attempted burglary and sexual offender charge. But now it's either act as Detective Hanson's eyes and ears or school expulsion. At least I'm out of jail and on my way home.

Esmeralda keeps her eyes on the road, yet I sense her energy locked-in on me. She is searching for answers. A clue in my every movement, every vocal influx, and every breath.

"I know what you're thinking," I say. "Why didn't I take the deal? When the video evidence clearly showed my doppelgänger at the scene. Why risk expulsion before my senior year?"

Esmeralda laughs. "Doppelgänger? Yeah, that's not going to hold up as a defense. Try again."

She might be right, I've shit the bed with this one! A surge of mixed drinks scorches past my Adam's apple. I roll down the car window as fast as I can. Come on, come on, come on. As soon as the window is low enough, I plunge my head into the turnpike wind. I vomit it all out, the disgust, my previous resolve.

How did I even get on school grounds? According to my phone's GPS, the party was on the other side of Hawk Union. I didn't walk or drive, and my Uber account shows no sign of usage besides arriving at the party. Even more random, *why* did I end up there? Solo dolo. No car or anyone else in sight.

But let's say I did go to the high school. School doesn't open till Tuesday! The day after Labor Day. So why the heck would I go there and piss all over the main entrance!?

Esmeralda maintains her focus on the road. "Listen, Danny. One, you better not have gotten any vomit in or on my car. Two, I'm thinking about how this looks holistically." She pauses. "They got you good. And unless you want to throw away three years of Honor Roll and possibly Salutatorian—honestly, I'm impressed— you are going to have to comply with Detective Hanson. And come on." She softly backhands my shoulder. "What's an ex-girl-friend worth these days? You, yourself, rambled on about lusting over potentially underaged booty at the party."

I spit out the last remaining vomit. "Ha-ha, real funny." Although, thinking about it now, I am eighteen. An adult. Am I legally allowed to holla at freshmen and sophomores? Oh, *helllll* no.

"Hey, quick question. Before we get back to this whole setup job. I'm technically an adult, right?"

"Yes," she says, like I asked the dumbest question in the world.

"Is the whole high school off limits to me now? Besides other eighteen-year-olds?" Which there barely are any. I'm a year behind because I failed second grade. "For example, let's say I was…*you know*…clapping cheeks with a—"

"OH MY GOD," Esmeralda blurts out. "Danny, I didn't want to say it earlier, but you need help. A therapist. A conscience. A filter. And possibly constant legal guidance."

Alright. That was OD on her part. A filter? I can see it. I am a little wild boy. Some thoughts that cross my mind should never be said. But everything else? She buggin'.

"Stop playing. I asked a real question. Am I legally allowed to holla at incoming freshmen or na? I'm asking for a friend." I'm the friend.

"You can date anyone you want. But you can't touch anyone you want. In NJ, sexual consent is sixteen years old, but it's more complicated than that. But to be safe, don't touch anyone under sixteen, or at the very least, anyone four years younger than you—a close-in-age exemption does not apply after that."

Sixteen? Shit! Maybe I was hollering at underaged booty. But, if fourteen and fifteen are still in play...*I mean.* Na-na-na. What am I thinking!? Gross-gross-gross.

"Oh. If that's the case, I'm good. I'd never do that."

For the upcoming school year, I had some girls lined up. Girls whose names I put on my phone's notes as potential roster fillers for my two-girlfriend quota. They will all need to be reevaluated. I glance at my crotch. *Sixteen and up only, okay?*

"Keep it that way. If you ever were to...I'd resign as your lawyer."

"Glad we can agree on something."

A pause between us ensues. It's been so long since we've spent more than five minutes together that all the conversations we could have are bottlenecked at our throats. Too many conversations we never had, rushing for priority. Number one on my list is, "Are you back to being my sister?" But it's easier to revert to the professional matter at hand.

"I can't take the deal because I love her too much. There. I said it."

I may be hungover, confused, and possibly still drunk, but that is how I feel. Just never thought I'd actually say something like that. I guess that's what happens when you date someone like Ida. They change you to become more communicative, more loving, more self-assured. And then when you lose someone like Ida, you're forced to find self-assurance in other places, like remembering what your dead father would approve of. Like going to a party, not for fun, but instead to bag shorties.

"As I said, from the bits and pieces I remember, last night was a movie. Inhibitions were coat-checked, blue jean stains on every wall. The music primed for the sandungueo and bellaqueo; a few mami chulas grinded on the Danny Salami Express for quality assurance. Something light. None under sixteen, of course. And Ida showed up with some herb-ass, punk-ass bitch. But still—"

I can't believe I'm about to admit this.

"—seeing her was the best part of my night."

I yank the car seat back the furthest it can go before the incoming *gay* joke. This is so embarrassing. A man acting this soft. Our father would be sickened by those words. *El hombre-hombre no llora por mujeres.*

Esmeralda cocks her head back and squints. There it is. The look of resistance before the *you're such a little bitch.* But instead, a short smile sneaks out. "Oh, it's one of those exes. Who was she?"

Who was she? More like, who *is* she? Or *what* is she? I swear there's never been a girl as tempting as Ida, not even Eve.

Ever since I was old enough for my uncles to ask, "Y las novias?", I've been infatuated with women, especially those with booties that jiggle like a good flan. But Ida wasn't infatuation. She was a blessing. Different. The only one I've viewed and still view differently, besides family. And those first words she spoke…it was love at first syllable.

Freshman year, during an emergency student-faculty assembly. A used condom—supposedly with enough jizz to fill up a test tube from chemistry class—had been found in the boys' locker room. Till this day, no one knows whose it was. But accompany that with the influx of pregnant students, one could only assume it was another baby in the making. 'Cept thinking about it now, the use of a condom is the opposite of baby-making. Ohhh, *so that's* what they meant with the "I'm glad students are using condoms" speech. So yeah, that speech happened, and it ended with an elephant-sized "*but…*"

For the record, I thought the principal's—Dr. Jones—speech was hilarious. It spoke volumes about Hawk Union. An Arnold Palmer type of town on the outskirts of the New York City Metropolitan area. The town half rich, half broke. Half urban, half suburban. Half liberal, half traditionalist.

"…but sex on school grounds will not be permitted. Ladies…" Dr. Jones paused to look at the section of pregnant students.

After being slut shamed, all five of them (one freshman, three juniors and one senior) clumped together for strength in numbers.

"—we need to do a better job at resisting our temptations and keeping *it* closed. Boys will be boys."

The speech caused an uproar amongst half the parents, but a year later, Dr. Jones based her mayoral campaign on that speech. She won!

Ida, though. Wow!

Up to the end of Dr. Jones's speech, I was indifferent. A few big internal laughs here and there, but I was busy. My fresh-man-head was on a swivel, filling in slots on my mental I-would-smash list. Ida was an easy yes for inclusion. Which didn't mean much because a five out of ten rating was the cutoff. Sometimes even a three out of ten made the cut. I was horny as shit. Didn't give a fuck. Even at that, the list was useless. It came in handy in conversation with the fellas, but I never pursued ninety-nine percent of the girls on it.

Ida, though. Sheesh! What a speech. During the assembly's Q&A, she hit savage-goddess mode.

"*Keep it closed?*" She took a deep breath. "You found a used condom in the boys' locker room, yet you assume a girl was involved? Gay guys exist. And they use condoms."

"While that is true, the odds suggest—" the principal said.

"The only thing you're suggesting is that men—and apparently grown women too—are allowed to normalize the sexualization of my body. I'm done with that crap! In the streets of Hawk Union, boys and *fathers* have no filter. During gym class, guys stare. At school dances, boys try to reach a hand between my thighs. When I'm minding my own business, boys move me aside by putting their hands on my hips…and they let it linger." Another deep breath. "*It* lingers. As soon as I step outside my home, I'm considered an object. And today, you expect me, us, to also be considered as the perpetrators? That doesn't sit right with me."

I clapped without realizing—though at one point I thought she was talking about me. I stopped clapping after I received a few male sneers.

My uncles and older cousins taught me that women enjoyed the attention she described. How else are women to be enamored? They all want an aggressive tiguere. They all loved *Fifty Shades of Grey*.

I internalized her words as a challenge. While the other guys called her prude, I saw her as a test of my game. If I could bag her, I could bag any girl at Hawk Union, including the members of the Celibacy Club (yep, that's a thing here).

I proved my game was tight. Shot up the social hierarchy. But then I fell in love. Allowed her to change me. I became the person I pretended to be in order to get her to like me: a man willing to support and uplift a strong young woman like her. Unfortunately, if you leave a lion in a zoo long enough, it forgets how to hunt. She made me soft. And after the breakup, I remembered my dad's words, "It's a man's world." And being with her alienated me from the world I was to dominate. It was embarrassing to tell my uncles, over and over, that I only had one girlfriend, even though she was all the woman *I thought* I needed.

She changed me. But not into a man. Yet, I still love her.

Esmeralda backhands me, snapping me out of my thoughts. "Don't avoid my question. Who was this Ida, huh?"

"Just some girl that tried to reform me. That's all," I say as nonchalant as possible, but those dismissive words lag past my

Adam's apple like a cold I can't shake off. All summer, I couldn't shake her off. Esmeralda needs to drop the topic.

"Well, you know what else tries to reform people? Jail. And by the looks of it, jail may do a better job of reforming you than this Ida."

"Whoa-whoa-whoa, what do you mean jail?" I yank my seat forward.

"You urinated on school property. And you're eighteen now. That's a sex offense. Now Detective Hanson said he would let those charges slide, but I'm sure if you don't change your mind, he'll suddenly remember to. And something tells me he's desperate enough to put you in jail. So, he'll likely force you to reconsider. Luckily for you, I told the detective that you were still under the influence and that we'd give a definitive answer by Monday night."

"Why you do that for? I'm not going to spy on Ida. I won't. And why the heck does he even want me to spy on her anyway? He was vague as fuck."

"You will." Esmeralda tilts her chin high. By the looks of her flexed jawline, she really means it. But she doesn't understand. I truly can't. I won't.

I made a promise to myself. Ida being the centerpiece of that promise. So, if diming her out to the cops is what I need to do to save my own ass, then I'll pass. I just can't.

"I'm sure we'll find out about the why when we agree to take the deal," she says.

"What's this to you? Why do you suddenly care so much about me? You show up out of nowhere and want to be my lawyer *and* big sister?" I focus in on her now filling eyes.

Am I being too harsh? Maybe my questions are misguided.

She did rescue me from jail. And it only cost me my one phone call, right? I don't remember if I called her…

She abruptly smacks the steering wheel. The car swerves enough to stir my stomach. "You are FUCKING accepting the deal. And *we* are going to spy on this little ex of yours until Detective Hanson is satisfied!"

The car revs along with her emotion and my heart rate.

"The truth comes out. Detective Hanson. Or, like you said, *Handsome*. You just want to wake up on his bed, wearing one of his big and tall button-downs."

Shit. Those words came out before I could think them over. And are likely the wrong words for this situation. I focus on her hands, eyes, and lips. Searching for an increase in tension, but hoping for a decrease. De-es-ca-late.

Esmeralda relaxes her shoulders. "While he is handsome, he is not my type. I just acted all ditzy so that he could be more lenient. Because nothing softens up a man more than the prospect of casual sex. But Danny, li-sten to your-self. There is no slick-talking your way out of expulsion and possible jail time."

I believe her, but something is off. The abrupt arrival. The abrupt tantrum. This is not like her at all. The Esmeralda I know doesn't give a damn about me. And from what I've collected off social media, she has full control over her Latina craziness. But her hands are now trembling again, her foot just slammed on the acceleration, and at this rate, she'll veer this car off the turnpike if I refuse.

I clutch onto the coat-hanger hook and brace my free hand on the airbag. No way I'm going out like this.

"How-how 'bout this? I'll consider it."

She ignores me. Eyes possessed by the yellow water jugs in the middle of the upcoming fork.

"I'll do it!" I say. Rather it be me saying those words than her.

"Really?"

"Yes-yes, now slow down."

"Cool." Esmeralda nods. "I'll call you first thing Monday morning."

Jeez, talk about dramatics. Suddenly, she seems level-headed and relaxed. I unclench the coat hook. She's either crazy or manipulative. And speaking of dramatics...

"We are almost at your new house. Which I have to ask, how did your mom afford it? I mean, being a single mother and all. I assume you chipped in with your inheritance," she says.

Inheritance? More like a responsibility. After the funeral, I've tried to tell Esmeralda that the only thing Pops left me was the deed to his childhood home in the Dominican Republic—or better yet, the wooden slabs his father shaped into a house. The property's only worth comes from the avocado trees, which I admit, fruit the most buttery aguacates in the world. Here, those aguacates would be a gold mine: I'd charge the rich side of Hawk Union (where I live now) twelve dollars for an avocado toast, something no one in DR would ever pay for. Yet I inherited fool's gold, and she doesn't understand it.

However, if Esmeralda thinks she'll squeeze some chisme out of me, as if this recent incident isn't good enough for her next trip to the unisex salon, she got me fucked up. 'Cause unlike Pops, my mother's most expensive vice is telephoning every Dominican in the tri-state area, whenever she catches a whiff of a pot-smoking relative or when somebody's husband has been taking the long way home after work.

"She worked two jobs and hoarded her money to purchase the house. That lady is something else. Under the right lighting, she glistens like Superwoman. And like Superwoman, she going to WHOOP my ass when I get home. Unless…she doesn't know about this." I elbow-bump Esmeralda. "Wink, wink."

"She doesn't know."

Okay, okay, good looking out, big sis. I see you.

She smirks. "But she could find out. Wink, wink. Monday, Danny. That's Labor Day, so don't go off celebrating. Because *we* shall be laboring on this case. That *I'm* not getting paid for. Your mom may or may not find out after then."

Worrrd? An ultimatum? Okay, I see how we're playing this. I exit the hooptie and give Esmeralda a stern look. "She better not find out."

CHAPTER FOUR

I quietly slip off my shoes just outside of the front door. I carefully grip the doorknob, pull it towards me, and enter the key as slowly as possible. I exhale. No rattle. I turn the doorknob and push past the initial resistance. I hold my breath. So far, so good. No creaks. I swiftly enter the house before the outside noise rushes past the living room and funnels into the kitchen, where I see my mother standing at the sink. Whoa! She bumping Camilo Sesto. Must be in a romantic mood. I laser my eyes on her back and side-step up the staircase until she is out of sight.

"Maaa! What are you cooking? It smells BANGING," I shout, midway up the steps. I can't smell jack-shit, but I know she cooking if the music on.

"Muchacho, cállate la boca and get down here already. You know what today is."

"Yeah-yeah, I'll be down in a bit."

Let's Gooo! I fist pump all the way up the stairs and into my room. When we lived in the apartment complex on the poor side of Hawk Union, the fire-escape was the only means of sneaking in and out. But this house-life got its perks. Wait. What's today?

I throw on the first clean pair of sweats and white tee I find. But where are my Adidas slides? I swore I put them next to the closet door. They're not under my bed, nor under my desk. I walk to the bathroom. Not here either, but what's with the third toothbrush? I walk into my mother's room. The bedsheets are wild off the bed. But por fin, there are my slides.

The romantic music, the third toothbrush, my slides in her room. She also didn't notice I was gone all night and most of the morning. *Ayooo.* My eyes open wide. Na-na-na, my mother isn't like that. I'm trippin'.

"DANNY! If I gotta go to the backyard and fix it up myself, you might as well stay up there writing your will."

"Chill, chill. Ahí voy."

I glance at my wristwatch. Damn, I'm running late. Good thing the guests are running even later.

"Hurry up, Danny! By the time you finish, the barbecue will be over," my mother yells from her second-floor window.

Yeah, aight. Her hair is still rolled up in a tubi. By the time *she* finishes, the barbecue will be over.

"Relax, lady. To be late is to be early; to be late-late is to be on time." I drag trash bins across the backyard. Some for garbage, others as makeshift coolers for the beers.

The annual family shit-show, officially known as the annual family barbecue: the Met Gala of Bulto, the Latin GRAMMYs of Chisme. It's the first time we host the spectacle, which is fitting because my mother and I moved in a month ago and never had a housewarming. Pero coño, don't volunteer to host, then have me do all the work. I'm already going to be doing a ton of chores in jail: beautification, polishing cement walls, possibly stirring lard. But I admit, I rather do this all by myself than to be in the bad ol' days. The days I was the centerline in my parents' game of tug-of-war called 70/30 custody. Neither one scared to rip off one of my limbs if it meant I'd end up on their side. Surprisingly, as long as my father kept his affair with my mother distant enough from Esmeralda, adultery didn't mean much in court.

Pops was a wild man, though. He dead-ass waited until I slid out the womb to inform my mother he was a married man with a whole brat named Esmeralda. Still, it brings me more pride than hate. If he didn't act like a man, I wouldn't be alive today. And that is what it comes down to. I wouldn't even be having this thought if my father wasn't out there propagating. So imagine if he was bound by marriage. Yeah, my mother suffered, but my life is worth way more than her pain. I mean, I still am my mother's pain. I chuckle. Eh, whatever. She is Superwoman; that woman can endure anything.

I put my headphones on and brush the grill rack my mother bought at a flea market. Momma dukes is funny, though. I shake my head. Always bringing up her forever impending death. "What's going to happen when I die? That's when you really going to appreciate me," she often says. I'm surprised she didn't say it just now. Damn, I should flip it on her: *What are you going to do when I'm in jail?* I sigh. I mean, what can I—

Slim, rough hands blanket my eyes, and a hint of a familiar body spray trespasses into my personal space. "Guess who," muffles through my headphones.

Who the heck could this be? J-Lo, Beyonce, or the mami chula with the fatty from the bodega on Park Avenue? She's usually off on Mondays, and I often wonder where she goes when she isn't making a top-five ham and cheese in the tri-state area. But I won't get my hopes up.

"Guess who," she repeats with more attitude. "Stop being wack."

"Give me a hint."

Her weight shifts, launching a jolt up my spine then around the other side until electric-sliding off my penis. I mindlessly toss the grill brush. Well, well, well, look at what we have here. A possible OD horny, twenty-four-seven nipple pleasure seeking freak-nasty. There was a nipple ring in that graze. I'm sure of it. I bop a little and clasp my hand. Let's go, Danny. You still got game… wait. What am I thinking!? It's a family barbecue. PLEASE don't let it be one of my aunts or worse, a little cousin.

"Just guess, pussy." Her Puerto Rican accent jumps out at me, as well as an overwhelming cherry and peach scent. Victoria's Secret Love Spell, a chonga's favorite hex.

The legend goes, at night, if you stroll down Bergenline Avenue or near Rainbow in Journal Square, you can hear three-inch hoop earrings pinging like wind chimes, and Love Spell can be tasted in each breath. My knees wobble. I free myself from her blindfold, jump forward, and turn around with my fists up.

Shoulder length, curly black hair. Stank face and hoop earrings, but with no name on them. Who is this? She looks a good five to ten years my elder.

"Ma! One of your single lady friends is here," I yell.

"What? Boy, you so stupid," the stranger says. She playfully slaps my shoulder with her hand holding a pack of Newport 100s. "You gonna make me look dumb crazy in front of my future mother-in-law."

My eyes retract backward. Future mother-in-law? Her nipple ring may be my type, but she is not. I scan her up and down. She got home-wrecker vibes too. My ex-boys cheat on their beautiful, faithful girlfriends with her type. The type my female cousins often show me pictures of before asking, "*Danny, do you find her cute?*" The answer always being no. "*Well, that's who Fulano cheated on Fulana with.*"

Before I could get a third look at her, my mother's room window screeches open. With only a bra on and the jumbo-sized hair rollers still tucked under the tubi, she says, "What I tell you about yelling?" She studies the stranger in an investigative manner. "Who is your friend?" She fake smiles.

"My friend?"

"Hey, Ms. Sosa." She straightens her back and waves excitedly. "My name is Jaslene."

Jaslene? How she know my mother's last name? Even if she knows me, she shouldn't know that. My last name is Estrella.

I tiptoe behind Jaslene's peripherals and frantically shake my head to gesture stranger-danger to my mother. But she's fixated on Jaslene.

"Jaslene, nice to meet you. I'm so sorry, I'm kind of busy, but make yourself comfortable," she says with her white voice. The voice she often uses when she is being fake-polite to one of my amiguitas. "Danny, be a good host now and make sure the lovely Jaslene is taken good care of."

The heck? She isn't a guest; she's a stranger.

Jaslene blushes. "Thank you, Ms. Sosa," she says, all bubbly. Her feet shifting and twirling.

As my mother's window shuts, Jaslene snuffs me into confusion. "Is this how you treat your future baby mama? The mother of your kids?" She hooks her claws deep into my armpits and yanks me into her. Her nails stab through my pecs like knives a second away from piercing out of me. "And why doesn't your mother know my name?"

"Chill, chill, chill." I gently lower her claws, resisting the pain.

What's going on is beyond me at this point. But now I need answers. Future baby mama? What's that all about? She clearly knows me, and my mother approves of her staying…

"My bad. Let's start over." I lean in to kiss her on the cheek, only to be intercepted by her palm.

"Hey, dummy, don't you see I got makeup on?"

Yeah, I see it, and it's spooky. Looks like it was done in the shower. I also see there is no baby bump. No way I got her pregnant unless she talking Immaculate Conception. I know I'm special, pero ni pa' tanto. But let's see if she got potential. With all this sass, she gotta have a nice ass.

I unfold a plastic chair for her. I gulp a breath and hold it just past my uvula, anticipating the moment I am clear to check out the booty—inch by inch, my view transitions from hip to backside.

I lick my lips. So far, so good. My new friends in jail are going to get a kick out of this headline: UNINVITED GUEST SHOWS UP TO A FAMILY BARBECUE, LATER PEELS HOST'S PLÁTANO.

SLAP, her open-palm slides across my face. My chin smacks against my collarbone.

"That's for last night."

"AYO! What. The. Fuck?"

The veins in my eyes throb at her. I lick my teeth in search of a faint taste of iron. I'm tempted to place a hand over her likely handprint on my cheek, but now this is about pride. Can't show pain after a hit like that.

"You a'ight? Need me to call your therapist and tell them it's happening again?" Because something had to have happened before. I clench my fists. Who goes around slapping people?

I exhale loudly. Something is seriously wrong with this girl. I might have to call my cousin, Rose, to yank her hair all the way to whatever psych ward she crawled out of. Rose would Stone-Cold-Stunner this bitch for much less than a slap 'cause she my female ride-or-die: Rubio's gender counterpart. Cousin by relation, but sister by cradle.

"I'm good. Thanks for asking." She smiles cheek to cheek, using all ten-plus facial muscles required.

I look up at the sky.

I'm a lover, not a fighter.

I'm a lover, not a fighter.

She is not cute enough to slap me around.

But not cute enough to stress over.

"A man without two girlfriends is not a man," I imagine my father in the sky saying to me.

I exhale loudly again.

Lucky for her, the overall context of her being here is in her favor. Prospective jail time and a Saturday night I don't remember. Also, that nipple piercing bought her some time. But if the booty is flat, I won't hesitate again. I'm calling Rose.

But that was for last night—the party, huh. Was this the vampire who bit my lips and left them tender? I tap my lips. There is no way she'd know if she was pregnant since then. I should ask her questions, but I gotta play this smart. Another slap like that will knock out my dental crown. That's an easy two Gs out-of-pocket. And in jail, at that.

I look her up and down. It would help if I knew what jeans she wore at the party. It's easy to forget a face, but not a booty. Is she Fashion Nova? Colombian Jeans? No, I don't think so.

There was one girl with a yummy pink thong peeking out. It played peek-a-boo with my thoughts. I can't place the timeframe, but that ish belonged in the "Thong Song" music video.

Eh, Jaslene's thigh-gap doesn't match the overall description.

There was another girl. Pobrecita. Her ass looked like calves squished together. I haven't seen Jaslene's calves yet, but her shins are a healthy width. Can't be her.

"Jaslene, I'll be right back. Just need to shower and change before my family arrives."

"Yeah, you thought. Get that ass over here. You not leaving without a shot."

From her purse, a personal-size Bacardí Superior bottle sings,

"Que bonita bandera," as it is unveiled. The untwisting of the bottle cap gives me goosebumps.

"Open wide, mi bebé."

I spit out on the third gulp and wince in disgust. "Damn girl, you trying to get me drunk?"

"That's for later." She winks. "I want that Bacardí dick." Her eyebrows dance up and down.

Wow, that was bold. Scary…but sexy.

I nervously laugh and limp away towards the sliding double-door that leads inside. Looking down, her aggressive behavior inflated big-little Danny. My mind and gut scream, *"Run! Kick her out. She can't be any good."* But my penis stands up for its needs. There won't be any female ass in jail. And today, an uncle is bound by manhood to ask, *"Cuántas novias tienes?"* She not the best looking, but—I turn around—she will do.

Jaslene lights a cigarette.

Gross.

CHAPTER FIVE

Riddle me this. Who shows up to a family barbecue uninvited and slaps the host, after claiming to be his future baby mama?

Jaslene from Saturday night, that's who. It's not a very good riddle. Impossible to solve unless you were there. Or in my case, unless you weren't drunk as fuck.

I button up my short-sleeve shirt, taking intermittent glances outside at Jaslene in the backyard.

Who is she?

She tosses her finished cigarette into my mother's flowerbed.

I shake my head. If my mom finds that, she gonna think I smoke.

My laptop!

I shuffle to my desk and accidentally toss my desk chair to the ground. I'mma google the shit out of Jaslene. Let's see.

Hunched over my laptop, I have no clue what to type. I don't know anything about her beyond her name, Jaslene. She's Latina, so that could be her first or middle name. Don't even know if it's spelled Jaslene, Jazlene, Jasslene, Jaslin. If she's half Dominican, Jazzlean is also a possibility.

"DANNY. COÑO. Ese muchacho," my mother yells from the backyard. Following her yell, I hear glass bottles and heels click and clack.

I glance at the search bar and out the window. Back and forth, forth and back. Damn it. I shut my laptop.

My uncles haul twenty-four packs of Presidente pequeñas on their shoulders, my little cousins double-team bags of ice, and my aunts carry bandejas full of food. I rush outside to help.

"Who's that?" my uncle-cousin, Tío-Primo Martín, half-nods toward Jaslene, Jazlene, or Jaslin. "One of your…" He snaps his fingers. "What do you guys call it now? Sidepieces?" he whispers.

I open two beers.

Well, at least this confirms Jaslene is not a cousin from either side of the family…or maybe not. Tío-Primo is from the los-primos-se-'primen era; a penis knows no familial boundaries.

I smirk and nod. Some lies are better said humbly.

"I see the family genes didn't skip a generation. How many you got now?"

There it is. The always urgent and pertinent, *Cuántas novias tienes*, question.

"To be honest, I've been struggling lately. Once you turn eighteen, you're supposed to hop on these phone dating apps where you swipe left and right. It's polluting my ocean."

I observe Tío-Primo to make sure he is buying the load of crap I'm feeding him. He seems engaged. Which means my manhood is still intact.

"You see, I'm old school like you. I talk to girls in person, not behind screens. So right now, I only got two. My girlfriend is sick, so I invited her instead," I lie, purposely omitting the ex in front of girlfriend.

"Listen." He looks around the backyard, locating his wife. "The other night, I told your aunt I was working deliveries late. Ended up at this spot on JFK Boulevard, by a car dealership. The women there," he chef-kisses, "that's the solution to your drought. I wish women were built like that in my days."

Yikes. I wonder how much money they took him for. Two to three-hundred dollars? Enough bills to fill up his smirk. I nod and sip my beer, stalling my response. He'd have to pay me in disinfectants and antibiotics to go to a spot like that, where all the fake-booty chapiadoras from New York hustle at. I only know about it because the guys at school know that at 10PM on Fridays and Saturdays, a flock of *bad* mamis unloads out of these black cargo vans. They're not my type, but it's an easy way to stay in good standing with the fellas at school. Just pull up across the street and watch. Someone from school is bound to confirm they saw you there on Monday.

With my masculinity confirmed with Jaslene here as my side-piece, I won't judge Tío-Primo. No need to crumble his manhood; age is already crumbling it for him. Plus, I'm too young to enter a bar, and that's my way out of this convo.

"I wish." I fake sigh. I swig my beer for added emphasis. "But I'm only eighteen. Too young for the big leagues."

He pats me on my back. "It's a shame, because some of the girls there…are eighteen, too."

My dad never mentioned if paying for women's attention counts in the two-girlfriend quota. Must be how older men keep their numbers up to par. That's kinda dirty, though. Too much scheming. And thinking about it now, what's an old man gonna do with two girlfriends? Aren't our libidos supposed to hit all-time lows after forty? Yoooo, it just hit me. My penis got an expiration date. So that's why a man needs two girlfriends. Gotta make up for the back-nine?

"Sobrino, you know what women like? You young, so you probably already know."

I chuckle in anticipation. Unsolicited advice from a fifty-seven-year-old wearing baggy Pepe jeans, an Aeropostale polo shirt, and the same old Curve cologne from like 1995. Or is that Egyptian Musk I smell on him?

"To get their butthole licked." He swigs his beer.

Oh, what the…

My beer races down the wrong pipe, carrying with it the image of my aunt moaning to the flick of his tongue. An image that should never poop into my mind.

"It's true." He shapes his free-hand into an O, placing it on the rim of his beer. "This is how you practice. Grab a beer, point your tongue—"

La-la-la-la-la.

"—never flatten it. Soft, precise strokes. Practice with each swig—"

La-la-la-la. Shut the fuck up.

"—because if you don't, that little, thin connecting muscle under your tongue will tire out before her moans do."

I hold my beer in front of my face and contemplate if I should chug it.

My aunt sneaks up from behind us and side-hugs Tío-Primo Martín. She wiggles her nose into his cheek and stumbles a bit as her feet fail to find proper footing.

Tío-Primo Martín winks at me.

"El amor, Danny," my aunt says. She leans her head back to better bask in his eyes. "It solves all."

I chug my beer and grimace. "That's beautiful…really beautiful." I look away in an attempt to erase the foul images manifested in my mind.

Still sitting, Jaslene mouths and bops to Karol G's "Ahora Me Llama," which plays off the speakers. Locking eyes, she starts mouthing it even harder, as if I were a cheating ex-boyfriend of hers. As if she was Ida.

Hmm, I wonder if licking her ass would calm her down? Shiet, would licking ass keep me alive in jail? I scratch my head and shrug. There is nothing gay about survival, right? My father never got to that lesson of manhood. We were stuck in the chasing girls lesson plan, up until his death.

"You know what else women like?" Tío-Primo Martín says.

Na-na-na, we not doing another round of this. "Hold that thought, Tío-Primo. I gotta get the grill going."

Black, short-sleeve button-down with flamingos and six-inch salmon-colored shorts, the color scheme plus the knee-to-thigh exposure begging for a gay joke, but just how I like it. Black penny loafers with quarter-inch heels and four-hundred dollar Prada sunglasses standing ready for a bougie comment. By now, I should have received at least three unsolicited roast attempts, but none of the cousins have said anything.

"Rose." I wave her over.

She has just finished a ten-minute round of saludos, but my greeting awaits her. Her freshly done box-braids my target or perhaps her flats, which clap like tap shoes.

"Diablo manita, let me get this straight. You went to Boca Chica, got your hair done, and you bought flats at a Charlie Chaplin Museum. Or did you buy the flats first, then galloped on them all the way to DR?"

"Hey, Danny." She hugs me.

Rose biting her tongue? Throwing the fight? "You a'ight?" I say.

"I'm good. Shouldn't I be asking you that? Your mom said you were depressed and on suicide-watch since the breakup. I would've hit you up, but I had to deal with my own drama at home: my dad found out I'm still dating Taj."

My mother would exaggerate my life away. "Well, that's ridiculous. You know that lady is a walking telenovela. I can splash water in my face, and she'd claim I'm drowning."

"Word?" Rose's eyes light up. "If that's the case, speaking of Boca Chica, I heard you didn't go on a vacation, but your ex definitely sent you packing." Painful yet healing, she redefines love, one clap-back at a time.

Our parents' romantic relationships were turbulent; money and infidelity being the major issues. But there comes a time when a man must make the tough decision: being a father, husband, or provider, never all of the above. As a result, us cousins roasted each other to express love. A downplay from our parents' constant arguing. If we didn't know any better, we'd think arguments were a love-language. Whether it is or isn't, roasting is definitely the primo love-language. It's just the way…titties.

A thousand shooting stars flash past my eyes, granting me my wish of possessing four hearts. One to love her innocent smile. Another to love her perky tetas. The third to love the outline of her hips. The last to pump blood into my inflating penis.

Standing alone, searching for someone, is love and marriage dressed in long pants. She probably didn't shave her legs today; I respect that. They're white pants too, signaling she isn't on her period; better yet, signaling that she surrenders her hard-to-get disposition, and today her coochie is open for business. A red Bebe tank top, the logo written across her milky pillows; the engine to my motor-boat. Her hair in a bun, she is smart to not waste her effort in this humidity. And her eyes have found their way to mine! She quickly turns away, as do I. She looks like an angel, but I hope she is a diablita.

"Who ordered the Popeyes?" I say to Rose.

"Popeyes?" She turns around and lets out a robustious laugh that attracts everyone's attention.

"Ayo, keep it down."

"Pero estúpido, that's my friend, Gloria."

"Gloria? I don't doubt it. She looks like glory. She got a—"

"Before you even ask, it's a no. N-O."

"No, as in, she isn't single? Or no, as in, you not gonna put me on?"

"No, as in, I won't let your toxicity near any of my friends."

"Damn, here I was thinking of you. Your bestie can come to

all the family barbecues from here on out…as family. Wouldn't that be nice?" A white lie because there won't be another family barbecue for me after I confirm my decision to Detective Hanson.

"Yeah-yeah-yeah. Nice try. Let me go introduce her to the fam." Rose walks away.

"Mmm, whatchu grillin'?" Jaslene says.

She must have seen me peeping out Gloria. Either that, or she saw Gloria and saw what I saw: a closeted freak-nasty angel from the open borders of heaven. Sheesh! I would have strutted over here myself if I was a girl not looking to lose out on dick. But little does she know, I'm in the market for two girlfriends.

"Nothing crazy, hot dogs and burgers. You want one?"

But Jaslene feels guaranteed at this point. Almost gifted. Bagging Gloria's phone number is now the mission.

"Eh, not really. What I want goes between a different kind of bun." She slaps my ass. "It's also a different type of meat." She grabs my hips and thrusts her pelvis onto my butt, something I'll likely experience frequently in jail. Never been much of a fighter.

I jump forward, hitting the grill's knobs. "Chill, girl. You buggin'. Don't you see my abuela over there?" I block my crotch with the spatula. Part of me feels weird. Violated. The other part, curious.

"You're no fun," Jaslene says. "Where's the bathroom? I need to wipe myself down, you got me…" She tiptoes to my ear. "Wet."

I let out a slight moan. Oh, she's good. She knows what she is doing. My penis can't take it anymore with all this up and down between her and Gloria. How am I supposed to think with all my blood flowing to the wrong head? And oh, her butt is decent. More hip-torque than ass, but I can definitely get with that.

From a distance, Tío-Primo Martín dribbles his eyebrows at me while tonguing the rim of his beer. This guy is ridiculous. Oh snap, is that who I think it is behind him? Shit, I need to get on my A-game.

"Loco, where the hoes at?" my cousin, Broncaulio, said at the arrival gate last week. He leaves in late September or early October—I forget—and has one goal: catch the return flight having smashed at least one gringa. If he doesn't, his first trip to the United States will be a bust...or lack of. But not like it matters whether he does or doesn't. Upon return, he will tell his friends he got some American pie. Probably describe multiple girls—one wouldn't be enough for storytelling—as the Dominican Wet Dream, an American tres golpes: white, nice eyes, and blonde. Gloria only checks off the first two requirements, but when she giggles, her aura shines like gold. Jaslene, on the other hand, is only blanquita, but Puerto Rican is American enough. I need to work fast. He is Dominican-Dominican.

"La cerveza más fina, para una mujer fina." I extend a beer to Gloria. "Rose, you should go get yourself one."

Yeah, she needs to get a beer and get as far as possible. Instead of sitting here like Gloria's watchdog.

Rose stands her ground and side-eyes me.

"What did you just say? I only speak un po-qui-to," Gloria says.

I melt into her non-rolling tongue. First, it was the white pants to signal she is not menstruating. Then, it was the shirt with Bebe written on it, calling me like the Batman sign. And now she expends her whole Spanish vocabulary to flirt with me. It's like she doing everything in her power to seduce me. Doing everything to change my mind—spy on Ida—so I can spend more time with her.

"My apologies. My name is Daniel, but everyone calls me Danny. What's your name?" As if I don't already know it.

"Gloria."

"Gloria?" I lick my lips. "Such an accurately descriptive name."

Rose turns away to hide her ballooned cheeks full of laughter.

Gloria laughs in a shy manner. The cute laugh, the freckles, and the white yet tanned skin like the crust of bodega sandwich bread. What a glorious moment it will be when I bag.

"Where you learn Spanish?"

"Bachata." She scoots to the edge of her chair and straightens her posture. "I love the sultry lyrics." She closes her eyes and dances her shoulders. "The passion. The emotion. I love it."

"Oh, *you do?* Give me a sec." I swag my way to my phone next to the speakers, doing my best Denzel impersonation. My bachata playlist, my forever wingman. I bite my lip an instant before extending my hand to Gloria. As the rush of vulnerability and fear of rejection hit my psyche, my hand in mid-air never touches hers like Michelangelo's Creation of Adam. My gay cousin was a step ahead of me. He pulls her to dance.

Rose busts out in laughter, no longer holding back, curling sharply into her chair. "It hurts." She grips her stomach.

I smoothly spin onto Gloria's chair and backhand Rose on her shoulder. She is laughing way too hard. My face reddens and reddens. A whole bunch of primas desperate to dance, and this gay ass mofo chooses the one girl at this barbecue that I crave to slide my thigh in between during a bachata. The one girl on the verge of changing my mind about my Ida decision. No offense to Jaslene, but Gloria got this innocence in her demeanor that elevates her to forbidden fruit status. Una vaina exótica.

But no. Instead, like clockwork, here comes one of my primas to ask me to dance, knowing damn well I'm going to say no. "You guys are so worthless, son to' pariguayos," she says after I brush her off.

When I was younger, dancing with my cousins was no biggie. But now I only dance with girls I'm trying to bag.

It's mind boggling too. They all have boyfriends! But with how *in* the primas are dancing, you would think it's hot-girl-summer for the second year in a row. Where do the boyfriends go?

"Remember when I invited Taj?" Rose says.

"He is Black, though. What did you expect? These old school Dominicans don't know how to hold up a mirror."

"Okay. Name a boyfriend that meets these viejos' standards? There is always a far-fetched reason to not welcome them."

"Oh! The white boy, Aden. How 'bout him?"

"That's completely different. He is this girl's fiancé." Rose shakes her head. "Look at him over there, basically part of the family."

"Aight. But before he was her fiancé, he was obviously her boyfriend."

"Yeah, when he was her boyfriend, they thought he had money.

Green is always welcomed into the family," Rose says. "Moncy and green cards."

"Well, the boys don't have it much easier."

"Who that over there then?" She points at Jaslene. An uncle, whose wife is barely ten feet away, is entertaining her with tú-sí-eres-bonita lines.

"She is an amiguita. Just a friend."

"Tato, let me introduce a guy as un amiguito. Catch me on *Primer Impacto* tomorrow afternoon." Rose pauses, likely wondering when Taj, her boyfriend of three years, will be accepted. And since she mentioned she got into it with her father again over Taj, that won't happen anytime soon.

"Sooo…" I play with my fingers. "Your friend Gloria. What's up? You really not going to put me on?"

Rose chuckles. "Bro, you are so annoying." The four magical words. "She's nineteen and in college. I doubt she would hook up with someone like you."

I catch a glimpse of Gloria's ass as she performs a spin move. I sneak a peek, again and again, every other time to reconfirm that she is indeed fine as hell. She nineteen, huh? That's extra-extra legal. I'mma make Rose bite her words.

"Hold my beer."

"What!?" she says, as I force my beer into her hand.

Without their approval, I step into Gloria and my gay cousin's dance space. He glares at me, then sits next to Rose, folding his arms with a why-you-always-gotta-ruin-the-fun facial expression. Rose does the same.

Diablo. The powder-soft hands. The torque of her rocking hips. The French-manicured toes, no bunions or cuticles. Her timid face asking for me to be gentle. Probably singing Alicia Keys's "You Don't Know My Name" inside her head.

I now understand why my gay cousin looks so agitated. She turned him straight, no doubt about it. I spin her once, but not again. I keep her facing me, so I could admire her quivering lips. Shit. I skip a dance step.

Gloria stops dancing. "What happened there? I thought all Dominicans were supposed to be master bachata dancers."

"It's been a while since someone forced me to keep up. I may need you to give me a master class." I bite my bottom lip.

Her eyes shy away. "Anytime. I love dancing."

I puff my chest in confidence, knowing exactly what I must do. "My phone is playing the music, but I'd still like to get your number later. Is that cool?"

"Is that all you want?" She gently pries my hands off her waist and steps backward. "You should have asked for more." She smiles with a slight head tilt that says, *be bolder.*

I watch her butt jiggle all the way to her seat.

I need that.

Fuck it. As superficial as this sounds, I'm taking the deal.

CHAPTER SIX

Guilt arrives only after the fact. And the fact was, we knocked the sheets off that pay-by-the-hour motel bed. The coochie, so grippingly tight, that when I slid it in, it got stuck like King Arthur's Sword. Only I could wield it out. And when I did, it was fall-off-the-bone tender. After, only the feeling of disappointing Ida remained. As well as the taste of heeding Tío-Primo Martín's advice. Gloria, Gloria, Gloria.

I still don't know how I pulled it off. Broncaulio didn't make it easy, and to think I'd still have that much game after years locked up in Ida's cage. But this feeling of guilt. It's odd. Like I'm remorseful for erasing everything Ida taught me in our relationship. And at the same time, it feels like she was holding me back from being the wild boy I'm born to be. It's odd. Confusing.

My phone rings me back to reality.

It's Esmeralda again. It's the eleventh time this morning and the fourth within the last ten minutes. I can't stop staring at my white ceiling, wondering if my jail cell's will look the same. If so, as long as the ceiling is the same, I'll be at home.

It's funny, because if Gloria would have denied me, I'd be ready to take the detective's deal in order to further pursue her. It's very primitive of me to make decisions this way. It is what it is, right? Now that I've had it, the motivation is gone. No matter how bomb it was. It wasn't how it was with Ida, though.

With Ida, it was insatiable. Something about her kept me wanting more and more and more, no matter how much I took. Drove me nuts. Drove the possibility of two girlfriends out of my mind—besides that one time. My hormones were entangled around her name.

Ida.

I'm sorry. You'd think I'd learn the first time. Another one-night stand, leading to a sunrise of emptiness.

Esmeralda barges into my room, huffing and puffing. Her smeared eyeliner and extra lazy bun tell a story of desperation. She tosses a manila envelope onto my face. "You're a fuckup."

"And you ugly." Who does she think she is, barging in like that? Unannounced like…like she is my annoying big sister! Okay. This is the part I act unbothered and peep what the fuss is all about.

On the envelope, dated early Sunday morning, is the acronym, DNA. I hold in my W-T-F, as a *Maury* you-are-not-the-father highlight-reel time-lapses in my mind. Jaslene's name better not be on this! Matter of fact, nobody's name better be on this.

Esmeralda coughs to get my attention.

I peer over the top of the document. Esmeralda's face flushed red. An example of what my father says is wrong with women. Her posture and expression says, *read-my-mind*, but her mouth says nothing. I skim over the results. A chart of unfamiliar acronyms accompanied by random numbers that I cannot decipher. It might as well be blank.

"Keeping it frank, you played yourself by giving me this." I chuckle with a hint of arrogance. Just happy that I didn't see a you-are-the-father or anyone else's name on it. "You know I have no clue what any of this means."

Esmeralda pounces on me and snuffs me side to side. "It means I'm representing scum. A low life piece of," she snuffs me again, "of ugggghhh." She bashes my head into the pillow.

I bust out laughing like I'm being tickled. I grab Esmeralda's wrists, which are gripped loosely around my neck. "Chill, what's good witchu?" I continue to laugh. I don't know why I'm laughing so hard, but her anger is amusing for some reason.

Esmeralda regains control of her anger. "Your DNA was all over Ida's clothes. And I, Esmeralda Bonifacio, Esquire, might as well be your accomplice. An accomplice to the worst type of scum in the world."

"What?" I release her wrists. "My DNA was...*Ida?*"

Esmeralda rolls off me, sits at the edge of the bed, and stares at the pile of clothes mounding on the floor.

I would never, not even in my worst nightmare. Not even on my last day before incarceration would I ever. I scan the document again and again, and again for Ida's name, but all I find are words like subject and individual.

"There must be a mistake," I say. Esmeralda's face is now flushed red. I don't know what to do. Do I comfort her? Do I clear my name first? I reach over to caress her back.

She squirms my hand off. "Don't touch me."

Oof, good. 'Cause that felt awkward as fuck. I'm no good at emotion. "Okay. But you must believe me. This can't mean anything. Perhaps we had contact, we danced, or something. I was drunk. Maybe I slurred some saliva on her."

"Danny, did you do it?" she says hesitantly.

"Do what?"

I wish I knew. I wish I could replace last night's wet sheets with the memory of Saturday's party. I wish I could twist some nerve ending or push a button on my head that could unlock the memories. That way, I could confirm my innocence to whatever is going on. Because I'm bamboozled right now. I thought I pissed on a door. Nothing more.

Esmeralda remains silent. The short hairs on her arms porcupine out. She must think I'm guilty.

"I didn't do it. I'm innocent. And I'll say it again. I would never ever *ever* do that. I'mma prove my innocence. I don't know how, but I will. And then, I'mma find the real piece of garbage that did whatever I did. My doppelgänger is not safe. I'mma find his ass." I grip the bedsheets.

"Danny, this doesn't look good. But the results aren't definitive. The truth is, there was no DNA found in the vaginal and cervical samples. So we can still make a case. But again, this doesn't look good. The results do confirm that you and Ida were in close contact between Saturday night and Sunday morning."

"But I have no clue what you're talking 'bout."

"Of course you don't; that's what they all say. Get it into your head. Innocent people go to jail too. You need to start taking this seriously. This isn't *Caso Cerrado*. This is real life. And in real life, we have a victim and multiple witnesses saying they saw you and Ida enter a room. Y'all spent some time together, alone." Esmeralda stands. "For your sake and for mine, you better not have done it. I'm going to keep giving you the benefit of the doubt, but…" She stares vacantly at the bare, white wall—I haven't gotten to decorating yet, besides the Sammy Sosa poster—until a shiver shakes her awake. "Okay, I'mma get going. I had a long night, and…look at me. I can't believe I rushed over here like this. I gotta fix myself." She looks at herself in confusion before regaining focus. "Listen, I'mma continue working on the case. And you, mister, better get to your electronics store job—your mom informed me on the way up to wake you up for it. We can actually use that for your defense—Danny, a responsible employee. So don't be late. After your shift, we'll meet up and discuss more as we agreed on the car ride. And again, I haven't told your mother anything."

"Wait, before you go." I gulp. "Ida? Is she like…okay?" My gut shrivels into a rock. My Ida Frida was…assaulted? Maybe. And I couldn't do anything. I couldn't do my job as a man; I couldn't protect her. I'm such a waste.

"She is safe at home. But honestly, I don't think you'll ever understand her emotional and psychological injuries. You would have to be born again a woman." Esmeralda sighs. "My heart goes out to her."

"You are wrong. I may not understand Ida's exact thoughts, but I know how she suffers. I've made her suffer. Which is why I won't spy on her. I've vowed to myself that I would never do her wrong again. And a man that can't keep his word to himself, is not a man at all."

Esmeralda sits back down.

"Freshman year, Ida, although still a bit chonga, was the flyest girl in school. Hair always slicked back in a ponytail, thin eyebrows, and two-inch hoop earrings. I liked that shit. She was both hood and pretty, hood-pretty. My two-for-one special. My trophy-chonga.

"The more we dated, the more she embraced her natural beauty. She shaped her eyebrows thicker and let her long curls flourish. She was a walking Macy's Day Parade, July 4th Fireworks on the Hudson, the Super Bowl Halftime Show—but not the one with Janet Jackson.

"Year one was smooth sails. Year two, though, there was a new flyest girl in school. Year three, another. I had an outdated model phone that worked perfectly for my needs. Meanwhile, all my friends were thotting on new girls each year—buying into the upgrades. All the stories my conquistador buddies shared glorified the single scene. I loved Ida, we even talked about eloping after graduation, but I was missing out. Dad would definitely agree with that."

Esmeralda nods and lets out a fleeting well-you're-not-wrong chuckle.

"One drunken night, I was gone off an Everclear and Kool Aid concoction I made with the fellas. I effortlessly bagged a girl's number from a different school. At first, we just texted, nothing serious. But flirting again excited me. On another drunk night, I cheated. It was like I was on auto-pilot."

I glance out my room window, locking onto the barely visible church chapel in the distance. Maybe there is a demon inside me. One that is never satisfied with the treasures at its feet.

"Sad thing was, it wasn't an accident. It wasn't bad luck. It was a mistake made in bad judgment. I know guys who cheat on their girls on the regular. On top of that, a quarter of my family is out of wedlock. Shit, I'm out of wedlock. Cheating may not be right, but it is definitely expected. Who was going to judge me? It's welcome to the club, and all men are the same, right?

"Ida found out because women always find out. So I told her the truth. I convinced her it was a onetime thing. But that didn't mean an apology accepted. Ida said something like, 'I can take you back and forgive you because I love you. Lord knows I want to be with you. But if I take you back, I'm not sure I'd love myself. It would be my weakest decision as a woman.'"

Esmeralda poetry-snaps. "And this girl is in high school? Yes. Queen. I like this Ida. She could definitely be my friend." She nods continuously. "Well, now that we got that out of the way—"

"I'm not done. So one day, she proposed an idea: a nail drives out another. I was to grant her a one-cheat pass. Correction, she was going to take a one-cheat pass."

"Oh." Esmeralda looks pleasantly surprised.

"She heard it in a Romeo Santos song. I didn't agree at first, but after a few weeks of standstill, I gave in. I loved her. I fucked up, and if this made it right, then I'd take the L. At least, I thought. After she got even, a Titanic-sized jealousy emerged from inside me. Chills ran through me like a never-ending ice-bucket-challenge. Worse part is, she didn't actually go through with it. During our last meetup—the breakup—she told me she lied because I was not gonna turn her into a cheater. But she wanted me to experience the hurt she had endured. The numbness hurt more than the pain.

I didn't know a heart could stop beating. I didn't know love lost can disintegrate every molecule in one's body. Although I know heartbreak is emotional, it felt equally physical.

"You know, sometimes it feels like being a man is about making dumb decisions," I say. "And you know what? That dumb decision led to this horrible event. If I had still been with Ida, this would have never happened. The…whoever…would have thought twice. This really is all my fault." I smush a pillow onto my face and scream into it.

Esmeralda busts out laughing.

"What is wrong with you?" I launch a pillow at her.

"How can you be so smart yet dumb enough to fall for this trick?" She laughs. "Nothing happened to Ida—that I know of. I told you that already. You pissed on a door, albeit the last door anyone over eighteen would want to piss on. Detective Hanson even read you the potential charges."

"So Ida is okay?"

"Wow, you really couldn't read anything on that chart. You must have a wildly guilty conscience because this is your toxicology report. You, little brother, were roofied."

Esmeralda points to a line on the report, Benzodiazepines (**Positive), and then another line, Flunitrazepam (**Positive).

"Forget about Ida—by the way, she sounds way too out of your league. Consider me impressed—by her, not you. Also, I doubt you know anything about love. Shoot, *I* don't even know about love. But listen to me. You were roofied, which means an argument can be made that you were a victim of a crime. Anything you did Saturday night into Sunday morning was a result of that."

Roofied? Men don't get roofied. But more importantly…I spring off my bed. "So I don't have to spy on Ida!? Detective Hanson can kiss my ass?" My shoulders float high.

"Not quite. Before I can make this defense, I need to do more digging. But it's a good start. So tonight, take the deal and co-operate until that happens."

"Tonight?"

"Yep, we're meeting with Detective Hanson to discuss the deal. So after your shift, I'll pick you up. I'll prep you on what to say and not to say. Then we'll meet with Detective Hanson. Don't mention this report, though. At all. This is our trump card and we need to use it right." Esmeralda grabs the manila envelope and stops at the door. "Also, I don't know what being a man is like, but cheating, chasing skirts, and other dumb decisions are not it," Esmeralda says. "Okay, now I really should go, and so do you. But can you promise me something?"

"Sure."

"Don't wait till you feel desperate, lonely, or against the wall to communicate your thoughts and emotions. I purposely wrote DNA on the envelope to trick you into telling me the real reason you're second-guessing Detective Hanson's deal. I didn't expect my plan would work this well, but now I *know*-know who this Ida is to you. And she is definitely not some girl that tried to reform you. She is your North Star. The first person to show you the way. And now I also know that there is a boy inside of you, confused, trying to become a man."

I chuckle. "Got it. Ida always said communication wasn't my thing."

"That's a lie. Remember when Pops, you, and I would spend weekends together? Each night, you'd hop on that shooting video game. The one you and your friends constantly shouted at each other in. I've heard you coordinate complex on-the-spot assaults like you were a SWAT captain. So I think you can communicate well. You just don't know when to. Think about that. And take the deal, Danny. I'll send you the details tonight. Now go to work or wherever your mom says you must go to today. I couldn't quite understand her. You know how she speaks Spanish like time is running out." She opens the door.

"ESME'! Antequetevayasvengaayudarmeconestedocumento…" my mother yells from downstairs.

Esmeralda shakes her head. "I have no clue what she just said."

I laugh. "She probably thinks I work today, but the store is closed. So see you tonight 'cause I'm sleeping in. Also, Happy Labor Day."

I plop myself back onto my bed. Hmm, communication. I guess she makes a good point. This white ceiling. Perhaps it's not meant to look like my jail cell's. Maybe it's a blank slate. And the deal is the path to it. Ida, my North Star.

CHAPTER SEVEN

Detective Hanson's reasoning for *employing* me is fundamentally sound. Ex-boyfriend likely to know the inappreciable details of Ida's pattern of life. If caught spying, would look obsessive-ex-boyfriend crazy instead of investigative. Someone who is out of the picture but very much in it. The new Ida, possibly my creation. And now I'm bound by societal duties to save humanity from the monster I unleashed. But I'm not sure what Ida has done. Detective Hanson claims it's need-to-know, and to him, I don't need to know. And honestly, I don't think I want to know because as far as I know, I just need to pretend to go along with the deal until Esmeralda can make my defense. So any more details may invest me more into this—whatever this is—a lot more than I want to. But still, what the heck has Ida done? And is this all a huge coincidence? I land in jail and BOOM! Detective Hanson has a deal ready faster than Esmeralda could show up to the precinct. This is all so weird. And WHO. THE FUCK. ROOFIED ME?

Initially I was delighted that I had a way out of this mess. Until I realized that being roofied is likely *how* I got into this mess.

As Detective Hanson munches down on his hash brown, the setting becomes more and more contradictory. This dummy picked the only diner in Hawk Union, where every student comes when they got the munchies. All the booths in a single file, and anyone can sit on a stool at the counter next to us. What he knows is a secret, but what I need to know is not?

"This is how it will go down. Every Friday, you will report any new information on," he waits for the server to pass, "*her*. I want to know about anything different, new job, new hangouts, new friends, new boyfriend…" Detective Hanson pauses to lie-detect my eyes. "You don't *like* her anymore, right? If so, that would be a conflict of interest that I can't have."

Of course I don't *like* Ida. I love her. Safety from expulsion and jail time are merely bonuses compared to the license to stalk her without actually feeling like a stalker—a point Esmeralda illuminated to me.

"I cheated on her. And I had greasy sex with another girl this past weekend. What do you think?"

"DANNY," Esmeralda blurts out. She has the same face on from when I asked her about clapping freshmen cheeks. But Detective Hanson's presence prevents her from saying more. And from his nonchalant reaction, he seems to not care, confirming that he is a manly-man. Accustomed to that kind of talk.

"Greasy, huh." Detective Hanson rubs the fingers that held the now devoured hash brown. "I'll assume that's a good thing." He nods at Esmeralda, reconfirming the deal is still in play. "Okay, I think we can start immediately. Friday, you'll report all information to Esmeralda, no matter if you think it's relevant or not. And Esmeralda will report to me. Think of her as your handler."

Great, give her more reason to power trip. From elder sibling to lawyer; from lawyer to handler. Soon she'll have all five infinity stones.

"So, where do I sign?" There isn't any paperwork on the table: only elbows, heavily-scratched silverware, and rough napkins.

"Esmeralda and I have come to an accord. First, a test run. If you perform well, then we'll make it official."

"Danny, Detective Hanson has given us a generous offer, especially with all the evidence against us. I think it's fair we prove our worth." Esmeralda awkwardly winks at me.

Some people can't master the proper wink. Luckily, I know she's weird. Probably hinting at what we discussed earlier about the roofie defense.

"Well, someone better at least sign the check. I think we all know I'm broke back mountain."

"What?" Esmeralda gives me a baffled look. "You've seen the movie, right?"

"Na, but some kids at school say that when they got no money."
Esmeralda slowly shakes her head.

"What? What's with the hating?" I say.

"More like someone's back got broke. If you know what I mean." Detective Hanson chuckles.

"Wait. The two dudes? Naaaa. *Chill.* Not the Nightcrawler and the Joker." I've been saying that for years. It kinda just stuck with me. All the kids with older siblings and cousins say it too.

"Don't worry. The check is on me," the detective says.

After he paid the check, me and Esmeralda were the first to gesture our impending departure. But Detective Hanson yapped and yapped, like my mother, who can turn good company into a hostage situation: you can't leave until I tell you this story, you can't leave without eating dessert, you can't leave until Danny gets home so you can see how much he has grown, you can't leave until your sister catches STOCKHOLM SYNDROME! He kept talking directly to me, but glancing at Esmeralda after every sentence, noting her reactions.

And Esmeralda just giggled and smiled through all the corny jokes. This whole bimbo routine that seemed performative at first but got hard to distinguish. I didn't know who was macking game to who.

"Hey, before y'all go, I must ask. What made you change your mind? You seemed full of resolve the first time I made you the offer, albeit you were intoxicated."

I glance at Esmeralda. "You said it right there. I was…" wait a sec, I don't recall him hitting me with underage drinking, "I wasn't thinking, that's all." I adjust my response.

Also found out I was roofied. Which is what I really need to be investigating, but satisfying the detective is the more pressing matter.

"And you know what?" I can't hold it in any longer. I erupt off my seat. "I gotta ask. Is Ida safe? This shit is sketch." I press my fingertips into the tabletop. "You've talked and talked about everything else, except her. As if Ida is just a detail. Surely, you can at least answer that."

Detective Hanson glances at Esmeralda. "She is safe," he leans back, "but only as safe as your performance. Are you sure you're not into her anymore?"

His reply puts a lid on my worries. "One-hundred-million percent. And say less."

If she is as safe as my performance, then she safer than the Capital Building during a presidential electoral-vote assembly.

Bro, where is she?

It's been three days and she hasn't visited our secret spot: our corner table in the microforms section of the school library—where relics for side-scrolling newspaper reels are buried—frosts with dust. On Chicken Parm Wednesday, she wasn't standing in-and-out of the lunch line, calculating the right timing to land our favorite lunch lady, who always slides us extra food. She wasn't in the *make-out* stairway; the only silver-lining to my failing search.

We were supposed to take Intro to Feminist Studies together, a new weekly elective offered by the school, but during attendance, the teacher never called her name. And since the course required parental approval, I can't switch it without a reasonable explanation. Ain't that some shit? The whole reason I signed up was Ida. And you know what, I articulated this exact situation to her: what if we break up and I end up in a class that I don't want to be in? But that only led to a "And why would we break up, huh?" Talk about speaking things into existence. That argument foretold our demise.

"Daniel, what is a heartbeat?" Mr. Greene asks.

Who? What? I was so lost in thought thinking about how much of a sucker I am for being stuck in this class that the teacher's question feels abrupt. I mentally retrace his words. What is a heartbeat?

I look behind me and side to side in hopes that another Daniel, Danielle, or anybody but me will respond. "Can I phone a friend?" It's not that the question is hard, it's that the answer to it sounds too easy. So what's the trick?

Instantly, the room squeezes in tension. All eyes on me as if I called the teacher a bitch or something. I've heard stories about Mr. Greene running a tighter ship than his shirt, but *Jesus*, what did I do?

Mr. Greene glances at his wristwatch. Bulging forearm veins tick with each pulse. "It only took five minutes this year. Class, I think y'all set a new record. Usually, the class clown takes a week or two to get comfortable."

I nervously laugh and sink into my seat.

"But Daniel, the question is easy enough. Also, class, there are no right or wrong answers. Actually, let me rephrase that. There are wrong and right answers, but it's more of a range instead of something concrete and specific. And this range changes depending on location and time period. Sometimes we ourselves are the location and time period. We all carry our cultures and experiences into this room. For example, let's say our parents come from the same hometown, Hawk Union. My parents raised in the sixties; yours in the eighties. I'm likely to be raised with some norms of the sixties, and you with some norms of the eighties because our parents replicate—to a degree—the way they were brought up.

Everyone present is a reflection of their parents' upraising, mixed in with our experiences of today. I don't know the particular demographics of the class, nor am I willing to assume. But *hypothetically*, some of you carry the norms of 1970 US; 1940—if raised by a grandparent—Peru; 1980 Italy; and so on."

What the heck is he saying? Got the class glossy-eyed.

"All this to say, right and wrong can get very subjective at times, because we define right and wrong with our own lenses. Correction, it is subjective."

Can it be, or *is* it? I bet the answer to that is also subjective.

"So class, don't be afraid to take educated guesses. If everyone knew the answers to my questions, then your attendance in this course would be pointless. Be wrong today, so you can be right tomorrow. Now Daniel, your answer? What is a heartbeat?" He slowly paces down the far-left aisle, ensuring students aren't texting, doodling, or showing any sign of not paying attention.

I sit up on my chair. "A heartbeat is a—" A giggle squeaks out of a student somewhere behind me. You see! This is a trick question. Shit. What could it be?

"Today, please."

Ahhhhh, I don't know. I want to say it's the pulse of the heart, but I'd be falling for the trick. "It is a…bum-bum bum-bum."

The class erupts in laughter.

Damn, the dumb shit that comes out of my mouth. Even Mr. Greene is doing something closely resembling a laugh. His lips want to curve up, but it's like a weight is nudging them down.

"I love the enthusiasm," Mr. Greene says. "And surprisingly, correct for the example I'm about to give." He walks down the center aisle, pausing in front of a student on his phone. He clears his throat. "Now Daniel, Texas has passed a new abortion ban, nicknamed the heartbeat bill. What do you think that means?"

Damn, there gotta be twenty to twenty-five students in this class. Why am I being spoiled with all the questions? "I don't know." I shrug. "If the baby, well, fetus has a heartbeat, *then*…it can't be aborted?" I look around the room for reactions.

"Excellent."

Oof, I'm a beast. Pulled that answer out of my ass.

"But it's wrong. Under the abortion ban, any fetus detected to have cardiac activity cannot be aborted. Which does not mean, like you said, a bum-bum bum-bum. So why call it a heartbeat bill, instead of a cardiac bill?" He halts his step and narrows his eyes on me, signaling that this may also be a trick question. "I'll give you a hint. It's the same reason my mother tells me it's about to be 11AM, when it's likely 10:15ish."

Now that's funny. My mother does the same thing. It's her way of getting me out of bed. As well as her way to get me to move faster on a chore or to get dressed. "To get people to move faster?"

"Why so?" he rapid fires.

"I don't know…support?"

Mr. Greene abruptly claps, then rubs his hands. Grinning like I imagine a mosquito would at the scent of sweet blood.

"And there, my students, is the power of words. We associate a heartbeat with life. If a fetus has a bum-bum bum-bum—which I'm pledging to use that for as long as I teach this course—then it creates the imagery of life."

True. I can see that.

"And if something has a heartbeat, then ending its life is an act of killing. Whereas the word 'cardiac' doesn't invoke anything in us. A heartbeat is a call for action. Cardiac is just a strange word to use any day of the week—unless you are in the medical field. And for clarity, we are not discussing what is right or wrong. What is life or not. The verbiage is what I'm highlighting."

Hmm. Interesting.

"A swap of synonyms or very similar-meaning words can change everything. Words matter. And when we begin learning labels, gender, sex, and more, I want you to notice how the words make you feel. What words trigger a cringe. Which ones offend you. Which make you feel included and excluded." His words begin to rise in excitement. And his grin has expanded to a housefly at an unattended buffet. "I'll leave it at that. Next week, we will go more in-depth on the subject of framing. Now open your books to page one."

Whoa, whoa, whoa. He really going to change topics like that. I look around at the other students to see if I'm alone in my internal reaction. Everyone else is shuffling into their bookbags, others already have their books open to the page.

Okay, guess not.

"Last one to open, reads first."

Anda el diablo! That's me, again. I slowly lift my eyes off the book.

"Daniel, don't worry. You'll catch on quick." He chuckles.

For the remainder of class, we took turns reading out loud. Asking and answering questions. Mostly going over terms like feminism, gender, and sex—all of which had slightly different meanings than I thought. And all had completely different meanings than my father would think. His voice rang and rang in my head during the passages.

It's a man's world, feminism is propaganda.

God made woman for man. No such thing as equality.

No such thing as bi-, tri-, quad-, or whatever new invention has been made up. You either hombre-hombre or maricón. Hembra or hembra-macho.

And it made me cringe, hearing his voice. Full of conviction. But was he wrong? If humans have been around for centuries, why does this feminist wave sound so recent? I've watched too much Discovery Channel to know that hierarchies in most species are instinctual. Patriarchy came naturally to humans, right? Instinctual. Not imposed. I must ask.

"Mr. Greene—" The bell rings, cutting off my question. And I'm not about to be that guy who holds up class for one last question. "Never mind."

"Next class we'll discuss the politicization and de-politicization of feminist topics," Mr. Greene says above the ruffling and shuffling. "Class dis—oh, before I forget. Allies for All. It's a student organization that holds meetings every Monday after school. You can earn up to five extra points for your final grade. One point for each meeting attended. I'll talk about it more next class. Now scram!"

As I mosey out of class, pretending to not be in a rush, because to be late is to be cool, until Mr. Greene pats the soul out of my back with his brolic hands.

"Good job today, Daniel."

I cough a bit. "Thanks…"

In between class, by my locker, I approached one of Ida's friends, the one that used to laugh at my jokes. Figured she'd be the most open to talking to me. But as soon as we made eye contact, she saw red. Eyes opened wide, then narrowed in on me like a homing beacon. And like a matador, I dodged her with the quickness. She stopped in front of my locker. I performed a Barry Sanders spin move on her and went to my next class without the proper books. It's the first week of school. One can get away with a *I-forgot-my-book-in-my-locker* till week-two. But one can't get away with hallway drama. No grace period for that. Already heard that a freshman got asked out by a senior (a potential crime in the making). And one of the teachers got caught glancing at a student's butt.

This search is a dead end. I know Ida hasn't moved out of town. I admit to taking the long way home sometimes. Her house is along that path. No moving trucks all summer. But I'm not stalking her. It's merely out of habit. Always took that path when we were together. And now that school has started, I can't be caught walking by there. That too would end up as hallway gossip. *I heard someone saw Danny walking past his ex's house. He doesn't even live that way. What a stalker.* The gossipers can miss me with all that. I got a rep to safeguard.

If Ida doesn't want me back…cool. But I'm not losing out on other mamis because of a *creeper* rumor.

What to do, what to do?

Can't even stalk her on social media. I deactivated all my accounts and the emails associated with them because I couldn't last three days without requesting a recovery password. How could

I not be curious about my Ida Frida's whereabouts? If not out of love, out of habit. If not out of habit, then out of jealousy. I always had to make sure there weren't any new boys in her posts or comments. At least not until I replaced her, an impossible task. But while I may not have social media, I know someone who does.

CHAPTER EIGHT

After school, I stopped by Rubio's house. His mom let me in. And seeing that I know Rubio's secret, the fact that she lets me in without hesitation confirms that she doesn't. The logic being, my mother would slap me at the door if I came home with some girl. Boys are not supposed to have girls as friends. And gay boys aren't supposed to have boys as…damn, I'm confused. If Rubio were to come out to his family, would boys not be allowed over? Only girls?

I pause mid-way up the steps.

If others know Rubio is gay, will they think I'm sus for going to his house?

Naaa, fuck that. He is my best friend. I'll hook off with whoever starts that rumor. I march up the steps.

"Open sesame, bitch." I storm into his room. Wish I hadn't though.

Rubio, on his bed laid out on his stomach, feet up in the air, panics to collapse whatever phone app he was on. I bet it was that Grindr app, lurking on some nearby pee-pees. Whatever it was, though, he did not want me to see it. His "I didn't expect you to come over today" was shakier than a vibrator, or maybe he uses one of them flesh-light thingies, but instead of a vagina, it's a butt hole. Found himself an Adam at Adam & Eve's.

"Bro, if you are going to watch porn, at least lock the door. It's masturbation 101."

He side-eyes me in annoyance. The look I'd expect after I roasted him five or more times for no reason. But I just got here, so he can't be at his annoyance limit yet.

"I need a favor. Would have texted you it but…" I give him the good ol' confident steeple hand gesture, hoping he would finish the rest for me. Last time I asked for this favor, he said to not ask him again. This time, I'm not *asking*. I'm *insinuating*.

"Not again. We've gone through this before," Rubio says with a concerned voice, which always rings gay in my ears. Like a man caring for another is a gay characteristic. Is it gay, though? I can say a *stop-being-gay-bro* right now, and it would fit perfectly into context.

Regardless, my father and uncles never talked about anything emotional. And when they did, it was about their favorite baseball teams or political debates on who was the biggest Dominican crook of the 2000s: Hipólito Mejía or Leonel Fernández. To this day, I still feel kinda gay—I mean weird—for telling Rubio that I love him like a brother. I've never said the L-word to another man. That's why Rubio is my best friend. He's heard me say one word too much.

"I know what I said. I'm the one with borderline Hyperthymesia, remember? I don't forget. But think of the circumstances. It's been almost three months, and I'm in a new space." I swagger across the room towards his Aaron Judge poster while pretending to hold a pimp cane.

"Nice try. Your rhythm is off."

I'll give him this one. Ida once forced me through an episode of the old *Queer Eye*, when she was prepping to watch the reboot. They assess everything from the clack of the boots to the jiggle of your balls in boxer-briefs. Rubio likely got that queer seventh sense for aesthetics. Wait, is queer and gay the same thing? And would a gay guy have an Aaron Judge poster, the same way I'm soon to put up a sexy Rihanna poster up in my room?

"Yo, you still like baseball, right?" I blurt out.

"I'm literally on the baseball team," he says. "But don't change the subject." He sits upright. "I'm not letting you use my social media to indulge in your obsessive misery again. You need to move on. I'm doing this for your sanity before you end up in a loony-bin or jail. I'm not an enabler."

I may have asked to see Ida's page one or twelve times before. So what? *I'm doing this for you. This is best for you.* All phrases I'm familiar with. Everyone seems to have a big picture plan for my life that I'm never made privy to. When I was eight, my father forced me into my first kiss, the first step to becoming a man. My mother obliged me to go to Catechism course, *we all need God.* Esmeralda encouraged me to take the detective's deal. And now, Rubio, dique knows best. For whatever reason, everyone keeps winding-me-up and marching me to their directional placement like a wind-up toy. At least Rubio got the jail thing right. If I don't get news on Ida, the deal never solidifies. I'll be forced to pimp

Esmeralda out to Detective Hanson until we can make the Rohypnol defense. And with how she flirts, I'll be in jail in no time.

I glance at my wristwatch. Each tick strums harder than the *Mad Max* blind guitarist. "Listen, I don't have time for this. If you want me to remain your best friend by the end of tomorrow, you'll have to give me your phone. Or else…"

"Or else what?" Rubio crosses his arms. His biceps flex, bulge, twitch, and wink at me, all at the same time. If he thinks I'll say, "I'll fight you," he's wrong. I'm a lover, not a fighter. And I know better.

But do I have a choice? I'm not supposed to divulge anything to anyone. Those were Detective Hanson's strict instructions.

"Or else I'll…open your closet."

Rubio looks at his doorless closet space. "O-kaaay. It's already open."

"So why you never tell me you were gay?"

"Now that's a conversation starter." Rubio shakes his head.

Yikes, I didn't mean to say that. Of course, I've been thinking about that question for a while now, but I had no plans to ask. I figured it would involve too many emotions that I'm not comfortable displaying.

"Were? I am. And for the same reason you never told me you are straight."

And whenever I envisioned this moment, I assumed he would immediately refute my claim. But as usual, he is honest; I've never caught him in a lie. "But then, why you pretend all these years?"

"When have I pretended? Name one time you saw me macking game to a girl?"

"How 'bout that party last year, when you drove that drunk girl home?"

"You mean that time y'all woof-woofed as I helped that freshman into my car?"

"I'm glad you remembered." I smirk. "Point proven."

"She was drunk and needed a ride. What does a favor have to do with sexuality or orientation?"

"But—"

"Okay, Danny. Let me answer all your questions at once. I'm not required by the Magistracy of Gayness to declare my sexual orientation like Puerto Ricans and their little flags on rearview mirrors. I'm gay. What's the difference between declaring it or not?" Rubio's eyes do not blink. "I've managed to stay under the *gaydar* without pretending or lying because my sexual orientation doesn't dictate how I act; it only dictates who I'm sexually attracted to. So, explain to me how declaring my orientation changes anything." He steps closer to me and clasps his hands. "Go ahead, explain."

I know this move. Shorten the personal space during an argument. Let frustrations become confused for sexual tension. If Rubio tries to kiss me, we fighting. I step backward, but I'm met with the wall.

"Ha. Don't worry, you're not my type, so stop getting shy now."

I don't have a rebuttal. I mean, he isn't wrong. I've never had to say I was straight, except for the occasional no-homo moment. And for a quick second, I wondered if he befriended me to gain access to my culito, which on any given sleepover is parked a stretched arm away, ready for the one night I'm too drunk or sleepy to defend myself. It's almost an instinctual fear. Gay guy around, cover your butthole. That's locker room etiquette at school. Even the idea gives me the grossest of chills, like a spider landing on my cock, then itsy-bitsying to the other side to web my booty hole tight. I squirm. But if he has never pretended, why do I feel deceived?

"You know what your problem is? Everywhere you go, you have sex on your mind. Everyone is either someone you wanna or don't wanna have sex with. Or conversely, everyone is either someone who wants to have sex with you or doesn't. You can get a little male-gazey at times."

"Chill—" What did I just get myself into? I'm supposed to be gaining access to his social media.

"Hush up. Let me finish. You wanted to play 21 Questions, so I'm giving you twenty-one answers."

But I hardly even asked him anything.

"If there is no closet to come out of, you assume all boys are trying to meet girls, and all girls are trying to meet boys. Fun fact, non-hetero people do not come out of closets, only creeps like R. Kelly do. And both the whole human reproduction and God-made-man-for-woman argument is stupid. If reproduction and human survival was an issue, I'd deposit my sperm in all the fallopian tubes necessary. The same way you would actually cook for yourself instead of waiting for your mother to, if you were genuinely hungry. My sexual orientation does not leave me incapable of reproduction, the same way your expected gender roles don't leave you incapable of cooking. Gay does not mean feminine. And also, with how global climate change is going, if you wanna continue with this narrative, for your convenience, gay couples could be seen as God-made population control. Regardless, surplus dicks and vaginas is not a global issue."

"But I never said—"

"Shh, my point is, you think with your penis too much. All the other stuff was a rant I've built up for years. Locked and loaded for the day my father asks me what you just asked. I'mma pop off on him. Watch." Rubio exhales louder than Esmeralda's hooptie. I can tell he is full of exhaust.

"You really believe I only think about ass and tetas?" I say. "You know that's not true." I definitely think about other things. How eggplant is a dumb name for a plant that doesn't lay eggs. Or how people that care for the environment decide to live in the wilderness instead of cities. Like bro, the writer, Henry Thoreau, was wrong; the whole idea is to leave nature alone and not emit carbon into it.

"Oh, yeah?" Rubio nods his head with a menacing smile. "Remember the first night with our fake IDs? The Lesbian Night we stumbled into? There was a huge banner hanging off the entrance and posters on every wall announcing the event. I told you, let's bounce, but you insisted on staying. For thirty minutes, I watched you breathe into every girl's ear, one by one, talking 'bout, *it's never too late to try dick.* At no moment did you stop to think that trying dick likely affirmed their sexual orientation. At no moment did you stop to question if you were sexually harassing them."

I laugh. "Okay, okay, you got me there. But to my credit, that night felt like a challenge was made to me. I wanted to see if I had enough game to make one of them like me." Same was with Ida after her infamous speech. I wasn't trying to sexually harass her. My intent was to test how much of a man I am. Because anyone can be a man. But not anyone can be *The Man.* Another lesson my father instilled in me.

"Dumbass, sexual harassment is never a challenge to accept. You made that challenge up yourself." He paces around the room, bouncing ideas in his mind. "Enough of this. I know it's a school night, but let's hang out tonight. I know of this event, which would make the perfect venue to test my you-think-with-your-penis-too-much theory." He snickers. "You like challenges, right?"

"Bet." I'll just sneak out or tell my mom I'm sleeping over because we got a project due or something. "And if I pass your challenge, you will let me peep Ida's social media profiles. You better still be friends with her. You know she private." He thinks he knows something that I don't know about myself, not possible. Unless he has been observing me in detail, which would be sus… Chill, Rubio is my only real friend. If anything, I owe him an apology.

"Wear something with style tonight." He smirks. "You rolling with me, and I can't have you bringing my flavor down."

"What?" I squint and cock my head back. "You know I got the sauce. I'll show up looking like Juan Gabriel or that Del Rio person from *RuPaul's Drag Race*, if it proves my point." I nod, waiting for him to ask if I watch *RuPaul's Drag Race*, which I definitely don't. But I've caught a clip or two in passing.

"Okay there, that's very unnecessary." He chuckles. "Just be ready by 8PM."

"Yeah-yeah-yeah. I'll be ready." I shake Rubio's hand, solidi-fying the deal. Welp, I would stick around to shoot the shit, but after that convo…I grab my bag off the floor and prepare to head home. I wonder, though… "Wait a sec, I got one more ques-tion."

Rubio sighs in anticipation.

I plaster on a genuine face of inquiry. "Do you still pee standing up?" The question is bound to rile him up.

A stern expression of disdain glues onto his face. He doesn't budge. A staring contest ensues until his smile squeaks out. "If you sit, you can't miss."

We both bust out in laughter.

CHAPTER NINE

"Que lo que? What-up, matatan?" my barber, Michael, says. "It's been a few weeks. I thought you were cheating on me again."

I swear barbers are clingier than any girlfriend I've ever had. I mean, he's not wrong. It's been a few weeks. But what he really got him salty is *Michel*—mi chelitos. I don't doubt for a second that since I've been gone, the haircut price went up from twenty-five dollars to thirty. That's how it's been since I was twelve. You miss more than a few weeks and he'll up the price on you. Inflation being his favorite reason. But I've never heard of a twenty percent inflation until him.

I fake-laugh. Something light to keep our fake-friendship cordial.

"Never, man. I told you. Last time, I was letting my hair grow out, but the curls got too 1980s for me." I clasp my hands and tilt my head in endearment. "You, my Edward Scissorhands, will forever be my barber."

Yeah, aight. He's my barber till he passes the thirty-dollar mark. At that point, I'll find a cheaper alternative.

We embrace each other.

Michael smacks the hair off the chair with the barber's cape.

A young boy, likely in his pre-teens, walks in. He glances at the three barbers in the shop, looking a bit lost. Perhaps all the posters of Pedro Martínez and Big Papi, the muted TVs with the Yankees-Mets game on, and the beers in some customers' hands got him thinking he accidentally walked into a sports bar. That's what I thought when I first stepped into a Dominican barber shop, after a decade of my mother giving me haircuts.

"Big boss, how can I help you?" Michael says to the boy.

"I'm looking for," the boy glances at his phone, "Michael. Someone recommended him."

The whole barbershop goes silent.

Michael shakes his head. "It's Mi-cha-el. Not Maicol. Not Michael like Jordan. It's Spanish. Mi like me. Cha like cha-cha. El like the letter L. Mi-cha-el."

Michael wraps the cape on me, wraps a tissue around my neck, and snaps the cape's button.

"The English name, Michael, translates to Miguel in Spanish. Man, who recommended me? Now you got me all fired up."

"My sister, Sharice."

After a pin drop of silence, the barbershop erupts in laughter.

"Ay-ay-ay." Michael waves the shop silent. "Calm down. Y'all gassing it." He looks at the boy. "Sit down, young buck. You got two people ahead of you."

"Bro, now you gotta tell me. Who is Sharice?" I say.

"Some chick from the block that won't stop blowing up my phone," he says in a low voice. "Got me going crazy."

"That's good, though, right?"

"Na, she got me going crazy-crazy. She calls more than Spam Likely. I'm talking 'bout all times of the day."

"*Damn*, what you do to her?"

"Nothing." Michael pumps the barber seat up twice. "She passed by the front of the shop a few times last week and parked her dump truck for everyone to admire. I swear she was casting an audition for her next Romeo. So, Old School over there," he points at an older, bald man reading a newspaper, who by the look of it, hasn't needed a haircut since 2000, "bet me twenty bucks that I couldn't bag the number. So you know me. I stepped out and holla'd at shortie." He covers his mouth. "She sixteen, bro."

"What!?" I lean forward on the chair.

"Chill-chill-chill. Once I found out, I deaded it. We just texted a few times."

"You just said she calls you OD. Block that number. Case solved."

Why in the world would a grown man like Michael not have blocked her already? He's easily in his thirties and I'm sure they could block numbers back in his day.

"Na, man. *She* calls. I don't pick up. But sixteen with an ass like that. I'll wait the two years." Michael swags in place. "You feel me?"

I'd *feel* him if he was eighteen like me. But…sheesh! He got me confused for someone else. Why has no one in the shop called him out already? Instead, they just laugh.

He chuckles and nudges my shoulder. "Yeah, you know what

I'm saying." He grabs the clippers and buzzes the top of my head. "What's good witchu, though? What's the wave tonight?" Michael asks as if he forgot I was in high school.

He asked the right question, but the wrong person. What the heck am I doing tonight? Imagine it's a spin-the-bottle type of party or a circle-jerk, where I'll have no choice but lose the challenge. Or worse! An all-male orgy. As far as the other question—what's good with me—nothing. Life is an absolute shit show. Before I can go into a rabbit hole of reflection, my mind snaps me back to tonight's potential circle-jerk.

"While we at it, skip the eyebrows this time," I say. Too crisp might give off the wrong vibes tonight. "Also, skip the straight-edge."

"Whatchu mean? So you just want me to pass the buzzer?"

"I'm trying out this new facial routine. Face been a little on fire lately," I lie. "The edges extra sensitive."

"Oh, word? You know we do facials now?"

"Really?"

"Yeah, bro." Michael pauses. "We take the bitches to the back and SPLAT." Michael busts out laughing and fist-bumps the barber next to him, who overheard the conversation and laughed too.

Either I've ignored it or didn't pick up on it on over the years, but Michael has gotten pedo' as hell since my last cut. What's up with this guy?

I chuckle. "You stupid." I cringe inside. I don't know Sharice, but I hope she never turns eighteen.

"Na, I'm just playing. Peep the new wash station in the back. We tilt your head back, exfoliate and all that. Lady comes in

Wednesday, Thursday, and Sunday. But yo, where you going tonight? I'm free."

Coño, this man won't drop the question. "I'm staying in with Rubio. Remember him?"

"Now that guy is definitely cheating on me. Haven't seen him since…I don't know. Maybe last year?" Michael smacks his lips. "But I follow him on social media. Saw him post something like, *I can't wait for tonight. It's about to be lit.* And he put the fire emoji."

Michael pauses for me to explain, like soliciting party plans from me, an eighteen-year-old high schooler, is not enough explanation for my silence.

I scan the shop for another lie. I lock eyes on the toilet paper roll on another barber's counter.

"He must have posted that before he got sick. Diarrhea and everything."

I look at my reflection in the mirror. The face of a liar, someone ashamed of his best friend. Is the self-preservation of my manhood more important than Rubio?

"*Sooo* you free then? If he sick, you definitely free."

This guy. Why does he have no quit?

"All I'm saying is, where the bitches at?" Michael spins me away from the mirror.

Yikes. This must be why Rubio stopped coming. Michael is way too old to be asking, *where the bitches at.* Regardless, I don't know where the bitches at. But I do know where they won't be at: wherever Rubio taking me. But I need to tell this guy something so he can quit asking.

"Why you even asking that question? You got that Sharice girl on your phone right there." I point at his phone with my lips. Perhaps bringing that up again will get him off my back.

"You a clown." Michael chuckles. He leans back to inspect my hair.

Mid-chuckle, I lock eyes with the boy, Sharice's little brother. He chuckles too.

Damn. Has he already abandoned his allegiance to his sister in order to fit in with other men? Like I'm abandoning Rubio in order to save face?

Michael unclips the hair cloth and lightly tugs the tissue on my neck off. He passes the buzzer at the base of my neck. "Alright, now don't tell anyone I gave you this cut. Dique, no straight-edge." He powders a brush and smacks the hair off my face.

I stand from the barber chair and hand him twenty-five dollars plus five dollars tip. We dap each other up. Michael doesn't let go of my hand.

"Your sister Esmeralda, heard she back in town."

Oh boy. Here we go.

"She still single?"

"Man, stop playing," I say. "See you in a week or two."

As I exit, I glance at the boy. There he is, eyes open, ears sharp, soaking it in like I did when I first entered the shop at the age of twelve. Which begs the question…

What have we taught this little boy today?

It took a while, but I finally got it. I strut down the space between my bed and dresser, which I converted into a fashion runway. At the mirror hanging on the door, I scan for any defects in my outfit. Damn, I look good.

I avoided all the colors on the LGBTQ flag, leaving me with an all-black outfit.

Imagine a buff-linebacker type assumes I'm looking to give up the cheeks because I'm wearing a particular color. Fuck-outta-here, ain't nobody got time for that.

Wait, what if black is the color that signals, D-T-F?

What am I talking about? I look like a motha-fuckin' SNACK. With this Britney Spears buzz cut, I'mma look like an icon in that bitch.

Call me Danny Día-de-los-Muertos because this outfit is killing it. I wipe off a smudge on the mirror and toss a nod at my Sammy Sosa poster in the reflection. My outfit almost as black as he used to be. I laugh at my own joke. I grip my belt buckle and kick out like Michael Jackson. "Hee-hee," I sing in a high-pitch voice.

I kick my leg out again. "Annie are you okay?" I say to my imagi-nation. I pump my pelvis out. "'Cause that ass gonna get hit by—*a smooth criminal.*" Alright, I'm buggin' out now. But sheesh! They gonna wish I'm D-T-F, but no señor, I'm closed for business.

Man, who am I fooling? What did I get myself into? What if it really is a circle-jerk, a spin-the-bottle type of party, or an orgy? Na, Rubio wouldn't do me like that…would he?

Shit, shit, shit. I gag on my thoughts.

Breathe, breathe. I focus on my eyes in the mirror.

Hombre-hombre o maricón. A man without two girlfriends is not a man. God made woman for man.

"Shut the fuck up!" Oh, shit. I said that out loud. And the fact that I did, brings me back to reality. No way I'mma go crazy this young.

Calm down, Danny.

I reach under my bed and roll out a Mamajuana bottle that I've aged since Ida and I started dating. A gift from my father on my fifteenth birthday. "Men drink. So you need to get used to the taste now," he said when he handed it to me. Tío-Primo Martín said it's an aphrodisiac, so I promised Ida we'd drink it when she turns eighteen. Part of me thinks that promise will be fulfilled. But it's unlikely. I need a drink to calm my nerves.

I take a swig.

Okay, okay. I raise the bottle towards the ceiling light, inspecting it. Smooth, weird tasting liquor. Okay, okay. I see you.

Ah shit! I screw the top back on. Now I'll be horny as hell at whatever event I'm going to!

Images of men in black-leather-studded sailor-hats, roasted-pig apple-gags, and whips flood my mind.

No, no, no, no. I can't do this.

A car vrooms in front of my house, Beyonce on blast. The music abruptly changes to a dial tone. My phone rings. Must be Rubio.

"Yerr, I'm downstairs, bitch. You ready for some gay shit, or you chickening out?"

"How 'bout you take me off the car speakers," I whisper.

"What? I can't hear you. Stop speaking like a little bee-ATCH— use your chest, please. *Cum* downstairs and hop into my gay mobile," Rubio says with an extra flamboyant tone. He is doing the most. He never talks like that. I must stop this madness before my mom hears him and starts assuming shit.

I rush downstairs and grab an icepack in the kitchen before sprinting outside.

"Took you long enough."

"Oh, now you wanna talk normal?"

I jump into the passenger seat of Rubio's white '92 BMW 325i Convertible. His pops gifted him it on his sixteenth birthday. We've been to many parties and fast food drive-thrus in this car. The back seats littered with burger wrappers and gym clothes. Even if Rubio is gay, he still got a lot of hombre-hombre in him.

"Relax. Just having some fun before the other gays get a hold of you."

"Man, stop playing." I buckle my seat belt and shove the icepack down my crotch.

"Ummm"—Rubio points at my crotch.

"Bro, just drive." If I gotta keep whatever this event is on the down low, I gotta keep something else lower. Who knows when the Mamajuana will kick in. Never had an aphrodisiac before.

"You got your fake on you, right?" Rubio smiles devilishly.

CHAPTER TEN

Dope lights, music lit, a roped-off middle section with a stage and runway. Several high-top bar tables sprinkled around with no seats. One long bar top with two mixologists, both with very, very, VERY well-touched eyebrows. Shits look drawn on. Overall, the venue seems cool, though. Although I feel like management is slacking because I'd figure they'd use the space in a way to maximize profits. But Rubio, what the fuck? The majority of the people are dressed in costumes, while we and a few others look out of place. If I had known, I would have gone to Party City. I even bussed it to the mall for this matching black fedora. Took me forever to get this outfit wrong.

"Come on, man. Why didn't you tell me this was a costume party?"

"Costume party?" Rubio laughs and begins pantomiming around his face. "This is a ball."

I brush eye contact with someone dressed like Lady Gaga at an award ceremony. "A ball?"

"Don't you see Cinderella over there?" He points at someone

with blown-out hair, a tiara, dramatic eyelashes, and a painted black jawline…wait…is that a beard?

"Like, drag?" I cup my mouth with both hands.

I scan and observe the room. One eye looking for Ida, because if she isn't in her usual places, then she must be somewhere she usually isn't, like here; the other one comprehending the situation. Suddenly, the room flips from a 6 to a 9. The women are now men. The men are now women. The lights are now rainbows. And my butthole potentially a pot of gold.

"Yep. Almost everyone here is either performing or simply cross-dressing for the fun of it. We lucky we got in, too. Look at this place. It's almost at capacity and we've only missed one event." Rubio smiles and nods, with a look that says, show me a little gratitude.

I mean, this is a bet after all. If getting me uncomfortable was his goal, he is succeeding.

My eyes zoom-in-and-out on the costume-wearers, their intense makeup, huge lips, and shoulders. As someone passes from behind, I jump forward and block my ass.

"Whoa there. You a'ight?" Rubio says.

"Yeah-yeah, just a cold shiver." I can fucking taste the rainbow in this bitch. Hairspray, weaves, and extensions mere frostings on top of the multilayered cakes of makeup. How am I supposed to protect myself? I don't got enough hands to cover my butt, dick, and mouth. I grimace. I'm glad my father isn't alive to even suspect that I'm here. I remember when I played Pee-Wee football for one week, a teammate slapped my butt after a play like they do in professional football. Yanked me straight out of the game.

"Oh, it's about to start again," Rubio says.

"Again?"

"Yeah, we arrived a little late. Had to get my fit perfect."

Rubio is dressed normal to me. Evergreen Banana Republic polo shirt, navy blue slim-cut chinos, dancing shoes.

"Sure, if you say so."

A man…woman…or person walks onto center stage. Purple Prince-type ruffled blazer, purple gypsy skirt. Right eyelash extended like a Chinese hand fan, left eyebrow reaching the middle of his or her forehead. What am I looking at? A transformer, an unsolved Rubik's Cube, Picasso's Weeping Woman? I nudge Rubio and lean into his ear. "Is that a man or a woman?"

"Danny," Rubio looks at me like a parent to a misbehaving child, "who cares? How is that relevant?" He shrugs me off his ear.

Okay, he may have a point. I guess in the grand scheme of things, it doesn't really matter what gender the person is, but I'm itching to know. "Bitch, I'm just making conversation. You know I'm kinda out of place here."

"How?" He flings his hands up in annoyance.

"Well," I scratch the nape of my neck, "people out here dressed differently. Come on, man. You telling me that outfit over there is normal? That person got a huge Lego block attached to his or her hair."

"Do you feel this way when you attend live football games, and people dressed differently, in massive shoulder pads and helmets? Did you feel this way when we went to that women's volleyball tournament? You were hella into it then."

I chuckle. Rubio got a response for everything. The most random comparisons, but it sorta made sense. "Aight, aight, I'll be quiet from now on." Rubio side-smirks.

Damn, now I wanna ask if this is a minority function. Hella Black and Latinos in here. "Okay, okay, my bad. One more—"

"Bro! You got Netflix. Watch *Pose*, and leave me alone."

"Are you bitches rested yet? Y'all been slaying this stage for a little over an hour now, I'm livinnnnnn'." The crowd erupts in claps. "Alright, alright, alright, I feel the l'amour. Next up is my favorite event, All-American Runway. So, after this short break, let's find out who got the BIGGEST. DICK. In the room." The person on center stage dangles the microphone by his feet—the audience hoots and hollers.

WHAT!?

"*Ayo*! I'm out of here. I'm not trying to see no dicks." I turn around and walk towards the exit. Half these people probably got fake dicks, and just like the chapiadoras, if you gonna have a fake anything, you might as well make it big-big. All these elephant dicks in the room, I don't stand a chance in a dick-measuring contest.

"You backing out of our deal already?"

"Bro, I'm not trying to see gigantic elephantiasis-sized dicks."

Rubio laughs uncontrollably, stumbling back and forth.

"There"—he crunches down in laughter—"there…there won't be any dicks showing, you idiot. It's a figure of speech. In this event, the performers present themselves as masculine. Typically it's queer men, but from what I read online, this place is lax with the rules and participants. So let loose, stop being so anal." He continues laughing. "Get it? Anal."

Solid joke, but not the time for jokes. I need to make sure I'm interpreting this right. "No dicks?"

"Yes, no dicks. Now get over here."

"Aight bet, 'cause you know I'm not about that life." What a relief. The exit might as well have had more locks than the state penitentiary. There was no way I could leave. One, it would scream homo- and transphobia. Two, and more importantly, I need to see this through and spy on Ida's social media. Again, somebody passes behind me, but this time I restrain myself from blocking my butt. Okay, okay, I'm getting better at this. Just gotta keep believing that nobody is going to sexually harass me.

I mean, it looks kinda safe in here. Besides the one contestant visibly arguing with the judges, it's all smiles and laughter around the room. And surprisingly, nobody has hit on me yet. Matter of fact, I don't think anyone in this room is getting hit on. Reminds me of my family barbecue, but without my uncles (I'm sure they'd still find someone to holla at). But as inviting as this venue may be, my body continues to tingle like an unceasing, silent alarm keeping me alert. I must continue to breathe and trust that no one will spit game to me or touch me inappropriately. "Ha!" A single laugh squeaks out of my inner voice.

"What happened? What's so funny?" Rubio quickly scans the room for what he may have missed out on.

"Nothing. Just thought about something." I've heard my cousin Rose and other girls talk about how they hate when creepy dudes spit game to them at parties, gyms, and basically anywhere. What I'm feeling may actually be the same feeling they describe. The feeling that I may be hunted by some predator who likes my culito. "Ha!" Another one squeaks out.

"Okay, you look crazy now. Whatever you got going on inside that tiny brain of yours, get it together." Rubio smiles and shakes his head.

A diss for zero reasons? He must be happy I'm here.

"Hey miss…mister, ah fuck." I'm never gonna get this right.

Rubio chuckles.

"Hey." I signal a server over. "Two shots of your cheapest tequila, please."

"Coming right up."

Rubio leans away from me, studying me. Suggesting I'm acting different. "Te-qui-la. You trying to get us bodied on a school night?"

"Fuck it, we here. I'm here. We might as well let loose and have fun with it."

Rubio reaches an arm around me and pulls me in for a light noogie. "Say less. Let's. Get. It. Poppin'."

Me at a ball. Can't make this shit up. Standing around is eventful enough. All the makeup, costumes, and guessing who likes penis and who has a penis is a mystery game in itself. The clues being Adam's apples, shoulder posture, and feet sizes. If she, he, or I-don't-know, is five-eight but got male size-ten feet and above, it's a dude or once was. (But don't quote me.)

A few mami chulas huddle near the armpit corner of the stage and runway, thicker than volleyball players, but maaaaaaan, it's not worth the risk. Sheeesh! I've never asked someone if they have a vagina or not. How do you even bring that question up? Before I can think to ask Rubio about proper etiquette, the host taps the mic to get everyone's attention.

"Alright, everyone, it's time for my favorite event. Like I said before, it's All-American Runway. DJ, let's make it happen."

BOOM! On stage, a Donna Summer look-alike erupts out of papier-mâché speakers, confetti snows from above, and the fast-paced part of "On The Radio" plays in the background.

My eyes burst open. I look around in excitement, making sure my reaction is normal.

"Security!" the host yells. The DJ stops the music with an erupt scratch of the record. "I said All-American. You know the rules, bitch. Wait your turn."

The crowd laughs and claps. I laugh too. It must have been a gimmick.

"Alright, alright, the fun's over. Let the real show begin."

The lights dim and the music starts. I observe the crowd's reaction, but part of my mind is still on the lookout for a potential Ida sighting. That's when I lock onto someone in the middle of the crowd. The single dimple on her left cheek reminds me of Ida's. Never seen another person with a single dimple. And honestly, that was at the bottom of the list of why Ida was so darn special. Simply unique. Hmm. I continue to observe the person. They indeed only have one dimple. I nudge Rubio. "Peep over there in the crowd. From this angle, doesn't that person look like Ida?" The wavy, curly hair matches. The slim-thick build not quite ready for a grandma's unprovoked you-are-getting-fat comment.

"Dead-ass? A new event just started. Get over her. Ida was awesome. You fucked up, now let's get fucked up and enjoy the show."

I glance back. The Ida look-alike is gone. "Whatever, man." I lightly elbow Rubio in the ribs. "And talk to me nice, bitch." Let's see what this All-American Runway is about.

Striding down the runway is someone in a Black Panther Party outfit, looking like he is about to storm the White House and slap Trump out of the Oval Office.

"My dude looking hard as hell," I say. "Is that really…not a man? I mean, not a straight cis-something man." I pretend to know what I'm talking 'bout. Truth be told, Ida taught me this stuff at one point, but I was never truly listening. Which made it even more of a miracle that we lasted three years. I guess as long as I appeared to be trying, she was okay with that. She would have loved to see me in a place like this. She loves people. Believes in this stuff. I'm still skeptical because, regarding gender, sex, and orientation, somebody has to be delusional. Is it my father, the church, or is it these allies and feminists? I refocus my attention to the stage.

At the end of the runway, the contestant raises a clenched fist. Huey P. Newton couldn't have done it better himself.

I nudge Rubio again. "Yo, I asked you a question."

"Just watch, please. You're distracting me," Rubio says, not bothering to look at me.

Again with that no questions bullshit. I bet someone took the time to teach him this stuff. Instead, he got me out here googling everything.

Another contestant walks on stage wearing a varsity-letterman jacket, denim jeans, and Air Force Ones. They juggle three leather footballs in perfect spirals like I envision Tom Brady would at his kids' Parents' Day. Then they grip one of them and point it towards me. We maintain eye contact one millisecond too long.

Rubio shakes me by my shoulders. "I see you playa-pimp!"

Without warning, the feeling of roaches stampede up my toes, settling on my shoulders, on Rubio's hands.

Keep it cool, Danny. It's not real.

Hombre-hombre o maricón.

Fuck, now I'm hearing my dad's voice. I inhale deeply, then exhale.

Get it together. You are not homophobic or transphobic. You don't want to be those things. Rubio won't win this bet. Esmeralda won't be right about you, either. You are not the trifecta: narcissistic, homophobic, and a womanizer. I inhale and exhale.

I'm good. Back to the show like nothing happened.

The contestant on stage turns around, and I unconsciously peep their ass. The sway of the hips. The jiggle. GROSS! What am I thinking? I grab my head. I'm so fucking confused.

Danny, you are here to get access to Ida's social media. Not to check out culos. Save that energy for another bar. And stop over-reacting.

I exhale.

More and more contestants man-handled the stage. To me, even after the awkward locking of the eyes, none surpassed the letterman jacket one. That contestant had the Chad vibes. Like *he* went backstage, good-job slapped some unsuspecting butts, and towel-whipped some teammate culo; good ol' no-homo fun. And I was right. She or he won. But I hope they don't think they won me over with that football point. But forget about that. The entertained crowd, the comedy, the music, the fierce movements, the intense facial expressions. Who would have thought?

"Rubio, this is aight. Like, real talk. This is like a fashion show. Or cultural exhibition." The best part, no one has hit on me (I'll say it loud and clear, that football point was nothing to see. It was performative. Didn't mean anything. Right?). *And* no tough guys around, mean-mugging me over girls that didn't pay them any attention.

That is the thing about regular parties and events. There is always some dude lurking for some ass. And when I slide through and mack it to the Cinnamon Apple of their eyes, they start party ending brawls. Dique, why you hollering at my girl? Dudes stay trying to fight strangers over a claim over another stranger. But at least here, I feel safe from that. Seems like everyone else is safe from that too. Like a colossal dance circle of death, preventing the creeps from accessing us.

Is this what inclusion means? A space with no predators? I'mma have way too many questions for my Feminist Studies class. All the girls in the class are gonna be like, *Danny, you went to a ball-slash-drag show? Wow, you are so open. Now tongue me down in the make-out stairway!* That would be nice. But then again, if I mention this, I'd have to explain how I got into a twenty-one and over establishment. So scrap that.

Oh, there is the Ida look-alike again. As she turns…the bubble gum lips, the lil' piglet nose that she hates, but I love.

"That's—" I frantically nudge Rubio. "That's Ida! No doubt about it."

Rubio clamps me by my shoulders and shakes me. "What are you talking about? Listen to yourself. You sound crazy, man."

"No time to explain. She's leaving!"

I machete through the dense crowd with no regard for my shoulders, maintaining a visual on Ida.

She leaves out the front entrance.

I follow. I bust out the entrance. There she is, turning the corner. That ass and walk are still as goddess as ever. I give chase and lunge an arm onto her shoulder. "Ida!"

The person turns around, startled. It's not Ida. I stumble backwards to show I mean no harm. I can only imagine how crazy the stranger must think I am.

"My apologies. I thought—what the—" Someone bumps me forward.

Rubio, who I didn't notice had trailed me, grabs me by a bicep, preventing my fall.

"Watch where you're…" The sparkle of the All-American Runway trophy blinds me.

"Danny, is that you?" the person says.

That sweet angelic voice. The one that hides a diablita in the sheets. The one from aquel viejo motel. Why is she holding this trophy?

And.

Why.

Is.

She.

Holding.

A Football?

"So you not gonna say anything?" Gloria says. She turns to Rubio to see if he knows what's wrong with me.

"A-Glory, I'm a huge fan. You absolutely killed it today," Rubio says, shuffling his feet, fan-boying.

"You guys saw me perform?" She/he…*they* happily nods. "I thought I was hallucinating, but it really was you in the crowd. But listen, I'm already thirty minutes late for my night shift. It was nice seeing you, shy boy." Gloria jogs off.

The smell of baked dough from the pizza joint across the street dissipates. The honks, from impatient drivers at the intersection, mute. My penis, full of dormant vigor, has shriveled into a chode.

"You okay?" Rubio says.

"Yes, maybe, sorta."

"Which one is it? You look kinda pale."

"Is. A-Glory. A man? Or a woman?"

"Come on, not again. I already told you that stuff is irrelevant. Treat everyone with human decency, no matter their gender or sexual orientation. Gotta start viewing everyone as simply human."

I impulsively grab him by his polo collar. "Listen, I don't give a fuck. Answer my question." Pins and needles ambush every layer of my skin. My eyes well up as I remember what Rubio told me earlier, "the performers are usually queer men, but this place is kinda lax."

Rubio pushes me off.

I land on a parked car. I forget Rubio can bench-press a lot more than me.

A small crowd forms, and a few phone flashes turn on.

"I don't know what's going on with you, but you're causing a scene. Let's go."

In silence, we walk to Rubio's car, then drive back to his house. It's late for a school night, so I'm sleeping over.

He might have spoken a few words, but the idea that Gloria is, or was a man, noise-cancels the world.

CHAPTER ELEVEN

Rubio's room smells like two dudes. The flamingo button-down from the family barbecue—which I lent him—hangs in his closet, still budding for that gay joke. Dust particles dance in the morning sun's rays; they flutter around me like glitter. There is a mustard yellow bandana knotted on the doorknob that, according to Rubio, depending on the pocket, once signaled to queer men something sexual off the Handkerchief Code—a covert system of non-verbal communication established to protect queer men. That (man's?) vagina that I thoroughly enjoyed; my raspberries soaked in that mimosa. Am I gay? It's a legit question. Like the legit connection I thought I had with Gloria.

"You were just a walk-in dick appointment." That is the reply my angry drunk texts got from her. To be that cold-blooded, she must have once possessed ice-veined cojones. And I want to be angry at that. But, "Women are entitled to sexual exploration," Ida would say whenever a girl at school was labeled a hoe. So I get that she doesn't owe me an explanation. But still. Is Gloria a man or woman? Rubio wouldn't say. Said that is something for Gloria to decide. But I can only assume the worst.

I turn my head up towards Rubio lying on his bed. The air mattress, with its squeaks, announces my movements.

Rubio quickly tosses his headphones to the side. Looks to have been up for a while now. "So, keep it G. How did you like yesterday's show?" Rubio's smile gleams like a toothpaste ad. Couldn't even wait for my freshly opened eyes to de-blur.

Oof, how I wanna grab his smile and use it as a punching bag. Have feathers fly everywhere. But that would make the room even gayer. "Toss me your phone first. How 'bout that?"

"I see someone woke up happy."

I glare at Rubio. Perhaps he meant to say gay.

One new social media post since our breakup: Ida and the guy from the party cheesing hard. Caption: My favorite Primo came to visit [airplane emoji]. Finally, some good news: the guy at the party was just her cousin. But damn. "I did this whole drag night challenge for this?" I mutter. "You know who this primo of Ida is?" I face the phone towards Rubio.

"Oh, that is Primo."

"I know, I just said he is her primo. But who is he?"

"No, his name is actually Primo, and he is also her primo."

A cousin named Cousin, that's too Dominican. Must be from her Italian side, which her mother often boasted about.

"And hey, I thought we bonded last night." Rubio faces the ceiling. Lips puckered out. Arms crossed. "So yesterday was not a waste." He smiles. "You know, I haven't been very forthcoming.

Yesterday was the first time I've been to a ball. I've only read about them and watched videos online."

No wonder he wouldn't answer my questions.

"I'm a straight-passing gay man. That privilege gives me access to hetero spaces, what you call normal society, yet, in a way, alienates me from the LGBTQ community. I'm the most undercover of the gays. A husky so big that I'm confused for a wolf, never seen as a dog." He chuckles. "It was fun to go to a ball with my best friend. I mean, you always drag me to all the straight events. Why can't I drag you to my LGBTQ ones?" Rubio nods to the ceiling. "I felt included in both worlds last night."

Hmm, when he puts it that way, perhaps I was a good friend last night. I don't remember the last time I did something altruistic. Definitely wasn't yesterday though. That was an exchange for social media access.

"You know what? Last night was different. Interesting, yet fun. Now I'm not saying it was my type of scene, but I'd be more than down for other events. It's the least I can do as a friend. I'm not sure I've been a good one to you." Especially if he feels I've been dragging him everywhere. That feeling sucks. Like when my mother used to drag me shopping before Saturday-morning cartoons ended. "But please, let me know what it is ahead of time." I laugh and toss a pillow at Rubio. "No more drag. Let's take baby steps."

Rubio hugs the pillow I threw at him. Happy. "Man, if you would have seen your face when I told you it was a ball." Rubio chuckles. "It looked like someone put a finger in your butt."

I laugh. "Chill, bro."

For almost an hour without break, Rubio divulged his personal identity-crisis, his invisible battles. Occasionally repeating himself, "Treat everyone with human decency because we are humans first. Everything else—gender, sex, orientation—is divide and conquer. Slick ways to decide who is more or less deserving of enjoying life as a human."

It was a contradiction to my father's words. *Hombre-hombre o maricón. Hembra o hembra-macho. Nothing else exists.*

The whole time he ranted, I stared at his Aaron Judge poster. What should matter is what Gloria identifies as. She was born a man, but was always a woman? I saw, felt, and tasted her vagina. It was there, right where it normally is. Like Judge, I hit home runs over Gloria's big-league walls. But a woman is supposed to make a man feel like a man: grandiose, in command, nourished, and alive. Gloria makes me feel…gay. Which is confusing.

There exists nothing more manly than conquering a new woman. Knowing one sperm can spread your seed. Another one of my father's words.

Is Rubio not a man? Surely he is masculine enough. But my uncles would say otherwise. A man's most prized possession, his sperm-filled balls, belongs in a woman. In combination with another man, it's useless. But what happens when our balls stop producing sperm? Do we cease to be men?

And if Gloria is a transexual woman, then that means she got no ovaries. I know because I googled it. I wish to have kids. Surrogate mothers exist, and I can do the manly thing: cheat and have children elsewhere. In the end, similar to what Rubio once said, Gloria's situation does not impede me from becoming a father. But I yearn to fall in love and create something out of it.

Perhaps I've already chosen between my roles; I wish to be a father, but not a husband. Ida had ovaries, and over time, she ended up making me feel less of a man. Even after we named our two future children.

The first, a girl named Autumn, after our favorite season; and for all the men that shall fall at her feet. Of course, like leaves, I will crunch them. The second, a boy named Daniel II, who will grow up to be a better version of me. Better life, better father, better decision-making. He won't repeat mine and my father's mistakes.

What do you think, Aaron Judge? All this dick swingin' has led to too many foul balls. And I know, I know, I shouldn't even be thinking of kids. But ever since my father's death, parenthood has been on my mind. His teachings that live inside my head are his last living remains. They deserve to survive, don't they? If not, he'd just fade away.

"Rubio, help me out. What are the gender classifications?" My mind and heart may be in a bowline knot, but Rubio's non-ceasing smile isn't. "The other day at my family barbecue, one of my cousins asked me if my pink shorts were non-binary. I still have no clue what she meant." Nobody actually said those words, but I figure it's a solid way to make Rubio feel seen.

Rubio laughs. "Let me guess, Rose said that?"

"You already know she be hating." She didn't say it, but she definitely would've if given a chance to add-on to her diss slash greet.

Rubio slaps his twin-sized mattress. "She stays with the witty comments. I love her." Rubio shakes off the last remaining chuckle.

"Okay, get ready because even I get confused. To start, you gotta understand the gender-binary system…"

Perhaps when he is done, he can answer one last question for me: Am I still a man?

CHAPTER TWELVE

Ever since Rubio and I found out that school policy allows for ten unexcused absences a year, we skip school from time to time. Sometimes they call but we've already added the school's number as Spam Likely in our parents' phones. And yesterday was the perfect day to use our first "PTO" day of the year. Plus, Rubio was schooling me all morning about LGBTQ stuff. School is also at home, right? But wow! Rubio was jumping topic to topic, and I don't remember him breathing once. I also used yesterday morning to ask about last week's party, but he said all he remembered was us getting absolutely obliterated. Oh, and also me embarrassingly approaching Ida at one point. Welp, it was Friday though, and I had to report something.

So in the afternoon, I told Esmeralda about how I haven't seen Ida in any of her usual places and how I haven't seen her at school this week either. I was going to tell her about how I thought I saw her last night—you know, work on that communication stuff we talked about—but I was afraid that would open a Pandora's box full of questions that I'm not ready to answer. *Why were you at a ball? You fucked a dude with a vagina?* I'm sure Esmeralda wouldn't ask it that bluntly, but I'd interpret it that way. Then I'd have to explain why I chased an Ida look-alike. Was it my anxiety? My longing for her? A mixture of reality, fantasy, and hope. In either case, I didn't report much. Yet, according to Esmeralda, Detective Hanson was pleased with that report. As the middleman or middle-woman—or perhaps mediator would be my teacher's gender-neutral word choice of the day—Esmeralda didn't question Detective Hanson's approval. She claims to have one job and one job only as my liaison (is that a better word?): to protect me from unintentional self-incrimination. And she did just that. She also said after witnessing the detective's low standard of information, we should break up any new information into crumbs. Keep Detective Hanson nibbling, week to week, for as long as it takes for one of two things: build our Rohypnol defense or graduate. Preferably the defense, because graduation feels a lifetime away. And I'm sure whatever Ida has gotten into can't be any good. That's the only thing I know for sure. Ida must be involved in something criminal for Detective Hanson to have me as an informant. But it also can't be *that* urgent if he has *me* as an informant.

But diablo, it's Saturday—the best day of the week—barely past noon and the bullshit has already started, ended, and started back up again. I went to my part-time job, where I'm basically king. Over the last year, my face has been plaqued high by the storefront so many times that I should be up for a promotion soon. Assistant Manager perhaps. But naaaaaaaa…

The five-time employee of the month clocks into work at noon. The former employee clocks out at noon o'five.

"Fuck you, you, I've never spoken to you before, but fuck you too," I say to ex-coworkers as I walk past the aisles of the shittiest, most undeserving of my talents place on Earth.

"Fuck me?" a customer, shopping in the world's biggest electronics retail scam, says. "What did I do?"

"I don't know yet, but you look like you deserve it." He probably feeds his kids ketchup sandwiches and hotdogs on sliced bread. The type to start a drama series with you, then binge the rest without you. Like he…what am I doing? That guy is struggling to get by. Look at him comparing twenty-four-inch televisions—at that size, might as well buy a tablet.

I stride back towards the manager's office and strike the doorknob with my best UFC roundhouse kick.

"What the heck?" The manager launches backwards in her rolling chair, hitting the wall. "You want me to call the cops?"

"Earlier, when I moped out of this dusty, smelly office, I forgot to tell you something."

She sniffs around the cramped office, still paying me half-attention. "I don't smell any—"

I lift one leg, and machine-gun out a string of farts. "Eat that." I dust out of the office. I'm sure that communicated my thoughts well. Esmeralda would be proud.

Behind me, I hear her say, "You see, this is why men are trash."

Trash or not, God only knew how much I needed this job and how much *we* needed it. Extensive work hours and tighter budgets were the price Mom and I agreed to, to escape the constant Pit Bull barks, emergency sirens, alternate-side parking, and dembow boinging out of old subwoofers at three in the morning. I've been scared to check my credit card too. All those cheap tequila shots. Now I walk out of here with nothing but a fading image of the new girl's ass. It's the least she owes me after getting me fired. Nobody told her to be so thick.

When the manager pulled up the video of me training her the other day, it appeared like I was harassing her. I admit, it did look a little sketch. But chill, it's not like I grabbed it. I was simply enjoying the view. What else was I supposed to do? Not look at her ass? It was right in front of me, completely unavoidable. She exercises day-in and day-out to build and maintain a body like that. She didn't seem to mind. But no, the self-righteous protector of female booties says it's sexual harassment. What a scam.

How the heck the manager even get that video? The store doesn't have shelf-level cameras. This shit was a fucking setup. Just like me pissing on the school entrance. I bet the manager took the video herself. *All men are trash*, huh? That ideology and her pixie-cut only say one thing, *I get no penis, not even on Tinder*. She blamed the playa, not the game. Tsk tsk.

But man, that felt good. It took a day, but I finally did it. I peeped a girl's ass without wondering if she was a transsexual. Because how the heck would I even know?

Hypothetically, my coworker with the booty could have been one, too. There is foul play going on these days. Is it even foul play? Like Rubio said, nobody *has* to announce their sexual orientation, so why would they have to reveal their gender or sex? What's the approach? It's not like I can go around looking up skirts, inspecting parts. And even if I like what I see, it could be another Gloria. Yooooooo, I'm sick. This is bullshit. But then again, women get surgery all the time for their butts, hips, and tits. Is that foul play too? I mean, it looks nice. Although original is my flavor of choice.

Do I just stop looking at butts? It is kinda pervy now that I think about it. The fact that I can solve my current existential crisis by being less pervy, less manly. Yet that option feels impossible. I love big butts and I cannot lie.

I need motha-fuckin' help. And I think Ida was that help—my North Star, as Esmeralda nicely put it. When I was with her pretending to be a man she liked, I never stressed about any of these things. But that's the thing. I know I was a better person when I was with Ida, acting all saint-like, but it was uncomfortable. Just didn't feel like me after a while. Which is ironic because sucio-me is what got me to pretend to be saint-me in the first place.

My phone vibrates.

Ha! I knew once I walked out the front entrance, Pixie-Cut would call me right back. I'm the best employee she ever managed. I slide my phone out of my pocket. Lame. It's Esmeralda.

"Hey butt head, you still at work, right?"

Butt head? How she know I was looking at butts? I look around the parking lot, then behind me at the double-door entrance. "Yeah, kinda."

"So as part of your defense, I was thinking we get an affidavit from your boss, stating your multiple employee of the month awards and your overall performance and conduct. That, along with an official transcript highlighting your GPA, will shed good light on your character. Simply put, it's to further assert that a model-employee and outstanding student would never commit the crimes that you committed, unless they were drugged."

"Not bad, not bad."

"At minimum, I think we can convince a jury that it was a mistake. A momentary lapse of judgement by a responsible individual who consistently shows a great work ethic and focus in school."

"Okay, okay. I like it." Although I don't exactly focus. My mind tends to hoard information on its own. It's easy to recall things I see and overhear. Another reason why the party incident is bugging me. I've never blacked out like that before. Then again, I've never been roofied till that day. My blood pressure skyrockets at the thought. WHO. THE FUCK. ROOFIED ME? At the realization that it would be almost impossible to figure that out, the question dissipates as quickly as it arose. The person obviously wasn't caught in the act and has gotten away with it.

"Alright, so request that affidavit. I say give your boss a deadline of a week or two. That way they can write it up and get it notarized without rushing. Capisce?"

"What if I can't?" Rather say my request was denied than admit that I got fired for admiring a coworker's ass. If that isn't one of the dumbest reasons to get fired, I don't know what is. Esmeralda would think even less of me—which is not much at this point.

"Why wouldn't they?" Esmeralda says in a mocking tone.

"Well, let's say I just quit."

"Well, let's say you didn't." Her tone rises with annoyance. "Where is this resistance coming from? Just ask your boss and that's it. And if you don't want to mention the case, say it's for, I don't know, immigration papers or something."

"But na, let's just say I actually did just quit…"

"Did you or did you not?"

"I didn't…technically."

"Danny! Stop testing my patience."

"I was fired." I wince, anticipating the cocotazo she wishes she could give me. I can visualize it now. A pristine knuckle flying out of my phone, slamming down on the back of my dome.

Esmeralda says nothing for five seconds.

I look at my phone to make sure she is still on the line.

"Send me the address. I'll talk to your manager. We'll change that termination of employment into a voluntary resignation. You won't like it, but I know someone who can get you a job ASAP. We will spin it as you resigned for another opportunity."

"Whatever it takes," a feeling of guilt speaks for me.

By the evening of my firing, Esmeralda had already set me up with a night-gig at a chicken patty processing plant. Something I never knew existed. It starts tonight, Monday, which means I need to take advantage of this extra-credit opportunity for Feminist Studies. Esmeralda claimed she would put me in jail herself if my grades falter too. And it's the class that is giving me the most problems.

The class contradicts everything my father ever taught me. So many new definitions, history, laws, and more. I can keep up with my other classes. Sleep will suck for the time being, but *you gotta do what you gotta do.* My mother taught me that. And not by saying it, but by living it. For that reason, she approved of this night-gig on school nights. She thinks the job pays more, but it's the same minimum wage (Esmeralda is giving me the extra two dollars an hour, out of pocket). Also, I'm legally an adult, and the mortgage is only two months out the bank womb.

Second Floor, Room 219. "Two for two-spirited. Nineteen for the Nineteenth Amendment," I mutter to myself, my way of studying on the move. Alright, this is it. I can't believe I'm attending this. Allies for All, straight students committed to learning about and supporting the LGBTQ community. I push the door open.

Mr. Greene, Mr. Greene, Mr. Greene, you sly fox. There are enough girls in here to fill up an intimate yoga session. Now I gotta take a front-row seat and appear astute, as dictated by the thirsty-dude paradox: a man sitting in the back of a female-majority room, counter-productively, makes women feel uncomfortable because everyone knows whoever sits in the back got ulterior motives, like the student that doesn't want to get picked on or is looking to nap undetected…or in this situation, the creepy dude who is trying to see some peeking-panties and tramp-stamps. Instead, sit in the front and be the last to leave. Peep all the culos exit.

"Excuse me, is this seat taken?" I say to the cutie with the sign-in sheet on her desk.

"No, not at all." She gestures for me to sit. "I've never seen you here before. This your first meeting?"

As I sit, I notice the thickness of her thighs. The seat has pressed them wide. Her jeans struggle to contain them. I bet she never finds jeans that fit both her thighs and ass. She seems tall too, but I also bet it's the extra padding that has her torso elevated. Her thighs and ass, her very own booster seat. Type of lap that would make every mall-Santa envious.

"I don't know." I lick my lips. "If I had been here before, would you have noticed?"

She laughs. "Let's bring that down a notch, Prince Royce. Look around. We don't get many guy attendees. Jeez, but nice try." She rolls her eyes.

Challenge accepted…ah, what am I talking 'bout. With expulsion, Ida, and my manhood all in limbo, another distraction won't help. I literally just got fired for my perversions. "By the way, my name is Daniel, but call me Danny." I extend a handshake.

"I'm Vicky, thanks for coming." From the ruggedness of her hands, I infer she has peeled a plátano or two in her lifetime.

"What brings you here? If you don't mind me asking," Vicky says.

Extra credit…and the pervasive question, *Am I still a man?* Better yet, *Was Gloria once a skilled urinal user?* The answer to that answers the first question. Because isn't a transgender woman just a confused man? My father made it a sport to point at all the *hombre-hembras*, when he suspected it. *Divos* is what he would call them. A play on the word diva.

"I got this friend, who confided in me enough to tell me he is gay. I realize that I've dragged him around to—quote unquote—straight events, but I've never participated in his world. And my other friends don't exactly agree with his kind, *if you know what I mean.*" I pause to study her reaction, hoping that she registers that

I'm not that type of guy to abandon a friend over his orientation. The type of guy that has a chance with her. "So, I'm here to learn how to be there for him. To support him. To be a better friend."

Was that my heart's honesty or my penis's slick-talk? Either way, I'mma have to thank Rubio for that one. Beats saying I'm here for extra credit. Perhaps I'm here to kill three birds with one stone. *Three: Article 3 of the Universal Declaration of Human Rights says, "Everyone has the right to life, liberty and security of person."* The last part is what we discussed in class.

"Thank you for your honesty. Sounds like there might be more to you than sweet-talking." Vicky chuckles. "I believe you are in the right place, but lesson one: there is only one kind, and that's humankind."

I smile and nod. Rubio would definitely agree. You know what, challenge not accepted. I didn't come here for the girls. And Rubio will not be right. I do *not* think with my penis too much.

Vicky looks at her phone and sighs. She stands and faces the attendees.

Let me not look below her neck because my peripherals are begging to show me…WOW. She is instantly on the I-would-hit list.

"Thank you, everyone, for coming. Unfortunately, today's guest speaker can't make it. But as usual, when a guest speaker cancels, we conduct an open forum. So, who would like to start?" she says.

Nobody raises their hands.

She fidgets her fingers, and after avoiding eye contact with everyone, her eyes latch onto mine, the closest person to her. "Daniel, would you like to go first?"

No. "Umm…what do I need to do?"

"Well, if you got any questions or anything to share related to the LGBTQ+ community, you share with the room. It can literally be anything."

"Uh…okay."

"Okay, everyone, this is Daniel, and this is his first meeting, so let's make him feel welcomed."

I stand, lift my jeans, and apply ChapStick.

The room claps.

What are they clapping for? Are they clapping because my name is Daniel? Because I managed to stand without falling? Because they can't see my boxer-briefs anymore? Because my lips aren't chapped? Because I'm soon to be the first person at this meeting to ask a dumb question?

"Yes, that's me, I'm Daniel, but y'all can call me Danny." I look beyond the back row, the safe zone for my nervousness.

Shit, should I ask? It would be too wild. "Umm…" I clear my throat. Damn, I should have sat in the back.

Vicky leans in for a whisper. "This is an inclusive environment. Feel free to ask anything, even if it may sound silly. None of us are experts. And we specifically asked for no teachers, so that no one can be judged or get in trouble. Ignorance is an opportunity to learn, it's not something we laugh at."

"Anything?" I whisper back, signaling with my eyes that she may regret her words.

She leans in again, this time covering her mouth. "Yes, now say something. You look like a little bitch up here—oops, I didn't mean that." She pats my back, nudging me forward.

Damn, she OD aggressive for no reason. I stand tall, regaining my previous position. Fuck it, she said I can ask anything. "So…" I clear my throat again and pace the front of the room. "I was thinking the other day," I pause my step, "and I think a lot." I walk in between the aisles like Mr. Greene would.

A few girls in the back laugh.

I glare at them. Probably freshmen.

"Ignore that, Danny. Keep going," Vicky says.

I pace. "By the way, I'm straight." I stick my palms up, the universal stop-sign for assumptions. "Just in case anyone was wondering."

The same girls in the back laugh again.

"Aight, what's so funny?" I tilt my head down towards them.

"You are such a…guy. That's the best way I can put it, and it's—I can't believe this is actually possible—refreshingly funny. I apologize, please continue," one of the girls says.

I'm such a guy? A man? You know what, I am. No matter what happened with Gloria. I'm still a guy…not a gay. Yet, I still gotta ask. "So I was thinking," I continue walking through the aisles, "if a straight man, like me, were to *for-ni-cate* with a transsexual woman, would that straight man be considered…gay?" I jab my head out as if the word gay was a taboo, the Lord Voldemort of sexual orientations.

Everyone bounces wide-eyed glances at each other. Must have said something wrong.

"Wait-wait-wait, let me rephrase that. Would dating someone that used to be a man make someone like me gay? I'm asking for a friend." Shit, that last add-on sounds even more suspicious.

The windows noticeably vibrate from the laughs, and the floor earthquakes from the smacking of the desks. Vicky played me; this laughter is not inclusion.

I grab my phone off my desk and head towards the exit.

"Wait!" Vicky says. "I think everyone here is just confused about your question. Don't leave. Don't you want your question answered?"

I inhale deeply. *I'll stay, but only because the laughing has convinced me to accept the challenge of having sex with you. I'mma get my revenge.* WHOA. I can't believe I'd think that. I've thought those words before, but now they feel strange, odd…creepy. Am I a creep?

"Listen, I'm just confused. Do we accept people for who they are now, or for who they were before?" I sit down. Is ol' Danny a creep? Is there even a new Danny?

Vicky fist-bumps me and smiles with her mouth sealed. Likely thinking, *Wow, this guy is a clown and a creep. No way he is getting between my thighs. But it's not like he was thinking it, because Danny is not like most guys. He doesn't think with his penis.* Yep, that's not me.

"Alright, anyone want to take a hack at Danny's question?"

Out of the nine girls that populate the room, only one doesn't raise their hand.

"Oh wow, that's a lot of hands. For the sake of time, let's do two. If you really feel like your response is a good one, keep your hands up."

All the hands extend even higher.

Vicky looks at me. "How 'bout we let Danny choose?"

"You." I point to one of the girls who laughed at me. "And

you." I point at the girl with the purple lipstick, the most likely to be an undercover freak-nasty.

"Your question is like asking, if my ex-boyfriend, after our relationship is over, gets a sex change, would I be a lesbian? Even when my relations with that ex is one-hundred percent over?" She shrugs. "We live in the present, not the past or future. What once was, is not what is. And vice versa. Don't expect perfectionism from humans. We all change."

Okay-okay, I like it. So far, that means I'm not gay.

"So Danny, what do you think? Any rebuttal?" Vicky says.

I think she exonerated me. I'm not guilty of a gay act. "I sorta get it. It's like the whole Bruce-Caitlyn thing, right? Kris didn't choose to stay with Caitlyn because Caitlyn was once Bruce. Nor is Kris now a lesbian because of Caitlyn's sex-change."

"That actually made sense. I think you get my point. By the way, I get the whole name-change thing, but how do you pick a whole new middle-name?" the girl who laughed at me says.

"Word. Mad random, right?" someone mutters.

"Let's not get off topic, please," Vicky says. "Next reply."

"Isn't a transsexual woman, simply a woman? The transsexual label is a heteronormative construct," the most likely to be an undercover freak-nasty says.

What the heck does heteronormative even mean? I don't think we've covered that in class.

"A transsexual woman is a woman. That's all she is. Doesn't matter if she had a penis before. I don't suspect anyone undergoes such a dangerous procedure that costs a ginormous emotional and psychological toll unless they truly believed they were born in the wrong body. Now, of course, someone may undergo it to escape the law or something, but I like to think that ninety-nine percent of the time, the sex-change is completed in good faith. That transsexual woman was always a woman, stuck in a man's body."

So Gloria is indeed a woman? By that logic, a gay man remains a man because he indeed is a man. No need for a sex change because they were born in the correct body. Rubio is a man. *Hombre-hombre.*

"But what if I want kids?" I interrupt. "Isn't motherhood an essential part of being a woman?"

"You asked about sex, not starting a whole family with the woman."

The room, again, shakes in laughter.

"Not marriage, not friendship, or anything else. But I assume the *man* that you mentioned—" She pauses to dribble her eyes at me.

No one else notices, so I don't bother to defend her correct accusation.

"—had sex with her because he was attracted to her. Now, if you are having sex because you are trying to trap someone into a future, that's on you. I hope she was a future sports star, musician, or actor. I know I would. I'm not trying to file taxes. Like ever." She chuckles.

"I'd be the first to admit, I've had sex with another person for much less than attraction," an attendee says. "A bitch got hormones. Sometimes it's a football player. Sometimes it's a chess player."

Jesus. She open as hell. Open as in sharing her TMI—not her vagina. Or maybe that too. Whatever. I'm not judging. Football players, chess players…can it sometimes be *me*, too?

"You can say that again," another attendee says.

A few laughs follow.

"I love that we can be open and laugh about these things, but I think Danny's question is an interesting one," Vicky says. "Does motherhood define a woman?" She glances around the room. "At our age—fifteen, seventeen—I'm sure a Latina grandmother has harassed some of us with the when-are-you-giving-me-great-grandkids question. If giving birth was a criterion, what happens to the women that cannot birth children?" She directs her question to me. "I feel like the standards for becoming a man are a lot easier. Let me ask you this. What if *you* can't have kids, because—I don't know, low sperm count, testicular cancer or something? Would you cease to be a man?"

"I don't know." I tilt my head and ponder. I don't have kids now, and I think I'm a man. One, I'm not a virgin. Two, I have a job. Three, I like girls. The only thing I'm slacking on is the two-girlfriend quota. "I really don't know. If I apply the logic that motherhood defines a woman, then fatherhood should also define a man. On a scientific level, a man with no sperm is a non-essential employee. The logic is there, but something about that doesn't feel right." Interesting. Again, what happens to men that get old and can't ejaculate anymore? So much emphasis on something we lose through time.

I've never really thought about it much. I simply watch other men be men, and by doing so, I know what it is to be a man. But fatherhood? There are a lot of men with kids that don't act like fathers. Didn't make them any less manly. Damn, I'm stumped again, like in Feminist Studies.

For the rest of the open forum, my questions hijacked the meeting. In the end, I found more questions than answers. Yet, the room's unified clap at the conclusion of the meeting lifted me on its shoulders. Perhaps this is my pivotal point of transition—between the Danny that was and the Danny that is—and the room celebrated it. Either way, I'm electrified with curiosity…or perhaps it's a rainbow that has colored inside me.

"You know what, Danny, maybe you have been here before," Vicky smirks. "Great job today."

"Wait up, Daniel, I mean Danny." The sound of thighs rubbing swiftly together bounces off the lockers that sandwich the dim after-school hallways. Vicky jogs towards me. "You left so fast, I didn't get a chance to thank you."

"For what?"

"For contributing. These meetings can get monotonous at times. Honestly, guys like you—good looking, ladies' man—are not too supportive. You saw the demographics. Looked like a gay guy with all his girlies—"

"*Chilll*—" I stop, realizing that it was kinda true. Also realizing that gay is not an actual insult. It just triggers me for some reason. But to think lesser of the word is to think lesser of Rubio. I won't do that.

"Your participation may be what our club needs. A different voice."

"*My* participation?"

"Not exactly. No offense. What I mean is, we need more male students to participate and bring up their questions. I realize that this is a tricky topic for most boys and men," she says confidently, as if she knows what it is to be a man. Wait, is she a transsexual too? "It's confusing. You're raised one way, told that it's a man's world, and you participate in it as if the fairy tales are true."

I nod out of courtesy. The only time I've witnessed a woman prevail is my mother. But she is the exception. And I'm not beat to start another debate. "Yeah, I guess that's true."

"And to be honest, I don't know what I'd do if I had a boyfriend who was born in a female body. But I know one thing, I wouldn't harm or diminish him. Which brings me to my next point," Vicky says. "You are the only one who determines how you feel and perceive the world. We all have some wild thoughts. But know that your actions and thoughts are two different things. And your actions determine if you are an Ally or not."

Wild thoughts? If only she knew that every pulse in me wants to press her against these lockers. Slide my thumb into her jean's belt loops and pin her hips. Wiggle a leg between her thunderous thighs, forcing a gap like a bachata dance. Get her to gitty-up on it a little. Get her to tip-toe a bit. And…shit! I'm getting hard. I swing my book bag off my back and position it over my crotch. I unzip it, pretending to make sure I have all my books. While my penis attempts to unzip itself out of my pants and aaaaahhhhhhh!

LeBron James's feet. LeBron James's feet. The mental image calms my hormones.

"*So*…you're not gonna say anything?"

"Oh, um. Thanks for that. I'm trying to be better." Am I really? I think I still love Ida, but I'm spying on her. I think I'm a man, but my recent sexcapade with Gloria puts that in doubt. Rubio is my best friend, but I'm only now seeing him for who he is. And I'm now seeing who I truly am. I'm a son of a mujeriego.

"Good." She glances behind her, then faces me again. "So, see you next week?"

"Can I continue to ask wild questions?" I smile.

"Uh, we can afford to be a bit less provocative." Vicky chuckles. "See you next week." She thigh-rubs away in the opposite direction as me. Even as she gets further away, the outline of her plump cheeks remains visible, like two moons in the night sky. Damn, that ass fat. As she said, it's my actions, not my thoughts. And my thoughts…*bruh*…can't help to be fresco.

You know what, I will come to another meeting. Beats lying in bed, thinking about a transsexual woman, Ida, being roofied, and jail. Plus, Vicky is fine—interesting is a better word.

I tuck my boner up against my belt, sling my book bag on my back again, and stiffly walk out of school.

The confused breeze, slapping me from each direction. The leaves dancing and swirling in private tornados. It's only mid-September, but the leaves have started to fall.

Outside of the school, my phone vibrates. Rubio.

Not now. I press ignore. Too much to think about. Too much to decipher. Too much to understand. I've been sitting on the school front steps for a while now. Just being.

He calls again.

What does he want?

"Yerrr. Guess what, I found some interesting deets about Ida—"

"Spill it," I sharply say.

"Talk to me nice, bro."

Oh my God. *This* guy. I exhale forcefully. His human decency, respectful bullshit is getting overboard. But I'll play along. "What's up, Rubi Rubes?"

"C'mon man, I thought we agreed to drop that nickname in middle school." He smacks his lips. "But aight. The reason we haven't seen Ida in school is not because she on an extended vacay or something. It's because she is not enrolled. She is being home-schooled."

That doesn't sound like an Ida move at all. And her parents are not the type to agree to such a plan. They love this town. Her mother sat on the School Board for years. Both born and raised in Hawk Union. 'Cept they did have beef with the principal becoming the mayor.

"And who said this?" I say. I need as much information as I can get. This is gold.

"One of Ida's friends. The giggly one."

The one that bull rushed at me in the hallway.

"She said you keep ducking her. So she passed the message along to me. She also said—"

Whoa-whoa-whoa. Who *the fuck* is that? High-tailing across

the street towards the high school, wearing a ninja costume: black hoodie, black sweatpants, and black sneakers. All of my senses lock onto the ninja. I hide behind a nearby light pole. Not the best hiding spot, but it covers part of me.

Into the school, the person goes.

"Yerrrr. Yoooo. What's going on?" Rubio says.

Whatever the ninja doing, there gotta be some chisme behind it. I hang up.

I rush into the building. First floor hallway, nobody. Our school is H-shaped, so if they are on the other side, they would've come down this side first. Second floor, nobody. I rush up the steps, again. Third floor. By my locker.

"AYO! What you doing by my locker?"

The ninja, startled, slips something into the locker's air duct or whatever those slits in the metal are for. And rushes off.

Panting, catching my breath, I walk towards my locker. "What the heck is going on with this school?" I mutter to myself. "Glad this is my last year. 'Cause God damn, people getting weird."

I open my locker. A note slips out.

A strong scent of Ida's favorite perfume, Zara's Pink Flambé, enchants the note. She wore it every time we met up.

I dial Esmeralda. It rings.

Pick up.

My foot jackhammers into the checkered red and black linoleum floor.

It rings again.

PICK. UP. You always on tu maldita phone.

It rings a third time.

"What you want?" Esmeralda says, annoyed as usual.

"Listen, I don't know what's up with Ida, but I just saw her dashing like Prancer and Blitzen in a Black Power Ranger, Black Panther-esque outfit. I think I heard her trip, but she must have popped up like the karate dudes in the movies and pimp-jogged away—the echoes of her strides were inconsistent. You should have seen her. She had her hoodie scrounged up, tied tight; only her eyes, nose, and lips were visible, like a fucking raccoon. *Sly Cooper*. But I know it was her. Are you listening?"

"You smoked laced-hookah?" Esmeralda says in her big sister voice. "Lay off those hookah pens. You never truly know what's in them."

"Ah hah, you weren't listening."

"No, that's not it. You told me what happened like a 3AM infomercial," Esmeralda says. "Everything sounded too good to be true. Slow down and make it digestible."

"Too good? And yo, I ain't repeating myself. Point is, Ida pulled up on me like a stick-up boy and left me a note in my locker. Something ain't right. She might need a crack-intervention or something. We need to save her."

"A note? What it say?"

"Are you listening? Ida is bonkers."

"I heard you the first time. But I need all the details so I can chop it into crumbs and finesse it to Detective Hanson for a couple weeks."

How is she so objective about this all? So calm and mission oriented.

The note says:

Dear Danny,

It has been a long few months without you. I still think about those long studious nights when you would surprise me with Banana Honey milkshakes from Tops Diner. As well as the monthly basket assorted with my favorite dark chocolates when I was on my period. How you strangely knew how to do knotless box-braids and would protest to be little spoon every once in a while. I miss watching you play video games with good storylines (not the gory shooting-ones, I still hate those) and how you used to rub my feet as we watched my drama-filled high-school TV series. You always seemed to like them more than I did. I miss how you always tried. I remember when you made me breakfast in bed that one weekend your mom was away and I lied to my parents, claiming to be at Cynthia's. Two honey buns with scrambled eggs in between, LOL. Point blank, I miss you. If you miss me too, meet me at the Wawa's by the mall at midnight Friday.

Love you more and most (ha, I win!),

Your Ida Frida
PS - I didn't know you were into drag!

Drag?

Does she know about Gloria?

"You see! I told you that box-braiding is a valuable skill, not just for women. And you thought it was just a line an older sister uses to manipulate younger siblings to do her hair. Your future daughter will be fortunate," Esmeralda says. "And *wooow*. So being in love is what it takes for you to be decent. She basically described a whole new Danny. Interesting."

"Maaan, it ain't even like that. I was pretending so that I could get some A1 ass. Plus, I treat a queen like a queen. Tis all." Oh boy, here comes the *you're-so-soft-body lil' bro.*

"Yeah-yeah, say what you want. Treating a woman right is a harder task than you think. Takes a strong man." She pauses. "Either way, this is great news. The meetup is huge. It can potentially set you free from Detective Hanson's hold. Friday, I will report that you saw Ida in an all-black outfit. If there are cameras around, he'll easily be able to confirm it. Also, he'll likely witness her place the note too. So we will say that the meetup is two weeks from now. We've been blessed with three weeks' worth of stalling. Which we may not even need if the Friday meetup proves fruitful."

Friday night…our reunion. On *Ida's* request, not mine. Suddenly I feel like I jumped through a gold star in *Mario Bros.* Invincible. *She* wants *me* to meet with her. She might want me back!

That whole ninja thing was just her being shy. This is the best thing that's happened to me in months. Maybe the only thing. Something doesn't feel right, though.

My Ida Frida misses me, and all I can do is snitch on her whereabouts.

Shit! I work Friday night.

CHAPTER THIRTEEN

Two days have passed, and I still haven't schemed a way to get out of Friday's shift. I *need*-need this money, but I also *need*-need to meet up with Ida. Welp, it's Wednesday, and the bomb is ticking. During tonight's shift, I gotta put something in motion. I got to.

I take a deep whiff. I won't smell fresh air again—if we can call Jersey air fresh—till I clock out. I scan my badge into the factory.

And there it goes, the now becoming familiar feeling of embarrassment cloaks me. Happens every time I step foot in here. Potential Salutatorian working in a chicken patty processing factory. With all these people that may or may not have a GED. But I remind myself of my mother's words, "Muchacho del diablo! A degree, like money and other pieces of paper, does not make you a better person than those without." Those were her words after I got my first college acceptance letter and started acting brand new. She humbled me real quick. I guess it was her way of saying what Rubio and Vicky said about humankind and human decency.

More humbling is that many of my coworkers believe they made it. Like how my aunts and uncles brag about their jobs when they call back to DR. Whether they are janitors, housekeepers, landscapers, or bodegueros, they've managed to uplift themselves from the worser form of poverty that awaited them in their homeland. Because you best believe, poor in America is nothing like being poor in DR. So I get it. They've made it in life. Still, I don't have that initial starting point to make me feel good about this job. It for sure will never appear on my resume. No matter if it pays the bills at the end of the month. I just wish my boss would give me Friday night off, though. But I just started, and it's not like I can say, *Hey, my ex wants to meet up behind Wawa on Friday, I need the night off.*

"Danny, you have a noviecita?" my coworker, Tijera, says as she plucks an odd-shaped chicken patty off the conveyor belt. (Yep, that's the job. Quality assurance, the fancy title for it. Me and Tijera work in tandem, standing along the final section of the conveyor belt, tossing out any chicken patty that appears aesthetically faulty.)

Tijera steps closer to me. Her short stature and wide back make her waddle more than walk. "A handsome boy like you always has a girlfriend."

"I have an ex-girlfriend, if that counts."

"Handsome boys like you always have that too." Tijera laughs. Her laughs always end in a sorrowful sigh. Like laughter is her break from life, and when it ends, she clocks back into reality. "My daughter has a boyfriend, and he seems a little sneaky. I don't know, something is off."

"Sneaky? That's very vague. What is it about him?"

"That's the thing, the reason for why is also very sneaky." Tijera plucks another odd-shaped patty, but it slips out of her hand. "Ay chingao! That's the third one today."

More like the eighth. On my first day, she was plucking them like piñata candy. Today, deformed patties avoid her like Whack-a-Mole.

"Sit down. Let me exercise my youthful hands while you explain to me what's going on." I point at the single chair allocated to us for brief breaks.

"Youthful hands, lazy minds. You better not mess up, Danny. Or it will be both our jobs."

"Relax, I got this. I've been helping my mother pay the bills since I was twelve." I pluck two patties like a Western double-pistol duel. "You saw that?" I blow my index fingers, rotate my wrists, and slide them into the imaginary gun-holster on my hip.

"Meh, that was…okay." Tijera leans her head forward to inspect the patties. "At your age, I could have done that with my feet." She starts a chuckle, but it dies prematurely.

"So tell me, what has this boyfriend done? Do you think he is cheating on her? Is he lying about liking your cooking?"

Tijera slides up on the chair and playfully slaps my hip. "Never, you payaso. All my recipes are over a hundred years old. Not like the crap we make here. I'm going to bring you some food one day, you gonna see."

Golazo! I pat my stomach. "I can always eat. But tell me about this boyfriend. Maybe I can help."

"Can you?" She leans in closer, ready to smile.

Only if you can help me out on Friday is what I want to say but let me not make my intentions known just yet. I'll ride along for the chisme.

"Whatever you need, Tijera." I've only known her for two days but she is cool peoples. Something familiar about her.

"To start, he reminds me of my husband." She stares at the ground, gripping her plastic gloves and hairnet.

"That can't be so bad, right? Your husband is the man you love."

"No, it's the worst. The man I love was him before he became my husband. When we were just niñitos who dreamt about the impossibilities of life. The man that became my husband lives in a different time era. In Mexico, he was like all the other husbands—a man that could provide survival for una mujercita like me—and I was okay with that. I needed him to survive in Mexico, and I thought a man providing for a woman was love. But since we immigrated here twenty years ago, he has been the opposite. Nothing to do with him, but in the US, I can work and buy my own things. I no longer need him to handle everything. Yet, he never changed. His views on marriage and women are still in Mexico and mine are here." She lifts her head. "The boyfriend is American-born, but I see a lot of Mexico in him."

"So what you're saying is that you are a time traveler?"

"What? No. That's a silly thing to say," Tijera says.

"No, check this out. Mexico, I assume, is like other Latin American countries, like my mother's native Dominican Republic. I remember reading an article for class that said femicide is high—and sadly, normal—in those countries. And women die for things that make no sense to me. Some are killed because they own land, even in places where female land ownership is legal. The men don't accept it. In the US, though, women fought for those rights over fifty years ago. In other words, when you immigrated from Mexico to the US, you skipped an entire generation of progressive movements. Mexico today is very much like the US decades ago. You get it?" I say.

"Are you saying I didn't earn the rights that American women fought for?" She anchors her hands on her rusting hips. "I get enough of that from the gringos. I don't need Latinos to say the same."

"No, not at all. What I'm saying is, your husband may as well be living in 1940 US, while you are in the present-day US. Get it? He lives with outdated ideas of marriage that are not compatible with today's American culture." Oof! Mr. Greene would be crazy impressed by my use of his teachings. On the first day of class, he talked about us all living with the norms of different time periods. I understand it now.

"Ay, you really confusing me. Say it again, but differently."

"Your daughter's boyfriend—whether American-born or not— was raised by Mexican parents to be a Mexican man. He believes he owns your daughter because that's the Mexican norm. And sadly, your daughter likely accepts that because…" Am I really going to tell Tijera that her acceptance of her husband's behavior is partially responsible for her daughter's situation? "Because…"

Tijera's eyes open wide. "No, that's not what I meant. I get that whole machismo thing, but I don't understand why you keep using the words, earned and future." Tijera braces her hand on her bulky knee. Staying too long in any position results in her aches and flare-ups. "Women don't *earn* the human rights that men hoard for themselves; we force them to hand over what was rightfully ours to start with. It's the pendejos running the world that think equality is something to be given, like monthly rations. You've ever seen an IV at the hospital?"

Before I can reply, she continues. "Picture that IV as all the things men have deprived us of, and the patient, women. Every decade, it drips a little. And every decade, we are given back a little more dignity."

Damn, the imagery. If she puts it that way, that's harsh.

"I can't believe it took half of my life for me to realize that. And the US may be a safer place for me and my daughter, but this is not the future. American men allow women to work because they care more about money than equality. Dual-income families mean more," Tijera rubs her thumbs with her middle and index fingers, "chelitos, chavo, mula. This isn't the future; this is more like American men found a better way to milk our cenos dry. Look at mine. They sag."

I glance at her breasts, but the thought of wrinkled nipples repels my eyes back towards the conveyor belt. I'm not up for conspiracy theories, but her words at least sound logical. Men let women into the workforce in order to bring more money into the household? "Interesting point."

"Move over, you let a bad one pass." Tijera bumps me over half a step.

"So what are you going to do about this boyfriend? You're surely not going to let your daughter keep dating him."

"My daughter is eighteen, not much I can do. By sixteen, I was already married. I don't govern her life anymore. Also, she needs to hurry up and give me nietos. In a couple of years, my knees won't let me play hide-n-seek. But you did say you wanted to help…"

"Whoa. Tijera, I'm not ready to have kids. I can talk to her or something."

She playfully slaps my arm. "Oh stop it, that's not what I meant by it. But since you said you were willing to talk to her…" Tijera looks away to gather herself. "We can be like Don Quixote's Lotorio. I'll hire you to seduce mi hija, but instead of running off with her, you just need to make her boyfriend jealous enough to break up with her. We'll be as sneaky as him." Tijera slaps her leg in excitement.

I chuckle until I realize she is serious about this plan.

Tijera snatches three patties in one swoop. "You see that?" Tijera pretends to lift a bazooka on her shoulder. She flips the bazooka's scope open, pulls the trigger, and jerks back from the recoil. "Ka-Pow."

I wonder if Ida's mom thought the same about me; *Ida, Danny seems sneaky. He is too Dominican.* What did she expect, though? I was raised by Dominicans. Destined to cheat on Ida.

Or maybe it was, *Ida, Danny seems sneaky. He is too much of a Libra.* I dated a Cancer once. She requested my phone remain visible at all times because apparently, Libras like to dabble in polygamy when the seasons change. Dique, I was bound to howl more on equinoxes and solstices. Never again did I dare date a girl who believed in horoscopes.

But am I too Dominican? So many years of my uncles reliving their playboy youths through me. Always asking how many girlfriends I had. Now I'm definitely not my cousin Broncaulio. That guy is Dominican-Dominican. But maybe even a little Dominican is too Dominican. I still remember my first catcall. What a day.

Mas Flow 2 was on repeat, the window rolled down, the slow down leading to the quick acceleration, and a thrill more heart attacking than the steepest of rollercoaster dips.

A month before my mother's unemployment benefits were up, she received a same-day interview and left nine-year-old me in the care of a seventeen-year-old cousin—the closest thing to an adult available midday. She gave him ten bucks to pay for my lunch. What for? I had to earn that back.

Once my mother was out of sight, we hopped into his old-gold '95 Toyota Corolla with black horizontal lines on the sides, a hand-me-down from his father. That junk huffed and puffed to the gas station like *The Little Engine That Could*. He spent the whole ten dollars on gas, speeding through yellow lights and stopping at his friends' houses for quick conversations.

After his rounds, at his boredom's peak, he asked if I had a little girlfriend. I never talked about girls, so I felt uncomfortable—half my friends still thought girls were oversized male ribs.

"You see that one right there?" He pointed. "Tell her something."

"Like what?"

"You know, something to make her feel sexy. Watch this." He

rolled down his window and hollered, "*Dammmn* beautiful, you too fly to be walking. How 'bout I give you a ride?" He sped off after she ignored him, unfazed by her rejection. "You see that? Too easy. Now let's see what you got." He pointed at an approaching teenager.

I gulped. My mouth sewn shut by fear; not a single word squeaked out.

"You must be gay then."

"No, I'm not," I refuted the claim with the quickness. The year prior, my father forced me to kiss a girl. So I knew I wasn't gay.

"Aight, you see that one with the stroller? Let's see if you *really* gay or not."

"Diablo mami, tú eres como un bacalao…te vez bien afeitao', muah," I said with my pre-pube' voice. It was something I heard Tío-Primo Martín say that one time he dropped me off at school.

Even though I butchered the pickup line, my cousin gave me a standing ovation. He wanted me to do it again and again. He laughed harder each time. I thought he was going to break the steering wheel with how hard he was slapping it.

That day, I was promoted to the big leagues. I hollered at five more unsuspecting women, each time less nervous. It was exciting, new, and manly. And what boy didn't want to become a man as soon as possible? The title of man is not earned by age; it is earned with other men's approval.

After, my cousin rewarded me with an iced-tea bucket and an egg roll from the Chinese-food restaurant. Not even close to a ten-dollar lunch.

By fourteen, catcalling outside car windows was child's play. I leveled-up to catcalling in front of my apartment building. My favorite was when the girls giggled, even though they were trying their best to hold it in. A close second was when a white girl had lost her way and made it onto the block. I would hit them with English, so the immigrant ol' heads thought I was killing it. It turns out the white girls were never lost. My old neighborhood gentrified three years later.

But man, I hated when they ignored me. Like damn ma, you see me. All I said was, *Let me talk to you for a sec*. Don't gotta be rude. I'm human too.

I was such a Class-A womanizer, Ida would say. She straightened me out. She knocked some of that Dominican out of me. Hopefully, I still got enough left. Me and Tijera settled on a deal: woo her daughter on a date (that Tijera has set up for tomorrow), and Tijera will cover for me tomorrow (while on the date) and Friday (while I meet up with Ida).

CHAPTER FOURTEEN

My date with Tijera's daughter is at 6PM, so I knew my mother wouldn't expect me home during my work hours. But *dammmmn* lady, at least act like you missed me. We haven't seen much of each other this week. By the time she gets out of work, I'm already on my way to my shift. And by the time I get back around 10PM, she is already in her room, ready for sleep.

"Explain to me why you're not at work? And even if you're off, why aren't you at Rubio's or at the park playing basketball? This is not like you. The sun is still up. So something else has to be up too," my mother rambles. She claims that since seventh grade, I've never once returned home before sundown. Which is likely true, gotta ball-up as much as possible before it gets too cold out.

"Calm down, I'm out once I figure out what shirt to wear. The Uber is already on its way." I swipe through my closet, halting at the shirt Ida bought me last summer, but I never wore because it was hella sus: short-sleeve button down, one side pink, the other baby blue. "I got a date tonight and I really need to impress." If the Mexican-American boyfriend is too manly, then I gotta be just manly enough. The pink and baby blue neutralize each other out.

"Perfect! Now that you found it, leave before…you got a date? Better be with Ida." She cocks her hand back. "It. Better. Be with Ida. I'm not playing la estúpida no more. I won't tolerate another one of your little cueritos like the one at the barbecue. Now leave before you're late." She aggressively nudges me out of my room.

"Ma!" I laugh, while resisting her push enough to stop at the staircase. "What is up with you?" I moonwalk away from the steps and spin around. "For your information, my date is not with Ida. It's with—"

She smacks the wall, leans on it, and pops her hip out for dramatics. If Captain Morgan ever made a Latina edition, I'm convinced it would be a woman in this exact pose. She turns her head to a family portrait hanging on the wall: just the two of us. "Coño, Danny, she should've been in this picture one day." Her fingers press into the wall before making a fist. Her face scrunches and scrambles through expressions of anger and disappointment, settling on the expression of motherhood. The face she makes when she questions if she raised *me* to be the way I am. "You know how many family recipes I've taught her? You think—"

I place my hands on her shoulders and gently shake her. "I miss Ida too. This date is just practice to get her back." I look into her eyes. "I'm even wearing the shirt she bought me. Same one I'mma wear tomorrow, when I convince her to go on a date with me."

"Mijo." My mother lets out a deep sigh, tilts her head, and

kisses the top of my hand, which remained on her shoulder. "Okay, Danny." She nods a few times. "I see I raised a liar. You think I didn't call Ida after the breakup? You cheated on her, you mother-flower." She wrenches me into a headlock and grinds her knuckles into my skull. "You said she changed after the summer started. And that you made the tough decision to break up. Who said you can lie to me?" She rubs harder. "Who taught you to lie to your mother, you mojon-del-diablo?"

I imagine this is therapeutic for her, letting out all her frustrations. Probably wishing I was Ida's Danny. The Danny from all the times Ida would come over and acted like a saint to impress her. The Danny that would volunteer to clean the apartment. All those dishes I washed, pretending to be the best son in the world.

"Okay, okay, my bad," I say.

She lets go of her hold.

I fix the button-down onto my shoulders and button it up. From the corner of my eye, I see my mother is not done. She shuffles her feet and changes position a few times until I give in and look.

"So…what do you think?" She steals my line and flirtatiously shows off her attire.

With all the violence, I hardly noticed her little get-up.

Looking like the Caribbean Erykah Badu. Hair still rolled up in a Dominican tubi, signaling today is a special occasion. Red spaghetti-strap summer dress with all my favorite fruits: papaya, mango, guava, and passion fruit. The dress hangs down just above her ankles, showing off her new coral ankle bracelet. Fingers and toes coated in an orangey mango-yellow. Scratch that, she looks like a lunch lady at a school dance, hairnet and everything. Although she still looks good for her mid-forties, perhaps not Halle Berry but definitely a runner-up, I am inclined to not gas her up.

"You look okay." I pretend to proceed downstairs, taking one step down.

"Excuse me. Where do you think you're going? You didn't even look." She flings a chancleta at me in annoyance. Nothing irks her more than an uninterested critique, her disappointed reaction reminds me that my opinion matters more than anyone else's.

"You look beautiful, Ma. Who you trying to look good for? You know I'm the only man in your life."

"Yeah, and you hardly that. But now that you mention it." She twirls, her dress showing off its colors. "Maybe I should find myself a man." Her eyes shy towards the wall. She trails a finger down the family portrait. "We may have to update this picture." The softest of sighs trails out of her smile.

"Yeah, right. *And you may need to update your empanada recipe to include raisins.* Two updates we don't need nor want," I say.

The doorbell rings.

"Hurry up! Use the backdoor." She nudges me down the stairs.

"What? Ma. What is wrong with you? Ma, stop pushing me. Who is at the door?"

She slides the backdoor open. "Have fun on your date." She shuts the door and hastily locks it.

"Oh, hell naw," I mutter to myself. Rushing to the front yard, I catch a glimpse of a man with a bouquet of roses stepping into the house.

My mother pokes her head out of the door to see where I'm at. *Go, leave*, she mouths, before shutting the door.

"What the fuck is going on here?"

An Uber notification pings my phone. Shit, driver is here. I'll handle this when I get back.

My father and uncles' vetted wisdom was correct; mistreatment, neglect, and superiority are the way to a woman's heart. It's always been that way—Ida being an exception. I should have shown up at the date, which Tijera marketed as new guy in town has no friends his age, like a tiguerazo. But no. Feminist Studies, Allies for All, Rubio, all had me thinking that respectfulness and human decency was what everyone needed. It's clearly not what everyone wanted.

I took Tijera's daughter to eat authentic Italian food from a spot that appeared on the Food Network. Yelp reviews were off the charts. She hated it. A pack of Nutella-filled churros would have satisfied her more.

I held every door for her. Pulled out her chair. Made sure to never place my elbows on the table. Never held the knife unless cutting. Made sure my legs were never opened too wide. Didn't slurp one spaghetti. And it was a shame I didn't, because the food was banging.

I ordered the fruitiest drink on the menu, a pineapple-mango juice with an umbrella, to signal I'm not one of those guys that claim to know what's manly or not. I told her I'm so accepting of people that I went to a drag show. Showed off my gay best friend, Rubio. I even paid the bill while she went off to the restroom to avoid the awkward battle for it.

Told her how much I loved Mexican food: Oaxaca cheese and chapulines. Loved the music: Natalia Lafourcade and Ana Gabriel. The historical sites: El Zócalo and the statue from *La Rosa de Guadalupe*'s intro, a telenovela I watched with my mother.

Then I told her how much I loved my mother and how she raised me as a single-mother, Superwoman. How, unlike most men, I learned to cook, clean, and do my own laundry at a young age (all facts). How I worked various under-the-counter jobs during middle school to help her manage rent. The Feminist Studies course I'm taking. The fact that I've made first honor-roll so many times that I've already received early-acceptance letters from various undergrad programs, one in Los Angeles, where I hear the tacos are bomb.

All while she didn't have much to say at all. She was dull, shy, or maybe I talked too damn much! Fuck.

Anyway, her ass was flat. Wide but flat. Two pancakes aligned side by side like a Venn diagram. And like ol'Danny, I'm back to dissing for no reason. I shake my head. Poor girl agreed to go on a friendly date, and I bombarded her with a TED Talk on why I'm a great person and why every woman should dump their current boyfriend to date me.

Welp. At least I know the shirt wasn't the issue. She actually said it was nice when we met in front of the restaurant. I took that as flirting. But nope. She was being nice.

What-to-do, what-to-do? I didn't fulfill my side of the bargain. May Tijera have mercy on me tomorrow.

~

Last night, after the date, I sent Tijera a text on WhatsApp, asking if she would still cover for me tonight, but oddly I got a "who's this?" reply. Why she do me dirty like that? It's definitely her phone number. We exchanged details for the date on it. So I have no clue if she'll cover for me, yet I have no choice. I can't miss this meetup with Ida.

Hence I'm in the Uber to Wawa. This time I requested no music. Instead, I ran romantic gestures with the male driver, who was highly entertained. We agreed that I should go with one of three options:

A, <u>a poem</u>:
Ida, your name rhymes with vida,
That must be why,
I can't live with neitha.

B, <u>an all or nothing</u>:
When in doubt, whip it out. Her note stated everything she missed about me, but she forgot the D. I need to remind her.

C, <u>plead the Fifth</u>:
Act like nothing happened, and hope she has forgotten about it or got over it to the point that the thought of me cheating on her is tucked deep away in a distant memory.

Before this mess, I was going to admit my wrongdoing. Tell her she was right and how foolish I was to cheat in order to fit in with the fellas. My summer was cold without her. I may not deserve a woman like her, but she deserved an apology. The real reason I went to that party in the first place. But the Roofie Bandit threw me off course. As well as her walking in with Primo.

I envisioned my entire life with Ida: old age, electric lift chairs, and life-alert buttons all over the house. It was as if when I dialed my dream future back to the present, I stumbled onto my future mid-life crisis. I thought I was supposed to experience puppy love in high school. Not full-fledged, once-in-a-lifetime, corta-vena if we break up, type of love.

"I wouldn't respect myself as a woman if I got back with you," she said.

Have her take me back and still feel like a woman, I knew where to start: a genuine apology. But how do I apologize? And how do I do it now, after months?

Estimated arrival, two minutes—three months too late.

CHAPTER FIFTEEN

I've never eaten a Wawa sandwich sober, but then again, I've never been to Wawa to meet up with a girl. Ida doesn't even like sandwiches, something about a gluten allergy. What a scam. It never bothered her when she scarfed them 5.99 two-topping pizzas. She rarely left me a slice. Where is she, though? The potholes on Route 7 slowed my Uber down, but I'm here on time.

I step further into the parking lot. My breaths billow out like Black&Mild exhales. A passenger van in an adjacent parking lot puffs with me; its dying engine shivers in the cold. The flickering light poles have been abandoned by most of the spring and summer birds. Only pigeons and aging birds, too fragile for distant travel, remain. The irony. Coldest night in September since 1912, such an odd statistic to remember, the backdrop of our meetup. Our love has gone cold, and the love that remains is scant. The parked passenger van lawnmowers away.

Okay, Ida. You know I hate being alone in open spaces. I pace back and forth, keeping a keen eye on the parking lot activity.

Plastic bags fly like kites and abandoned carts, surprisingly, are better parked than city folk.

…I should have showed up on Latino time.

SKRRRRT.

An Astrovan screeches into the parking lot, nearly hitting me from behind.

Could this be her? I pause my step, check my breath, and peek at the side-mirrors to catch a glimpse of the driver. I side-step to get a better angle.

Ida rolls down the window. "Hey, sorry I'm late. Hop in before you get sick."

My fingers tremble, my knees buckle, and every other part of my body feels detached from me. It could be the cold's numbness, or it could be Ida. I can't process anything. An Astrovan, Ida wearing the same black hoodie, and…I'm still in love with her? My heart is knocking to kiss her. To taste her. I knew I still loved her, but I didn't know I still loved-her loved-her. But she is here. Really here.

I tuck my hands into my armpits. I have the will to move, but fight-or-flight has taken possession of my legs.

"Get in, silly." She smiles.

I hope she has a hand-truck in the back because I'm like a Four Lokos right now; heart on a thousand, but my body is in full depressant mode.

And that smile. Its ability to brighten anyone's day and stun people in awe is still her superpower. I just wanna squeeze it and shake her in a rage of love.

"Don't tell me you're upset that I'm a few minutes late." She puts on a pouty face.

The face I can never be mad at for too long. My kryptonite.

"Hello, Danny. *Hello, Ida.* So nice to see you. *I'm happy you contacted me.* Now get in." She chuckles and blushes.

Long-awaited hellos are awkward. I'm typically Stefan Urquelle, but tonight Steve Urkel showed up. As soon as I regain composure, I scuttle to the passenger-side and grip the door handle. I yank, but it doesn't budge.

"Still the same ol' Danny. Instead of just asking me if the door is open, brute force is your first solution."

Is the car door open? Who would ask such a question? Does the new guy entertaining her in my absence ask such questions? Should I start asking such questions?

"Yeah-yeah, good one. Open up."

"You not going to say please?"

Is she…flirting with me? "As funny as ever, I see."

Option B is out the window, my dick is likely shriveled from the cold. Option A or Option C.

"Ida…"

She waits for me to continue.

"Your name rhymes with vida…"

"What? Boy, get inside." She laughs. "What kinda silly statement was that?" She reaches over and hands me a styrofoam cup. "Before you get in," she raises her own cup, "let's take a shot."

Oh snap, Ida trying to get loose. Perhaps Option B is still an option after all.

I look into my cup. Vodka? Oh, she trying to get loose off the

Goose. I chuckle. "This is so random." I shake my head and look at the clear liquid in my cup. "Bottoms up!"

Okay, that was definitely not vodka. Not even Ron Blanco. Maybe not even liquor at all. Water with salt? Holy Water!? I cough. "Damn Ida, what you give me?"

"Something to get your inhibitions down. I got a surprise for you." Ida bites her bottom lip. "Open the side door."

"It better be unlocked." I air out my shirt to cool off the burning tingle. I hope she notices it. I need her to know that I understood the assignment. That this meetup was serious.

The car-locks thump up.

I take a deep breath. "Open sesame." I slug the side-door open.

This. Bitch. "Ayo Jaslene, what are you doing here? Don't you know anyone else whose life needs complicating? And why it smell like Newport 100s back here? Ida, what's going on?"

"You never hit me up after the barbecue, so I decided to deliver my 'nani to you." Jaslene blows me a smooch. "And for the record, I complicated your cousin Broncaulio's life. He loved it. Talked about not going back to DR so that he can be with me."

I'm sure he said that. I'm also sure he didn't mean it. The uglier the Dominican, the better game he spits. Broncaulio is a lot of ugly and a lot of game.

"Ida, what's going on? Why is she here?"

"Don't you see the mattress?" Ida says.

I stick my head into the van. A twin-sized mattress lies on the van floor. Threesome? Imagine that. Never had one before. This would be *epiiiiiic*. I jerk my head back to reality. Na, this some ol' Danny mistake waiting to happen.

Ida hops out the van and walks to my side. She places a gentle hand on my back. We look into each other's eyes.

"Maybe if we would have cheated on each other, together, at the same time, it would have worked out better." Ida nudges me into the van.

I don't see how that makes sense, but…fuck it. This is her idea, not mine. I dive onto the mattress.

CHAPTER SIXTEEN

"Wake up, sleepy dick," Jaslene says.

The room spins and spins. My breaths loud and crisp, like something dragged across sand. It's blackout-curtains dark.

"You want some wet-wet, huh?" she says. "How does that feel?"

A warm stream drips off my middle and index fingers—the drops echo around me. No matter how much I try, I can't move them.

"How does this smell?" she says.

A rank fishy-smell parks above my upper lip.

"Smells like a vaginal infection, but don't get shy on me now. It never stopped me," I say.

…

"Yer, you still there? Jaslene? Bitch?" Women always respond to bitch. Easiest way to rile them up. "Ayo, bitch," I repeat with my best DMX impersonation. "Ayo, relax!" The second easiest way to rile a woman up.

A groggy haze overcasts between my eyes. My body aches.

Man, did these girls fuck me to sleep? The last thing I remember was hopping into the van. My bitch-ass must have tapped out. Now everything feels so dream-like. This can't be euphoria.

"You know I always find out," Ida says.

"What the—"

"Time to really get even," Ida says.

"Chill, Ida, it's not that deep," I say. "Jaslene was simply asking me a few questions. I didn't want to be rude, so I answered back. You-you know ghetto-fab is not my type. You the only one that can pull off hood and sophisticated."

Below my torso, something snip-snip-snips. A scissor? "AYO! Stop playing. What are you planning to do with that?" Anxiety invites fire ants to bite away at my nerve endings. A castrated man is not a man.

"Help," I yell, but no one responds.

"Help!" I yell again, but my voice doesn't vocalize.

...

What the heck is going on?

Could this be one of them nightmares, where my mind wakes up too soon, leaving my body paralyzed?

Wake up. Wake up. Wake up.

Cold water smacks my face like a facial cleanser commercial. So much water that it feels like slow motion. I involuntarily jerk forward and gasp for air. My heart races. Goosebumps harvest out of every pore.

In front of me, three dark figures stand side by side. From the right, a burning torch enters the darkness. It lends its flame leftward to another torch, illuminating Jaslene's face.

Jaslene lends her flame leftward to a torch directly in front of me, illuminating Ida's face.

Ida lends her flame to a third torch, illuminating Gloria's face.

What is this, *Inception*? My next dream, a creative *your one-night stand, pretend-sidepiece, and ex-girlfriend walk into a bar dressed as Little Red Riding Hoods* joke? Halloween parties don't start for at least two and a half weeks.

"You three chauvinists have been summoned as tributes for Jaslene Fuentes, Ida Monterey, and Gloria Cadena's initiation into the proud sisterhood of Daughters of Achelous," a voice behind me says. "Let the initiation begin."

I laugh. I would dream of a sorority. The name is kinda weak though. Isn't Achelous the Greek god of some river? He's also the father of the Sirens, I think. Okay, makes more sense now. Original. This is for sure a dream. Even fabricated last names for Jaslene and Gloria. And who the heck is a chauvinist? I turn to my left.

Eldon? I think this is the first time I've seen Eldon not in a party. It's Friday night too. This guy should be hosting a Hawk Union banger right now. And what's with the gag? Are those balls resting on his chin? Holy shit, that's a dildo in his mouth.

I quickly turn to my right. My cousin, Broncaulio, also with a dildo in his mouth, dances his eyebrows at me.

I look down past my nose.

What-the-fuck. What-the-fuck. What-the-fuck.

WAKE.

UP.

WAKE. UP. IDIOT.

I frantically fling my weight in all directions but barely muster a movement.

One by one, the dildos, drenched in our saliva, are unclipped at our necks and slipped out of our mouths.

"Guess y'all wanted more than just the tip," Jaslene says. "Oof, especially my little freak, Broncaulio. He nibbled on it."

Laughter within the darkness surrounds us.

"Loco." Broncaulio squirms in excitement. The saliva that had pooled on the edges of his mouth drizzles outward. "We about to have an orgy!" He looks around excitedly, squinting into the darkness. "Can't wait to tell my boys in DR! Wait, ain't that the blanquita from the barbecue? You won't get mad if I—"

"Shut. Up," Jaslene says. She dildo-slaps Broncaulio across the face.

Broncaulio's smile widens. A dog in front of a bone. No matter how many fake tosses, his tail waggles like a high-speed windshield wiper.

"Wake up, wake up, wake up," I mumble.

Ida cocks her hand back with the dildo in hand. "If you don't shut up…"

I gulp.

"This isn't a dream, you cheating bastard," Ida says.

I look down at my soaked chest. Water still drips from my chin. Ropes snaked around my wrists, sanded wood at my palms. My feet feel distant. Perhaps asleep. If this really isn't a dream, how would Gloria, Jaslene, and Ida's presence be explained? Only a brain could invent such a coincidence. Not to mention, strap-on dildos.

"Eldon, Eldon, Eldon. People describe you as Jamaican dude, throws all the bangers in Hawk Union," Gloria says. "Surprisingly, you are worse than these two knuckleheads." She sighs. "But for everyone's information, he throws more than just bangers. He likes to get girls drunk, too. Isn't that right, Eldon?"

"No. No. I only provide the liquor. I've told you this already," Eldon says. He lying on his dick. Eldon be scheming for the popola. By midnight, he usually got his arm slung around a drunk girl. Hmm, I wonder if he knows who roofied me? It *was* his party. Shit, it could have been him!

Gloria dildo-slaps Eldon on his ear. Saliva from the dildo whips onto my face. A droplet dribbles into my mouth.

Eldon yells in pain. "That was my eardrum, you bitch."

The droplet tastes like…ass. Not like real booty, but as in the universal description of something that tastes like…ass. I spit out. Wait. I've never tasted something so vividly disgusting in a dream before.

Gloria strikes Eldon again, this time tomahawking down on his coconut. "How many times do we have to hit y'all until y'all get the message? When grown women are talking, little boys remain silent." Those blows had to hurt. After all, Gloria was once a man (I think).

"Hit me," I yell. I've never felt pain in a dream.

Jaslene, Ida, and Gloria each toss a dildo at me.

As the dildos bounce off my face, leaving blotches of saliva, the pain inflicted confirms that this indeed is reality.

"That's enough. Put the dildos back on them," a voice behind me says. "Unless the tributes agree to hush up."

I hastily nod in rapid successions, hoping that the other two will follow my lead.

"Time to officially begin. From here on out, silence and discipline are required," the voice says. Her footsteps approach from behind. A flame briefly heats the nape of my neck as she passes by me. "Daughters, it's been a long journey to get to this point. You three have proven trustworthy, capable, and fierce; your tributes are evidence of this. Many others have failed. Some even risked our identities. But like always, we, the women of DOA, Daughters of Achelous, prevail. Because of your hard work, our mission to end machismo has progressed a bit further. Tonight, the war gains three additional Sirens. And loses three breeders of inequality. Your toughest test is upon you. Don't feel pity for these womanizers and chauvinists. Believe us, the world will be a safer place for women without them."

"Sisters, guide us with your radiance," Gloria, Ida, and Jaslene chant.

In unison, boot-steps encircle the room. Flames spark around us, illuminating more robed women.

Broncaulio loudly exhales.

I know what he is thinking: even if this was an orgy, no amount of Red Bull, Gatorade, Five-Hour Energies, and Henny would be enough for us to split up twenty-plus girls in one night. This must be something else.

"You were made for this. You can do it. Sí se puede," Broncaulio whispers to his crotch.

Shit. We're fucked.

CHAPTER SEVENTEEN

I've figured it out.

One, fall backward.

Two, transition into a backward roll as the wooden chair shambles into splinters.

Three, muscle through the sisterhood circle of flames like a running back at the goal line.

Four, the trickiest step, feel for a cool draft because that's where the exit must be.

Five, run through that exit like it's the last day of school.

Six, don't turn around if Eldon or Broncaulio scream. Every man for himself.

Okay, Danny. Let's do this. You a beast. A tiger. A man.

One.

Two.

…

Two and a half.

Okay, okay, let's start backward.

Three.

Two.

One.

A projector is flicked on.

Spiders scurry off webs that drape over a white bedsheet that serves as a screen.

Step-in-step, Ida and Jaslene march off from in front of us and halt next to Broncaulio. Besides the immediate circle and screen, I can't see much. There are loose blades of grass scattered on the floor. A feint scent of…goat? Horse? And judging by the size and high-positioning of the white sheet, the ceiling gotta be high.

"First, we have Eldon, my tribute," Gloria says. A headshot of Eldon and a list of accusations appear on the bedsheet. "Intoxicating women, hosting parties with strict 2:1 *queens*-to-*fuck-boy* ratios, and assaulting women on the dance floor."

"Any words in your defense?" Ida and Jaslene chant.

"I'm innocent," Eldon scoffs and looks around in confusion. "I never force women to drink. We all know, less guys equals less fights. I try to host parties, not royal rumbles. And lastly, I'm Jamaican. That's how we dance, you bomboclaat. We boom-boom on that poom-poom. Nothing is meant by it."

Gloria takes a few steps toward the bedsheet, turns around, sprints toward Eldon, and dropkicks his crotch.

I flinch—a mixture of dust and blades of grass blasts past my legs. From the sound of it, Eldon toppled backward in one compact motion. And now I'm in full survival mode. Flinging my weight everywhere. I need to get the heck out of here! But again, the chair doesn't move.

"How is that boom-boom for your poom-poom?" Gloria says

as she dusts her sides off.

Eldon thrashes around, drowning in pain. He can't breathe.

Shit, my plan won't work. It really-really won't work. The chair didn't even creak, but I can't say the same about his wood. I heard something. Shit, I felt something. After that blow, his face, wrinkled in agony, looks fifty years older—likely pleading with a higher being for a merciful death.

What the heck can they have on me? "Listen-listen-listen, I know it's not my turn yet, but I just want to say that I'm a new man. And I've changed since my breakup with Ida. Don't judge me on my past actions, as those actions do not represent the Danny of today. Danny would never, ever, not in another lifetime, make the same decisions."

"Oh, yeah?" someone out of my line of sight says. "Repeat that again."

"I said—"

From behind, mid enunciation, a dildo is shoved into my mouth—the click of the fastener vibrates in my ears.

"I think you're right. The Danny of the past would never have a dildo in his mouth." She giggles for a moment before returning to character. "And stop referring to yourself in the third person." She snuffs my head to the side. "Just makes you sound silly. Sirens, continue."

All those butts I've looked at over the years—gotta be over a million. The sexist banter that I engaged in with the fellas—*that's what she said* jokes aren't even that funny. I won't lie, when I saw the spiderwebs and how dusty this place was, I questioned how in a room full of twenty-plus women, none grabbed a broom or a vacuum. But I quickly rephrased that to, in this room full of twenty-plus people—because that is what Rubio would want me to think.

Just give me time. I'm starting to understand.

Gloria clicks to the next slide, a video of Eldon picking up a girl by her thighs, sitting her on his shoulders, and motor-boating her coochie before WWE-slamming her onto a beat-up couch.

"I went to one of your little parties. Let me tell you what happened," Gloria says. "To start, it smelled like sweaty feet in that basement. Do you even bother to clean the place before guests arrive? Would it cost you to get a few dollar-store fans?"

"Look around, this place in worse condition," Eldon says with an annoyed temper. "Smells like shit." That acute rage that crops up when someone asks you if you are sleeping, while you *were* sleeping. "And of course it would cost me. Isn't that what happens when you buy something? You pay a cost."

Gloria dildo-slaps Eldon. "The attitude, tone it down."

I frantically shake my head at him. He really trying to get us smoked, clapped, dusted, coffined, circumcised, or neutered.

Eldon notices my disapproval. "I apologize. I'll be more respectful." Eldon spits on the floor and communicates *this some bullshit* with his glare.

Can't believe my disapproval reached his common sense before Gloria's dildo-slaps did.

"So, it smelled like a locker room after a county track meet. I get it. You are gross. But that is, like," Gloria puts her hand on her chin, "number one-hundred and two on the list of gross things I experienced at the party.

"Fourteen, that's how many times I watched you squeeze past girls at your party. Now I'm not talking about, let me squeeze into the crowded bus type of squeeze. I'm talking about crotch on butt, hand on waist." Gloria squints in confusion. "Why? Why do you have to sexually harass women to walk past them?

"Nine, that's the number of times I watched you seize a girl's hand to dance. You know you can use words to ask someone to dance? If people snatched each other's hands every time they want to ask a question or get someone's attention, it would be so awkward." Gloria chuckles. "Toddlers do that.

"Six, that's the number of times I heard you round up the single ladies for shots." Gloria clears her throat. "*Ayo ladies, if your man at home playing PlayStation instead of treating you like the queens you are, or you plain ol' single, and trying to get turnt, it's shot time.*" Gloria tosses her hands up. "But you don't force girls to drink, right? You just encourage them to. Why did you need them to drink so much? Not once, not twice, but six times. Pfft, you didn't even offer the good stuff. And when some refused shots, you harassed them until they did."

Dang, Gloria is good. She hit the switch on her vocal cords and used her man-voice to impersonate Eldon.

Eldon always was a bit shady. Ida told me that she heard from a friend's friend that Eldon fills up empty Cuervo and Grey Goose bottles with cheaper alternatives. Pretty slick because I can never tell the difference between tequilas and vodkas. It's probably why we never got too-too along. Simply struck me as desperate—someone who did the most for some pupusa…or beef patty. Someone who may roofie someone…

"But that is not the worst thing I saw at that party," Gloria says. She clicks to the next slide: another video.

Eldon and a friend stand at the corner of the room, looking into the party crowd. Eldon, with his lips, points at two girls standing beside each other. His friend nods in approval. They then snake through the crowd and start a conversation with the ladies, but they position themselves in a way that forces the girls to have their backs to each other. Slowly, the two girls are separated. The one girl with Eldon turns around and looks for her friend, but she is already nowhere to be found.

Gloria fast-forwards the video.

Eldon's friend takes shots with the girl. At the same time, Eldon remains with the other girl, who is still seen occasionally looking around for her friend.

Gloria fast-forwards the video again.

In the darkest corner of the party, Eldon's friend is tonguing the girl's neck down. Slobbering on it like corn on the cob. Like a Mexican street vendor's elote. End of clip.

"Can you explain what happened in the video?" Gloria says.

"My boy got cuffed in the middle of the party. He owes me twenty dollars for that now. And I'm compounding interest on his payment."

This guy is ridiculous. They just told his dumbass to drop the attitude. By the time they get to me, they gonna be on a short fuse. One slip up, and it's **KABOOM** for me. I'mma be **BOMB**-oclaat for-real for-real.

I turn to Broncaulio. His eyes are closed, and by the movement of his lips, it looks like he on his second set of ten Hail Marys.

"You know what it looks like to me?" Gloria says. "It looks like y'all finessed a little divide-and-conquer." She stomps her foot onto the edge of Eldon's seat, between his thighs.

I can't help but look deep into her lunging position, wondering if a penis will slip out. I purse my lips and focus. I'm an idiot. I know she doesn't have one.

Eldon looks down, shaking. Even his 'locks tremble.

"Let me tell you something about me and my girls. When we go out, before we even arrive at the spot, we designate a responsible friend for the night. That friend agrees to be the designated driver. Agrees to take our phone away if one of us is tempted to text an ex-boyfriend or girlfriend. And essentially cock-blocks anybody that we wouldn't mess with when sober. I realize that I'm speaking for myself and my girls, but from the video, I think they had a similar arrangement in place. You distracted the responsible friend while your friend worked on the other. How can I tell? The girl you distracted had a water bottle in hand and was very attentive of her friend. You two just happened to be better at your little system than they were at theirs." Gloria pushes her foot off the chair and stands tall.

Ayyy, I see you. That was some solid detective work right there. And the camera work? She got better angles than an ESPN replay.

Eldon trifled with the wrong one. I knew some dudes be desperate, but that whole football play he ran is wild-disgusting. I shake my head. Scheming on girls is WACK!

"What you shaking your head at?" Gloria says. "I'm sure your ex-boss liked the video I sent her."

I look straight forward into the outer circle and stare into a flame. Evil, that's what she is. That bitch got me fired! And if she made that video, I don't want to know what other videos she may have. Our night together? Play by play, touch by touch, lick by lick. Ida will hate me forever. But damn, can't even be supportive before I die. These women ain't playing. Eldon is a sleazeball, and Broncaulio is Broncaulio. But me, I'll admit, I'm a bit misguided. Which is nothing to kill me for. (Do they plan to kill us?) It wasn't like I cheated on Ida with any malicious intent. I was being a man.

"Excellent work, Gloria. Next up, we have Jaslene."

Jaslene steps forward, makes a sharp right, then a sharp left. She exchanges spots with Gloria.

"I'm not good with slides, so I only made one." Jaslene clicks.

A picture of Broncaulio slamming a domino on a dominoes table…I jut forward to get a better look. It's me on the other side.

Is there anything these women haven't captured?

CHAPTER EIGHTEEN

"First, I'd like to thank Danny. What a headache you were. All fine and sexy, I was trying to have your babies from the moment you stepped out of that Uber. All nervous and shit. It was so cute." Jaslene clasps her hands. "Shrink you and blanket you under my pussy lips type of cute. You led me on, too. Told me you hoped to see me inside. Called me Bella. I was wit' the shits, but then you went inside and hollered at every girl in the damn party. How you think I felt, huh? Then you leave the party with some hoochie in a hooptie. Drove off to *I don't know where* to do *I don't know what*. So I followed the cheese."

Damn, Jaslene was a cigarette-fea!? Hoochie in a hooptie? Is that how I got to the high school?

"Overheard you mention a family party, so I pulled up. This time I knew to be more aggressive. Your manly butt is just so… ARGH…cheesy bread-like. No matter how many times I tried to diet, I had to grab it. And slap it. But *nooo*, here comes this white girl." Jaslene looks at Gloria. "You's a bad bitch. I forgive you. Just wish I would've known you was joining too."

Gloria crosses her hands over her heart and mouths, *I'm so sorry, boo.*

"Then this clown walked in." She points at Broncaulio. "There isn't much to say about him besides his perverted charm. He ain't no Danny, but he must have memorized every bachata and salsa lyric ever sung because he wouldn't stop flattering me. In all honesty, he might be the most respectful one out of the three tributes."

She is definitely buggin' with that statement. Broncaulio is the most sexually-optimistic pervert I know. Watch him at church one Sunday and you'll catch the father hesitate to hand him the sacramental bread because of all the choir girls he's tried to holla at.

Broncaulio finishes one last Hail Mary, looks up and grins. "Showtime, baby." He looks around. "What's with the picture? Hey, is that me? That's us at the barbecue." He devilishly smirks at me. "You remember that pela I gave you?"

A dildo is shoved into Broncaulio's mouth. He keeps talking, although no one can make out his words.

"Broncaulio doesn't put up a front. From the start, he told me he wanted the 'nani. And although I'd like to believe that I am the world's prettiest and most breathtaking angel in heaven, I know his game and flattery is patronizing. He views women as totos to be conquered in his kiss-and-tell stories. This picture is proof. It may look like a regular dominoes game, but it is far from it."

Jaslene is right. That was not a regular dominoes game.

"In this picture, these two bozos are playing for the rights to…"

～

After I snuck in that dance with Gloria, Broncaulio pounced on Jaslene. Made her a colorful cocktail with an umbrella—which he must have brought with him—and whisked her away from my grasp. Without my permission, he set up my stashed hookah—which, moments later, I gave away to him, after my mother asked whose it was.

"I see you met my cousin," I said while straining my eyes on Broncaulio.

To start, how he even know that Jaslene wasn't a cousin of ours? I know he approached her. Jaslene hadn't moved from that chair since she last harassed me. Or perhaps he didn't care.

"En verdad verdad, Broncaulio is super chill. He is a gentleman, funny, and very attentive." Jaslene fake-coughed. "You know he got an ATV in the Dominican Republic?"

An ATV? Broncaulio can barely afford gas for his moped.

"Yeah, it's dope. I did a backflip on it once," Broncaulio said. "Tell her." He winked at me.

"Oh, really?" Jaslene said. Impressed by his Meek Mill stunt.

Broncaulio winked at me again.

He really tried to woo her with some X Games feats. But I wasn't gonna help him spit game to my Gloria fall-back plan. "Broncaulio, come with me."

He passed the hookah to Jaslene and followed me to an equidistance between Jaslene and Gloria.

I glanced over Broncaulio's shoulder. Jaslene had this evil smirk on her face. She knew what she was doing. And now we all know what she was doing.

"Be careful. She is my girl," I said. It was a statement I never thought I'd say. But I was so horny, I wanted both Jaslene and Gloria. Higher chance to make one in the basket if you shoot twice. Something Broncaulio knew too well. Rejection was part of the game.

"My bad, matatan. She said you two were just amigos. I'm not looking for trouble."

But I should have known better. When a guy like Broncaulio is denied an opportunity, he jumps onto the next.

We embraced each other with a hug.

In my ear, he said, "She got a friend, though? A neighbor? A recently divorced aunt? Anything?"

"I gotchu one, just for you. We'll talk about it tomorrow," I lied. At the moment, I thought by today I'd be expelled, in jail, and/or a registered sex offender for the door thing. All things that my mother, herself, would kill me for. So tomorrow never existed.

He embraced me again, this time with a firm handshake leading into an even warmer hug. "You the man." He patted my back. "Always looking out."

I then went to G-check Jaslene. I'm not dumb, I saw her glance away as soon as I turned to her. She had been working hard to decipher my conversation with Broncaulio. "Broncaulio is a funny guy, right?" I said. I grabbed Broncaulio's old seat, placed it directly in front of her, and straddled it.

"Isn't he?" She slurped on her daiquiri. "This drink is on point."

"He is *so* funny that he-said-that-you-said we are just friends." I tilted my head and ran my tongue around the inside of my mouth.

"Oh hush, it's not like you out here claiming me." She took a puff out of the hookah. "Two can play that game. Don't act like I didn't see you and that gringa. What's up with that?" She blew out a few O's.

"What!?" I stood up. "That's my...third-cousin." I shook my head. "I can't believe you would even think that of me. Man, I'll be back in a bit. Gotta grill up another batch of burgers." I started to walk away.

"Excuse me! Where do you think you're going? You know the drill." She whipped out her Bacardí bottle. "Not even Broncaulio got a taste out of this. All for you, my love."

I thought I won the award for best actor by flipping the guilt onto her, but I guess that was never the case. She slapped my ass while I casually walked away. She was playing games. And I had games for her. But Broncaulio, man. Why he gotta be so sexually optimistic?

There he was with Gloria, who was now holding one of his signature cocktails. I should have just sent his ass home; instead, I confronted him again. "Loco, Gloria my girl too."

He crossed his arms, clamping hard on his biceps. "The cousins yours too? I got three weeks to score me una Americana. Let me borrow one. I'll give it right back."

"No," I said. And for some odd reason, I meant it. It was as if I had dated Jaslene and Gloria for years, instead of just meeting them hours prior.

"Then we got ourselves a problem because I was being polite. But now I'mma spit game to both, 'cause you selfish. And next time you in DR, I ain't taking you nowhere."

He had a point. He always looked out for me when I stepped foot on native land. And that's when I saw the dominoes table. I played for the right to keep both Jaslene and Gloria; he played for the right to borrow one of them. The picture on the blanket says it all.

Broncaulio hit me with a capicúa, the dreaded palindromic win.

"Now, initially, I was super gassed that these two papi chulos were fighting over me. But what if I wanted both? They took that option away from me." Jaslene shakes her head, then looks at Ida. "Sorry boo, just being honest. This was before I knew this was *your* Danny."

"Fair enough," Ida says. "Not like I ever talked about him until recently."

Jaslene makes a heart shape with her hands and flashes it towards Ida.

"As I said, I was originally flattered by the gestures, but this initiation process has taught me to value myself. My kitty is not to be gambled for. Only I roll its dice." She blows into her fist and shakes it. "Any final words, Broncaulio?"

Broncaulio glares at me as the dildo is unclipped. "Danny said this, Danny said that. I didn't know what in the Monchy y Alexandra was going on at the barbecue. But if I had to do it all over, I'd snatch you out of his tyrant hands again. Because for you, muñeca, I'd go to Cuba and shave Fidel's beard."

Jaslene's cheeks redden. She looks around the room. "Y'all see what I'm talking about?" She focuses her attention back on Broncaulio. "You get an A-plus and an Outstanding conduct-grade. Forever romantic. 'Cept Fidel is dead, and that pick-up line died with him." Jaslene extends her arm outward and releases the clicker. The clicker's batteries and back cover pop out in all directions—a few sisters in the outer circle mutter back and forth.

"Ladies, ladies, I get that mic-drops are a thing, but remember, this is an official initiation. Jaslene, please reassemble the clicker. And please don't drop anything else."

Ida steps forward, makes a sharp right, then a sharp left. She exchanges spots with Jaslene.

"Next up is Ida."

CHAPTER NINETEEN

Why am I here? Eldon uses alcohol and exploitive tactics to get women. Broncaulio recites chapbooks of poetic flattery to seduce women. But me? I cheated once. I made one bad decision. And the decision was not an attempt to sex more women; it was an attempt to regain my manhood. To do as men do. Liking women does not make me a womanizer. I'm the nice guy here.

Displayed on the dangling blanket are a bunch of squares listed under four categories: LGBTQIA+ Rights—when the heck did LGBTQ add more letters—Gender, Female Anatomy, and Other.

"For my tribute, I've decided to play a game of *Jeopardy!*" Ida says. "Danny is a cheater, but whoop-de-doo, most men are."

Exactly what I'm talking 'bout. I'm just your average man. Free me from this chair, please.

"So instead, I wish to highlight his disregard for the experiences, struggles, and rights of others," Ida says. "He is the prototypical machista male. It's a man's world, his mantra."

Machista male? I was most definitely a gentleman during our relationship. Surely the sisterhood can slice through the bullshit and realize that if I was a "prototypical" machista male, then why the heck did we last three years! Now if we talking outside of our relationship…debatable. And like Mr. Greene would advise, first we have to define the term machista, its parameters, and then establish who benefits most from the word and definition.

The dildo is slipped out of my mouth. I o and O, letting the taste of rubber that clings onto the back of my throat air out.

"Pick a category and I will ask a question relating to it. Understood?"

I understand Ida still goes all out for me. Eldon got a rushed criminal-rap-sheet slide and video. Broncaulio got one social media worthy pic. However, I get a whole game of *Jeopardy!* The effort, even if aimed at my demise, means something. I nod.

"By the way, I forgot to mention. Danny is an excellent student, potential Salutatorian. But he doesn't use his smarts to learn about the experiences of others. Instead, he spends his time enjoying sexist banter and competition with his friends. So let's begin. Choose."

Doesn't even matter the category; I have no chance. She did good by setting this up. A reminder that she cared for me and paid attention during our three golden years. Each square catered to my ignorance. A sign that I am more than a tribute. I'm a peer, perhaps even a rival. To her, I'm worth the effort.

Someone kicks my chair from behind. "Choose."

"Uh-Um, LGBT…," shit, that's a bad choice, "—Gender!" I exhale. Don't know why I bothered to hesitate. It's an L either way. Each square holds sweet, sugar-filled revenge. Ida's poisonous box of chocolate.

She shuffles through a pack of index cards. The cards scratch, scrape, and rasp like knives sharpening.

I should have gone with my gut. I've seen the movie *Milk*. Poor guy got assassinated. I should have gone with my gut with Ida, too. Cheating was wrong. I assassinated our love.

She finds her knife of choice and smirks. "What is the difference between Genderqueer and Gender-neutral?"

"She a savage. I don't even know that," someone whispers.

"Good thing I'm not on that chair," another person whispers. She knows me too well.

"The difference between genderqueer and gender-neutral is, genderqueer refers to someone who doesn't identify with gender stereotypes and expected roles. On the other hand, gender-neutral refers to someone who doesn't identify with the male and female gender classification, period," I say.

Correction, she once knew me too well. I do this now. I'm a motha-fuckin' Ally, bitch—I mean Ida, queen, princess. Feminist Studies, Allies for All—albeit one meeting—and Rubio the hetero whisperer have put me on game. *Cheater*.

"Oh, shit! Is that right?" someone murmurs.

Broncaulio and Eldon both snap their necks to look at me. They hop up and down and forward and backward as much as the restraints allow. Their excitement is one of a game-winning shot.

"WRONG!" Ida says. "Although the definitions were accurate, you did not answer with a question."

"But—"

"But nothing. It's *Jeopardy!* You must answer with a question."

"But you didn't—"

"I didn't what? That was unfair?" Ida grips my wrists and leans forward until our foreheads tap. She squeezes tighter and tighter. My wrists, her stress ball, crunch and grind. The pain is endurable for as long as she stares into my soul. Punish me, Ida. Punish. Then forgive. Surely, from this close, you can see that I have changed since our breakup.

"You know what's unfair? You throwing away my dream of a life with you when you decided to cheat." She pushes off my wrists and walks back to her previous position. "We had lots and lots of plans. Not anymore."

My Ida Frida, she must know that I miss those plans too. I'm sorry. Please don't give up on us.

"Next question," Ida says. "Choose."

What's the point? Just give me the maximum punishment. Don't stop at kidnapping and dildo-slaps. You deserve more revenge.

"Since you don't want to choose. LGBTQIA+ Rights," Ida says.

The knives sharpen again and much louder.

"Is same-sex marriage legal in New Jersey? If so, what is the court ruling?"

"What is a, yes, and Superior Court Judge Mary…Jacobson! 2013?" I say. *Cheater!*

A commotion incites amongst the outer circle.

Months after our breakup, I still unceasingly cause Ida pain.

I cause myself pain too. The tears that pool in my ears when I kick back and think of the future lost: proposal, wedding, first home, first child…

"Um, that is correct," Ida says. She stares at her index card, alternating between front and back. "It's what I have written, but how can that be?" Ida mumbles to herself. She slaps her index cards on her thigh. "Okay, the next question will be in the Female Anatomy category." Ida chuckles. "What are the five major internal parts of the female sexual anatomy?"

"What are the Fallopian Tubes, Ovaries, Uterus, Cervix, and Vagina?" If only I hadn't gone out with the fellas that night. If only I had better humans as friends. If only I didn't have to learn everything through experience. If only I didn't study the female anatomy in order to angle my strokes for maximum female pleasure. *Cheater! Cheater! Cheater!*

The clamoring from the outer circle overtakes the room.

Ida rapid-fires questions, "What is femicide? What is the difference between circumcision and genital mutilation? What is the difference between sex, gender, and sexuality? Difference between feminism and sexism? Benevolent Sexism? Marianismo? Why the FUCK did you cheat on me?"—until she runs out of breath. She hurls her stack of index cards at me.

Good thing she throws like a…I'm sorry. So much I want to say, but a golf ball of anxiety lodges in my throat. Never learned to express love. I glitch every time I want to. Every time I need to. Ida knew that, and she worked with it because deep down she knew I cared.

"Ladies, a huddle outside, please," the person behind me says.

Ida mopes out with her hands dragging on her sides, thumb awkwardly up.

The room dims as the torches exit behind us. A door drags on dirt, or maybe leaves. Its hinges grind shut.

Outside, the women deliberate over something too muffled to make out. Clearer is the word, cheater, that won't stop reiterating in my mind. I get it. I didn't understand most of those answers. I just remembered them from recent conversations and class. Information that my uber-hoarding brain stored out of habit.

"Let's get out of here while they're gone," Broncaulio whispers.

Young Sherlock forgot about the wrist and ankle restraints? "And how are we going to do that?" I say.

"We need to get these ropes off," Eldon suggests.

"Wow, two geniuses," I say. "How are we going to do both? Free ourselves and escape."

"So, we the Three Wise Monkeys now?" Broncaulio says. "Y'all didn't hear the other door in the back slowly open? Y'all don't see the light approaching? Or do y'all simply choose to not talk about it?"

I squint into the darkness. And that's all it is without the flames or projector, darkness. I don't even know what this room, dungeon, lair looks like beyond the cement floor and random blades of grass—the flames illuminated us but made everything behind them darker. "I don't see anything. You sure you're okay? The drugs must not have worn off you yet."

"Aight. Now you acting like you didn't spend your summers on the family farm," Broncaulio scoffs.

Broncaulio is a genius! We're in a barn. The concrete floor, the random grass, the smell of horse.

"The light approaching is the same distance from the back door of the house to la letrina. My guess is a phone screen," Broncaulio continues.

I turn to Eldon. His outline hardly visible. "He's tweaking out. I think we've lost him. The distance from the back door to the outhouse is easily like fifty yards in pitch dark," I say.

"Kiss mi neck back! Broncaulio is a bat?"

"Kiss? What? No, he just an idiot."

"Yeah, yeah, keep talking. Just wait."

Eldon spasms and jerks in his chair.

"You a'ight?" I say.

"Mm-hmm," Broncaulio mums.

Eldon's outline tips forward. A loud thud fills the room.

"Sh!" someone faintly hisses, like a ghost beginning its spook.

The women outside abruptly stop talking…then, after a brief moment, continue their deliberations.

"Ah fuck, my legs. They fell asleep." Eldon slaps his thighs.

"Shh," the person whispers again. The person pats and searches for my restraints—tugs away at them in a rough manner.

"Who are you?" I whisper.

The person covers my mouth with their hand.

I tighten my lips.

They release Broncaulio.

"Hold each other's hand and follow my light," a feminine voice whispers.

The door behind us swings open. A single flame peers in. "Anyone heard that?" one of the cult members says. "One of y'all go check it out."

CHAPTER TWENTY

"Stay low, and Danny, take off your colorful shirt before they spot your peacock-vibing self," our hooded rescuer whispers.

"Word, you look like a baby shower. Like a gender-reveal prop," Eldon says.

"Stay low also means shut the fuck up. Solid joke though. Remember, don't look back."

I glance back. It's as dark as the barn we came out of. No lights, except the stars. Only thing chasing us are the dark outlines of tall, slender trees. I shiver. Yeah, shirt staying on.

The cellar door swings open. "They must have escaped through here," someone says. "Alright, spread out."

We hasten our steps. My fingers barely cling onto Broncaulio's shoulder.

"Keep going straight from here. We aren't too far off the main road. I will distract the others. Now go."

"Not before you tell us who you are," I say.

"Almost forgot. Here are your phones. You won't have signal till you get closer to the road. Now go."

I guess it doesn't matter who she is. As long as we get the fuck out of here. We trek forward, Eldon leading the way with his phone light.

Faintly, behind us, our savior shouts, "Sisters, they're over here!" She flashes her phone in our direction.

What the fuck!?

"First one to catch them gets to do the chopping," she says.

The chopping? What the heck they chopping? Our…

Eldon pauses his step, causing me to collide with Broncaulio.

"Chopping? Fuck this, every man for themselves." Eldon pushes Broncaulio and dashes into the darkness.

"Mamague—"

I cover Broncaulio's mouth. "Hush up, genius." I search for Eldon, but his blackness is natural camouflage. Fuck it, we'll use it to our advantage too (although not on Eldon's level). I take off my shirt and shove it into my waist. Damn, which way is the main road again? Uhh… "Lead the way, Campo-Eyes."

Broncaulio shrugs. He's lost too.

These bitches are as relentless as these unforgiving leaves. Every time me and Broncaulio create separation between us and the cult, leaves fucking announce our position. A leaf crunches under me. FUCK!

"I think I heard something over there," a cult member says. From her voice, it's hard to tell how far she actually is. It's so silent out here amongst the trees. Even a leaf falling sounds like it crashed down.

"You still remember how to climb a tree?" Broncaulio whispers, referring to the mango trees and coconut palms we'd climb as children in DR. The older heads would send us up to fetch fruit, but I haven't climbed a tree since I became old enough to send the new ten- to fourteen-year-olds to do it—same way the older heads would send me and Broncaulio.

"It's been a hot minute. I don't know."

"You still got your shirt?"

I tap around my lower back, where I tucked my shirt earlier. "Shit. Must have fallen while on the move." I know what he was getting at: wrapping a shirt around a tree makes for an easier climb.

Broncaulio tosses me his shirt. "You climb first. Once you get," he drops his head back to assess to the height, "thirty feet, toss the shirt down. Grip that tree like it's the last time you'll ever jerk off."

Ha! Even under duress, this clown still says pervy shit.

"I've found Gender Reveal's shirt. The baby blue and pink one," the voice from moments earlier says, sounding a lot closer.

And the realization that they are close makes me not think at all. Adrenaline climbs the tree for me. Broncaulio quickly follows. And like the genius he has auspiciously become, he climbs the tree from the opposite side, ultimately using the shirt to pin my body against the tree, while also reducing his legs' load.

"I wonder what the whole chopping thing was about," a cult member says under our tree. Another member's torch trails behind her. The light dies out just below our feet.

"Wait. You didn't get the update? We chopping shit off now. That's the new org-wide mandate."

"Nooo way."

"Yesss way. We turning dudes into bitches now." The girls continue walking past.

What in the hell!? I can't even process that statement. But to our luck, they continue walking past us.

From their fading phone lights and torches, we can only assume that we are safe for the moment—the closest light appears to be at least…I don't know, far.

"Primo, we good. They are the distance between the outhouse and the rancho away," Broncaulio says. Translation: one and a half football fields. And in this darkness, that's plenty of separation.

As soon as my feet touch the ground, I notice that I have one bar. I call Rose, who has called me thirty times in the last two hours.

CHAPTER TWENTY-ONE

Jail it is. That's what I texted Esmeralda. No explanation, no summary of last night's whatever that was. Just those three words. Fuck that. They dique turning dudes into bitches. There aren't many ways to interpret that, and they all bad. So I quit. Esmeralda needs to accept my decision. And as for Ida…damn, I want to say she is a victim and needs rescuing, but if Calvin Harris and the Disciples approached me with a "How deep is your love?", I'd say, not that deep. Definitely not the motha-fuckin' ocean and definitely not like Nirvana. So I'mma just enjoy these last few days of freedom. I'm going back to sleep.

"Get your bitch-ass up, Snow White. It smells like the Seven Dwarves let their feet dry out in here." Footsteps vibrate the bed. The curtains swing open. "If you waiting for someone to kiss you awake, buy yourself a blow-up doll."

WHY IS SHE HERE? Living a little further away from family was supposed to be another perk of this house. Because when family lives in the same apartment complex as you, phone calls aren't expected. Just knocks of arrival at whatever time of day. A revolving door of aunts and cousins. 'Cept during dinner time. Mom and I always stayed hush and never opened the door during dinner hours. We don't like free-loading lambones.

With my eyes shut, I pat around for my phone—10:59AM, another eleven missed calls from Esmeralda. "Leave me alone. I got a solid seven more hours of sleep in me." I bury my face into the mattress and squish pillows over my ears.

I wonder if Mike Tyson walks softly in his mansion. Old habits from growing up in apartment buildings. Something Rose never learned to do. If it's not her flats clapping a rushed beat, it's her combat boots performing a drum solo. Crawl spaces empty out when she enters a room.

"Fine. I'll let you sleep a little longer. But we snatching these bitches' necks when I get back. We got work to do." Rose slaps my mattress before storming out. "Tía, pero ese hijo tuyo es un vagabundo…"

Sike! The only work to do here is an unpaid sleep study. And she dumb. How she gonna call me a vagabond if I have both a home and a job…or had (Tijera never got back to me)? Now I just want to live the rest of my life on this bed.

When Ida and I broke up, some days I'd sleep for ten hours and zero on others. The constant being this new room and bed. I would replay where I went wrong. Where I could have changed my words to better communicate my love. That way she would see that I did, and still, love her. I made this room my prison. But last night. How do I get over that?

Before last night, I thought there was a sliver of hope for us.

~

I slept through the morning and most of the evening—a mixture of the one-hour car ride home and the emotional toll of the drug-induced kidnapping. Would have slept longer, but my mother's love barreled through my nose.

Her pollo guisado with arroz con guandules; the sizzle of the stew, the clanking of the lid, the swoosh of her stirs. Walked into her hips swaying like a hammock between palm trees to the wind of 80s salsa—music that never gets old. I once attempted to go pescatarian, this exact meal brought me back.

"What a pleasant surprise. You woke up before sundown. Let me guess, you not staying for dinner? Where is the party at tonight? Where was it last night? Or should I say this morning?" my mother interrogates. She stands by the stove, dripping sweat over the Best-Mother-Ever apron I bought her when I was twelve. She inspects me up and down. "You look like you had a rough night. Ha, silly me. I meant, rough morning." She points the big wooden spoon at me. "You would think that the cutting of the umbilical cord was the end of our connection. Pero we on Wi-Fi now. No matter how old you get, I'll always know what time you get in and when something is not right."

I'll let her keep believing that. A lot has slipped by from under her nose lately.

She lifts the lid and stirs. "Come taste this."

Finally, something safe to respond to. "If I must," I say. And I must. I fear she has more questions lined up than Ida. "You do it every time, Ma."

"And what's that?"

"Remind me that I should have gone home quietly after little league baseball games, instead of crying for fast food."

"You can say that again, but Mijo, sit down. Tell me what's been going on." She increases the flame on the pollo guisado.

I slide out a stool from under the kitchen-island counter. "Well, first…" How do I explain to her that I'm on the verge of expulsion, jail time, unemployment, and sacrificial lamb duties without adding potential homelessness on the list?

I feel like Detective Hanson knew about this. Why else hide all this information? He must've known about the cult and figured that expulsion or jail would've been better than taking the deal. And now, I know what was need-to-know at the diner, when the deal was struck. Ida is in a cult. But why spy on her? That doesn't click. If he knows Ida is in a cult, why isn't he trailing her himself?

"Actually, let me start with these bizarre repeating nightmares I've been having," I say. "So I had this dream that I woke up in a jail cell, then—"

My mother dashes to the living room. From there, she shouts, "Keep going, I just need to get paper and pen to jot down your lottery dream-numbers."

"Really?"

"Found it! Keep going."

"Then Esmeralda showed up all lawyered out. I'm talking about suit, a leather cased tablet…"

My mother ponders at the ceiling fan for sec and jots a number down.

"Are you listening?"

"Of course. We winning the lottery, aren't we?"

The doorbell rings.

"Come on, who can it be now? If it's Rose, shoosh her away," I say. I know I should be welcoming Rose. She truly ride-or-die; my sister, rather than cousin. She saved me last night and like a hundred other times, but I'm just not beat today.

My mother throws a kitchen towel at me. "Boy, you know I would never." She chuckles and goes off to answer the door.

A dragged out kiss smacks its way to the kitchen.

Who the fuck? I stand and peek into the hallway. Oh, hell naw. Not today. "Ayo, we don't need extended car warranties, we not joining any new churches, and we definitely don't need another man in this house."

My mother's eyes hone in on me with laser precision. "Daniel Estrella, you better control your demons before I smack them out of you."

"I'm sorry." I bite my cheek.

"Danny, this is John. John, this is my son, Danny."

I know who this chump is. He's not John Snow, not John Cena, not John Legend, not even John Stamos. All the Johns in the world, yet, my mother ends up with John "La Mujercita" Nadie from the unisex hair salon. He is or was, Ida's hair stylist. And I remember the day I had to sit there reading fashion magazines while Ida got her hair done and he said something to Ida that had her laughing while jabbing glances at me. He must have clowned me because Ida downplayed it with, "It was nothing."

"Hello, Danny. Nice to finally meet you." John extends a handshake.

I hesitate. I can't believe this the guy my mother kicked me out of the house for. I scan him up and down, making further assessments.

My mother narrows her eyes on me again.

The third toothbrush, my slides in my mother's room, and a man with a bouquet of flowers Thursday night. For weeks they've must have seen each other, and she never mentioned him, but I know all about him. He volunteers at the local orphanage; plays hopscotch and tag with a few kids. Occasionally, I've found him at the artisan coffee shop reading a book. On days he can't stay long, he orders a matcha tea to go before his first hair appointment. Women go in and out of the salon, but his eyes never wander too low. I've spotted him at the free Pilates program at the park during one of my rare jogs. Thinking about it now, dude is basically omnipresent. I've seen him all over town. And everything I know about this guy tells me he is gay. No doubt about it. And I'm not letting my mother get caught up in a symbolic relationship; proof to his family and friends that he is straight. With fierce eye contact, I shake his hand. There will only be one man of the house.

"Get in here. I'm a hugger." He yanks me in for a hug and grips the back of my head. To think, it only took me eighteen years of life to experience how it feels to be a football during a QB to RB handoff. As he takes his paws off me, he faintly moans into my ear.

Ayooo. Hella sus!

"Enough. Let's save the formalities for later. Let's eat!" My mother rushes us into the kitchen. She lifts the lid; her love steams out of the pot; she stirs it with a careful eye; fills a bowl of arroz con guandules, and adorns it with the pollo guisado. She taps the wooden spoon on the rim of the pot before putting the lid back on.

I blow on my first spoonful.

"So, Danny, I hear you like to—"

Oh hell naw. No small talk today!

I drop the spoon into the bowl. "Wow, look at the time. Mom, I gotta go. Forgot I had to finish a group project with Rubio at the library. I would do it here, but you know what happens when I use the school laptop at home." I forget that it's my school laptop and get caught watching porn by the school district (that was not a fun parent-principal meeting).

I rush out the house before my mother could fully process everything.

I mosey into the public library, which is attached to the high school. I don't have a school project to complete, but I do need to research the hell out of this Daughters of Achelous cult. 'Cause while I may not care about the deal anymore, I do care about getting kidnaped again.

But what the fuck? As if there couldn't be more bullshit stuffed into one day: the school network claims my log-in password is incorrect. Impossible, because I've never changed my freakiton-aThongsong08 password. That password is bulletproof.

"Hawk Union School District NetID Office, this is Jaslene speaking. How can I assist you, sir or ma'am?"

"Jaslene?"

"Duh, Aristotle. I just said that," Jaslene says in her unmistakable ghetto-fab voice.

"Listen, you psycho. It's Danny. When I catch you—"

"Danny?" Jaslene says.

"Duh, Plato. I just said that. Now let me finish."

She purrs like a cat. "I knew you couldn't resist. You stalking me? You found out where I worked, huh? You little freak. Ida and Gloria weren't enough? You lucky I'm willing to share. I like that shit. Let's complete the trifecta."

"Whoa, calm down. I called because I need help with my password and apparently that help is you," I say.

"Well, what you gonna do for me? What does the quid-pro-quo look like?" Jaslene says.

I smack my lips. "This your job, babosa. You get compensated with a weekly or monthly check, don't you?"

"Tell that to the hiring manager, who tried to get a new-hire blow-job out of me. Like him, you think you gonna get something free from me?"

"Alright, stop messing around. This the number the incorrect-password-screen-thingy told me to call. You gonna help me or do I have to go down to your office and take out my anger and frustrations on you?"

Where is the office anyway? Can't be too far off. I peek above the computer screen and inspect around the library like a submarine's periscope, barely above water. No offices in sight, besides the circulation desk with a sleeping librarian behind it.

"Danny, although I do like it rough, I'm not feeling your attitude. Is that your final offer?"

I hang up.

She acting crazy wild, but damn, I need my password. I call the number again.

"Hawk Union School District NetID Office, this is Jaslene speaking. How can I assist you, sir or ma'am?"

"Coño, not again. Don't you got a coworker that can pick up instead? What time you get off so I can call this number then?" I say.

"You think you slick? How 'bout I block your number from the system? You not avoiding me."

"Bruh, kidnapping me wasn't enough?"

"I'm just messing with you, Danny-boy. You really are no fun," Jaslene says. "Good news, I can reset your password from here. Bad news, I ain't doing it for free." Jaslene's words chalk around my body.

"So, what was the good news again? Because good news is supposed to be uplifting," I say.

"Hey-hey, don't get snarky with me. I'm helping you, not the other way around," Jaslene says. "And now that you know what I'm offering, how about you take me on a date? I got a few spots on my Yelp list that I can't afford."

I got a laundry list of things I can't afford either. On the top of the list is adding more complications onto it. I hang up.

What demon is this cult praying to? First, they raid my family barbecue. Then, they get me fired. Kidnap me. Now they commandeer my password?

Esmeralda calls again. I don't have time for none of this. I send it to voicemail.

Who's next? My barber Michael asking where the bitches at?

My phone vibrates again. Fuck it, let's see what Esmeralda wants. I hit ignore, but scroll down the voicemails.

Sixteen voicemails and twenty text messages cursing up a storm. My resignation from the deal was not well received.

Latest voicemail:

"Danny, you asked me why I care so much about your situation, and I'm going to come clean. I think you are a piece of shit of a man…boy. And I know I blame you for the downfall of my home, my parents' constant arguments, and the neglect that came from it. But I've always been jealous of you.

"Pops never wanted me to become a lawyer. He thought women were too emotional, and for that reason, he never supported my pursuit of a law degree. Instead, he allocated every supportive gesture in his body on you. Teaching you how to play baseball and encouraging you to chase girls and all the dumb stuff he labeled as manly. He didn't even show up to my Bar Exam celebration, arguably the happiest day of my life. Three hard years, Danny. Three. Hard. Years. I don't know why I'm telling you this, but I am.

"After the exam, I didn't look for a job. Instead, I went straight to the blotter reports. Spent weeks combing for the right case. One that wasn't easy and would prove my worthiness as a lawyer. One that would hit home; a DUI case that on paper was a clear-cut guilty verdict. I took my first case by the horns. I was going to prove our father—I mean, our provider—wrong.

"I found evidence that the male-driver was actually a victim of a crime,

and the resulting DUI was not his fault. Sorta like what I'm doing with you.

"The day of the not-guilty verdict was the day Dad's liver spilled over from all the alcohol. That machine that kept him beeping teased me into thinking he would wake up for just ten seconds, so I can tell him, I am a lawyer, and no man will tell me otherwise.

"It's fucking sick. Here is this man on his deathbed, and I remained flushed with hate, devoid of any love for him. I've been a mess this past year. Everything feels so unresolved. I waited for so many apologies from him, and this was the only one I ever needed.

"I went out to earn that apology. Who does that? To think, even if he pulled through, he likely would've found another reason to not acknowledge me. But that small chance was enough to drive my tenacity.

"So, where do you come in? When I saw your name on the blotter report, I quickly understood that this was the opportunity to finally get that apology. I don't believe in spirits, but in the small chance his spirit is somewhere watching us, saving his son, his prized possession, from such a nasty situation would surely prove my worth.

"…I need this.

"Also, I know about Sister Clarissa. I've been doing a lot of digging into the past and what an idiotic thing to send someone to church rehabilitation for. And at such an age. I don't blame you for anything. I guess we are both victims here. But you're still a piece of shit." She chuckles.

"…call me back."

Yes, indeed, it was an idiotic thing to play House with my older sister and pretend to be a housewife, while she pretended to be the husband. We were tired of playing the same roles. Thought it would be fun to switch it up. But Dad was not amused. He grabbed the first belt he found—Esmeralda's old My Little Pony belt that she kept as keepsake—and smacked the rainbow out of me like a Skittles commercial.

It was another reason me and Esmeralda became estranged. My father thought that being around my mom when I was home and Esmeralda when I was with him was *too* influential. I saw less of her after that day. But I didn't know she had all this built up frustration. I always assumed she got the better childhood experience than me. If Dad was teaching me all these things, I only assumed Esmeralda learned more from him because she lived with him for most of her upbringing.

But Sister Clarissa. That's a memory I've tried to put in its own skeleton closet.

The truth is, Esmeralda and I got along just fine as kids. The age-gap didn't help, but she was keen on her big sis duties: protecting me from other bullies, while also being my bully. 'Cept an older sibling's bullying is more manipulative than physical—hence how I learned to do knotless box-braids. Every weekend when I was on Dad's watch, she'd have me braid her hair after she scared me into believing that *not* doing her hair would conjure a vicious demon that eats little brothers.

I chuckle. Esmeralda got me good with that one. And like Ida's note mentioned, I got pretty good at it. I guess I got the second but not last—laugh, 'cause those braiding skills probably show cased some feminine side of me that Ida found intriguing.

Sister Clarissa also found those skills intriguing. Further supported this notion that I needed saving. Every Sunday for two months straight, I spent an hour with her. We talked about my week, which was her way of seeing if I was *progressing*. And read the bible (Old and New Testament), taking special notice of passages that defined manhood:

Deuteronomy 23:1. No one who is emasculated or has his male organ cut off shall enter the assembly of the Lord. (And of course she ignored one of the following verses that claimed something like, a son born out of wedlock got no place in heaven.)

Corinthians 11:3. But I want you to understand that Christ is the head of every man, and the man is the head of a woman, and God is the head of Christ.

And her favorite, Ecclesiastes 11:9. Rejoice, young man, during your childhood, and let your heart be pleasant during the days of young manhood. And follow the impulses of your heart and the desires of your eyes. Yet know that God will bring you to judgment for all these things. (Her way of saying, *if you keep doing girly stuff, one day you will be forced to repent.* Sounds like Daughters of Achelous is just that.)

I arrive home again and lie on my bed. My eyes, heavy, shut themselves.

Esmeralda needs her little brother to act like her brother. Detective Hanson needs me to spy on Ida. Rubio needs me to be a friend. Tijera needs me to save her daughter. Ida needs me to repent. And I need silence.

"Danny!" my mother yells. "Come to the basement. You got guests."

I rage off my bed. Left hook. Right hook. Uppercut. WHY IS EVERYONE ON MY SHIT TODAY!?

CHAPTER TWENTY-TWO

Chairs arranged in a semi-circle. A whiteboard on wheels with pictures of Ida, Jaslene, and Gloria taped on it, a map, and the words, Daughters of My Fist in Their Asses. Broncaulio writes *cosplay* at the bottom edge of the board.

"What's up, *Taken*?" Rose says. She points at the whiteboard. "Me and Broncaulio already started. From what we know, y'all Vienna sausages were about to get minced off." Rose raises an eyebrow at Broncaulio. "Or y'all almost experienced a cosplay orgy."

Broncaulio drops his head back in frustration. "Say whatever you want to say, but I'm telling y'all, all we had to do was stay a little longer, and we would have left happier than Pepé Le Pew." He looks at Rose. "That picture on your phone looks like a Bang-Bus porn scene."

"Shut up. What the fuck do y'all want?" I say. I'm tired of this. "Wait, what picture?"

Rose hands me her phone. "I received it before saving you fuck-boys." In the photo, me and Broncaulio are tied up, dildo-gagged, and blindfolded on a mattress. "Dumb hoe sent it with a geo-tag and must have activated your location-sharing. Probably was that double-snake-trifling-fake-bitch Gloria. When we catch them, I got first dibs on her."

"Na, na, na, na." I hand the phone back to Rose. "Y'all can do whatever you want down here. Be my guest. But I'm laying low. They not kidnapping me again. This is something for the police or for some snooping white people in a horror flick to handle." I head towards the stairs.

Eldon rushes down the steps. At the bottom, he rests his hands on his knees. "Sorry I'm late." He catches his breath. "Every parked car looked suspicious, so I ran here." He looks at his wristwatch. "Where you going? You guys done already?"

"No, we just started. Danny was heading up to get us some snacks. Isn't that right?" Rose says.

I glare at Rose. "Yeah, I don't know about that. And how do we know we can trust this *every man for himself* ass mofo." I step towards Eldon.

"Chill-chill, I would have done the same if it wasn't for you clinging onto my shirt," Broncaulio says. "And it's not like he put us in a worse situation. We still got away, and…we still missed out on a cosplay orgy."

I grill Eldon up and down. Broncaulio has a point (I ignore the cosplay part). When I was scheming the backward roll that would shatter the chair, I had no plans on turning back if I heard their screams. But still. It's actions—not thoughts—that matter. "I don't know. It still doesn't—"

The doorbell rings.

My mother excitedly greets someone. If it's John back for a nightcap, we fighting. I pause to listen. By the sound of it, must be Rubio. She loves him like a second son. "Alright. Who else is coming?"

"Just us and Rubio," Rose says.

"Just us and Rubio? I'll pass. Y'all can play Clue all you want. I'm calling the police."

"Police?" Rose crosses her arms. "Since when do you trust the police? You may have have moved to the nice part of Hawk Union, but you still look the same."

"Facts, don't bother," Eldon scoffs. "I already went." He sticks out his arm and lightly rubs the top of his forearm. "I'm Black, so you already know them Babylon bwoys wasn't buying that whole dildo strapped kidnapping story. They was ready to hit me with a false report charge."

"Perhaps y'all got a point. But did you show them Rose's picture?" I say to Eldon.

"What picture?" Rose says.

I cock my head back and squint at her.

"The one—"

Rose smacks the back of Broncaulio's head.

Rubio clears the flight of stairs in one hop. "What I miss?"

"Oh my God, y'all doing the most. You bought into this whole vigilante idea too?" I say.

"Duh." Rubio lightly backhands my chest. "As far as I remember, only me and Rose are allowed to mess with you. Ain't that right?" He fist-bumps Rose. "By the way, since we saved you three, our Justice League name is the Blond Rose. As the muscle, Rose's codename will be Thorn. I'm the getaway driver, so I'm the Yellow Blur. And y'all three can fight between Wrench, Hammer, and Screwdriver, 'cause y'all a bunch of tools."

Rose and Rubio bust out in laughter.

I glance at Broncaulio, Eldon, and the crickets in the room. "That was corny." I grab the marker at the whiteboard.

Everyone sits.

"Task Force Redr. One, because I'm pissed off. A bull after seeing red. Two, it's our initials. Rose is big-boned, so she gets the big R, and Rubio's favorite phone app ends in a similar r. Broncaulio, you out to DR soon, so…" If I don't include him, he going to be butt-hurt. "You likely catching a red-eye flight, so Red is for you. Along with the dr ending."

Rose and Rubio lock eyes and exchange looks of discontent with a touch of compromise.

"Does this mean you are in?" Rose says.

"Not so fast. I'm angry and curious to see if we can catch these handmaidens of Gilead meet the "Children of the Corn" wannabe's…eh, I couldn't think of anything cleverer. But y'all know what I mean." My heart rate ramps up. "I'm a motha-fuckin' man, and these hoes are not going to further ruin my life."

"Whoa-whoa-whoa, Danny-boy. Let's be more respectful to the woman in the room," Rubio says.

I harden my eyes at Rubio. "How you expect us to respect these dumb bitches that kidnapped us?"

"Facts," Eldon says.

"I keep telling y'all. They meant no harm," Broncaulio says.

I throw the marker at Broncaulio. "Shut up, bro."

"Respect thy enemy. That's how," Rubio says.

"That's fi'yah right there. Poetic," Eldon says.

"Na, fuck that. I got no problem with you guys calling them hoes, bitches, tricks, or whatever. They fucked with the wrong people." Rose stomps her heavy foot like I've seen her do since we were in diapers. It's her way of signaling, *it's about to go down.*

I half-nod at Rubio's always-trying-to-be-politically-correct head-ass.

"Let's get this meeting going. First—" Rose says.

"Wait! Just so y'all know. I'm kinda already a confidential informant…" I look around for any looks of disapproval.

Everyone remains silent.

Rose chuckles. "We clearly didn't fall for your joke. Now you just reaching for a reaction."

"This guy." Eldon shakes his head.

"No, I'm dead-ass. Remember my first party as a single, handsome, eligible bachelor? Eldon, it was one of your parties. Rubio, you was there."

"How can I forget the End-of-Summer Bash," Rubio says.

"That party was jumping, right?" Eldon nudges Rubio's knee.

"It was a little *too* jumping. And a little *too* popping." I pay extra attention to Eldon. "Pill popping, that is." No reaction. "Apparently, according to what Jaslene said at the initiation, I left the party with some chick with a hooptie. Then, I ended up on school grounds." I scratch my head in embarrassment. "I pissed on the main entrance. I'm eighteen, so that's somehow a sex offense. And on top of that, I can confirm that I was roofied that night." Still no reaction from Eldon. Okay, maybe it wasn't him.

"WHAT!?" Rubio says.

Broncaulio wakes up from whatever daydream he's been having since he sat down.

"Can't explain it, but I ended up in jail. And I made a deal with some detective. Right now, Esmeralda is looking for clues about what happened that night."

"What?" Rubio says again. "Bro, I forgot to tell you," an apologetic look takes over his face, "I did remember something else from that night: you left the party *with* Esmeralda."

What the heck?

"Also, fun fact. Well, not so fun. Alcohol is the number-one date-rape drug in the world. And like I had already told you before, you was hella lit at that party," Rubio says.

A stern look overtakes Eldon's face as he processes Rubio's words.

Rose side-eyes Eldon.

I have no clue what the Rose-Eldon beef is, but that's unimportant. Rubio needs to give me more details. "You sure you saw me drive off with Esmeralda?"

"I mean, I didn't *see* you guys drive off, but I remember you talking to someone with Esmeralda's car. And you never came back to the party after that. So I can only assume."

"Wait-wait-wait." I'm still not getting this correct. "Did you see Esmeralda? Like you can confirm that, right?"

"Well, I didn't see her face. But thinking about it now, most of our classmates have hoopties. And I was hella saucy too."

I shake my head. This guy just said a whole lot of something and a whole lot of nothing.

"How about Ida? Do you remember more besides me approaching her that night?" I ask Rubio.

"Yep. That I tried to stop you. But you was in your feels." Rubio lightly backhands Rose's shoulder. "If only this clown was this adamant about her when they was together."

"Word. I liked Ida," Rose says.

"Wait, isn't Ida the girl on the board?" Broncaulio says.

"Y'all know I'm still standing right here? I can hear y'all loud and clear," I say.

"You and Ida went into a room, or maybe outside. I couldn't tell where that door led to. I was type-litty. I told you already," Rubio says, almost uninterested.

"Na, y'all went into the bathroom. Caused a long-ass line," Eldon interjects.

Ida. Okay, that part makes sense. But Esmeralda, though? "Do y'all think Esmeralda is the type to join a radical group like Daughters of Achelous?"

"Never thought about that. But yeah. Why not? I mean, what is the criteria? Ida is in it. She didn't seem crazy," Rose says. "Just stupid to mess around with you."

"Ha…ha." I glare at Rose. "Not the time for jokes."

"From the sound of it, even Rose could be part of it," Eldon suggests.

Rose launches off her seat. "If you don't shut your face…" She cocks her hand back.

"AYE! Everyone, calm the heck down. Something ain't right." Everyone gives me their attention.

"Ida and Jaslene were both at Eldon's party. Jaslene was then at my family barbecue. Broncaulio was there too. Along with Rose's friend Gloria."

"A-Glory was there?" Rubio interrupts.

"A-Who?" Rose says, visibly unaware of Gloria's side gig. "Oof! When I catch Gloria…don't hold me back."

"Can y'all just shut the fuck up? I'm trying to process this all." I pace around the basement, weaving in and out of the columns. "At the party, I talked to Ida for a substantial amount of time. About what, though? Also, Jaslene or Ida could have drugged me at the party. Then, for whatever reason, I called Esmeralda to pick me up. She leaves me near the school? And I stumble my way to the main entrance. Detective Hanson identifies me and connects me to Ida, who he has been investigating for her enlistment into the cult. So how does Detective Hanson know about Ida and the cult? And why didn't Esmeralda tell me she picked me up that night? Too much conflict of interest? And who helped us escape the initiation last night? At the moment, it looked like our hooded savior dimed us out, but she must have been the one to send Rose the picture and turned the location-sharing on. Probably bet on us to escape, while covering for herself. And that person couldn't have been Ida, Gloria, or Jaslene because we saw them go through the other door." I pause my step. "There are too many question marks. We need to split up our efforts."

CHAPTER TWENTY-THREE

Esmeralda's annoyed facial expression is the same as usual. The suit typical for her profession. Same curly hair that has a mind of its own. Her walk doesn't look different. Still more hips than legs. But do hips lie? If so, she a big-time liar.

Esmeralda slides into the booth. "What was so important that couldn't be said over the phone?"

The waiter rushes to our table with his order pad in hand.

"I'd like the three-egg omelet with applewood bacon and a side order of hash browns," I say.

"And for the lady," the waiter says, still looking at me.

"I don't know. Ask her." I chuckle. "She's right there."

The waiter's cheeks redden in embarrassment. "Oh, yes. She is. My apologies."

"No, I'm fine. Actually, a small coffee. Black." Esmeralda crosses her arms. "So…"

"So what?"

"What did you want to say in person?"

"That was it."

Esmeralda squints in confusion.

"You know I'm broke. I wanted to see if the hash browns were truly as good as Detective Hanson made it seem."

"What?"

"I'd like the three-egg omelet with applewood bacon and a side of hash browns. That is what I needed to say in person. I have no money and I needed you here to pay." I squeeze lemon into my water. "But now that you're here, what's up? Anything you been itching to tell me?" I tilt my head side to side, scanning Esmeralda's eyes for a lie.

"Are you serious?" Esmeralda smacks the table. Her rings ping like chimes. "You know I got a job, right?"

Perfect. Got her emotionally unstable. She bound to slip up now. Just like the movies.

"Yes, and part of your job is getting me out of this trouble I'm in. Have you discovered anything new about that night?" I nod. "Like, how the heck I ended up at the school?"

Esmeralda leans back. Looks outside the diner window. "Have you?"

"Have I?"

"While I'm busy trying to patch a defense for you, what have you been doing? Have you remembered anything new? Asked anyone at the party if they saw something?" She momentarily pauses to let me reply. "Huh, have you? All you've done is whine and quit. I thought you dragged me here to tell me you were continuing with the deal, or at least to fill me in on Friday night's meetup with Ida. But instead it's to waste my time some more."

Oh, she trying to flip the table on me. Like I haven't been putting in work. Little does she know, I've put in enough work to get kidnapped.

"Also, you never called me back the other day. Did you even listen to my voicemails?"

"I did."

She is doing this to prove herself to our dead father.

"Then you know why I'm here." Esmeralda stands and tosses a twenty onto the table. "Enjoy your meal. I have to get back to work."

"I'm continuing with the deal."

Esmeralda presses her hands onto the table.

Damn, she really has been working out. I can see every vein on her hand.

She exhales. "Good."

"But we are shifting focus."

"We?"

"Me, Rose, Broncaulio, Rubio, Eldon, and you. No more spying on Ida just to spy on her. We are taking this sorority, cult, sister-hood, or whatever Daughters of Achelous is, down."

I hold my breath to better hone in on any slip-ups in her act.

"Cult? Daughters of who?"

Damn, she didn't gulp, flinch, glance left, or nothing.

"I was kidnapped on Friday. The meetup with Ida was a setup. Broncaulio and Eldon were kidnapped too."

"What? Like Broncaulio, your horny cousin? And Eldon, who is that?"

She doesn't know Eldon either? Dang, I may be wrong about this all. Nah, nah, she just good at this. "Yep, the same cousin.

And Eldon, the guy I told you threw all the bangers in Hawk Union."

Esmeralda sits again. "What happened? Tell me more. So the note wasn't from Ida at all?" Esmeralda takes her purse off and waves the waiter over.

"How did you find me so fast that morning? The day I was arrested."

"You used your phone call on me. I ignored it because I thought it was Spam Likely. But then I got the voicemail, *'Do you want to accept this phone call for a fee?'* I googled the number. Bam! Put two and two together. Hawk Union Police, had to be you. I also confirmed with the blotter report," she says without hesitation.

She said that a little too fast. Almost rehearsed. But it's plausible.

Ahhh, fuck it. I just don't see how she would drug me and then abandon me at the school, only to legally represent me. Pissing on a door and getting arrested is mid-tier on the list of worst things that could have happened to me. That would've been a perfect time for the sisterhood-cult to kidnap me too. Save themselves the trouble of infiltrating the barbecue, getting me fired, and everything else, just to get me roped into a chair. Nothing points to Esmeralda being part of the sisterhood. "Why are you helping me?"

"Because I refuse to believe that someone as smart as you, raised by a hell of a woman like your mother, and someone who shares half of my blood, albeit the bad half, could be such a dick." She nods. "And, of course, the whole dead-pops-spirit thing."

"I've been thinking about that too." I glance away.

Esmeralda places her hand on top of mine. "Really?"

I instinctually pull away. "Chill. Not the dad thing, that's on you. But you know, why I let Ida slip away like that? She was the best thing to ever happen to me. And I won't lie, I was acting for the first half of our relationship. Doing everything I would never do, if it weren't for wanting to slide off her panties. The modern-day remix of that old school banger, Bobby Caldwell's 'What You Won't Do for Love'. In my case, it was 'What You Won't Do for Ass'. And in the end, I turned her into a monster."

Esmeralda gives me the same look of admiration as when I initially told her about Ida. "We are all worth saving. If she really is how you make her out to be, let's save her. Surely whatever she has gotten into is not her. And I have more than a hunch that Detective Hanson thinks the same. So tell me. What happened the other night?"

"Alright, order yourself a plate. We gonna be here for a minute. 'Cause you 'bout to think I'm lying out my ass."

"Yes, tell me more!" She excitedly takes out a notepad. "Better yet, tell me on the way to my apartment. I must show you something, too."

"Detective Hanson may not be investigating Ida after all." Esmeralda folds her arms and stares at her wall-mounted cork board full of case notes. The edges of the board are worn out, along with most of the apartment.

"I see you going for the hand-me-down look." I stick a finger into a small opening on the leather couch. My first time here at her place. Thought a lawyer's pad would look more expensive than this.

"It's called student loans and no fatherly support. One of which you will experience in five years. But I hope you get something to show for all that debt. Because college can be a scam."

I toss my hands up. "I'm not dissing. I'm just saying." Let me shut up before I offend her. To annoy and to offend are two different things.

"Does Ida have a brother or cousin that you know of?"

"She got a cousin, Primo."

"That was the guy at the party, right? Yeah, not him. Anyone else?"

"Na, her family is small. Why, what's up?"

"Nothing, just thinking. Detective Hanson may be working with Ida." She points at an index card with a question mark on it. It is connected by yarn to Ida's name and Detective Hanson's name. "It's just a theory, but this new," she writes something on a fresh index card, "Eldon guy. Throws all the bangers in Hawk Union. I think you told me those exact words in the interrogation room. Same words you claim Gloria said. That's odd because, a quick search revealed that Gloria is not from Hawk Union. She doesn't even live in Hudson County. And also, the detective may have been stringing us along. Not the other way around."

"As in, he wasn't macking game. You were?" I poke fun at their previous flirting.

"Yep." She nods her head.

"Oh." Okay, I wasn't expecting that response.

"This may be too much information, but seeing that you like

to tell pervy stories, I'll tell you one of mine. After sending you all those emotional voicemails, I was in need of company. That dad-spirit thing may be silly, but it's real to me. So I called up Detective *Handsome*, told him I had more information. We met up and I may have seductively rubbed my leg up on his. I was testing the waters. He didn't bite at all."

"Footsies!" I bust out in laughter. "Your game is weeeaaak." I slap the couch's armrest. A bit of cotton puffs out. "Let me guess. You winked at him, too." I slap the armrest again. "You walked him home, all the way to the door, too? Mailed him a love letter?"

Esmeralda jumps on me and tickles me. "You think this shit is funny?"

"Stop-stop-stop." I curl in laughing pain.

"Wanna keep talking shit?" She continues to tickle me to death. "Say mercy."

"Mercy-mercy."

"I didn't hear you."

"MERCCCYYY!"

She lets go and readjusts her shirt. "Like I was saying—"

"Wait. Jeez. Give me a sec." I clutch my ribs, waiting for the bruised-feeling to subside. "Okay, go."

"For all that flirting he had been doing, no way he would deny, ignore, or resist my advance. He is either gay or swindling me in order to keep you investigating for him. Perhaps you are his bait."

"Or maybe…" Perfect timing for an ugly joke, but I've barely recovered from the tickle-torture. "Maybe he is just *friendly*. Girls complain when men take friendliness for flirting, right? Could be the case here."

"Ha! Straight men are not programmed to be *friendly*."

If that's true then…

My phone's alert notification goes off. Someone must be in my room. After my slides mysteriously wound up in my mother's room, I set up a secret camera.

Oh. Hell. Naw. "I gotta go!" As important as this information is, fucking John is stealing my slides again.

…and that motherfucker is *friendly* as fuck.

"Yerr. I'm home," I declare as I step into my crib. Nobody responds, but I know they here.

I look to my left at the living room. Popcorn bowl half eaten. Oh, they put M&Ms in it too. Not-bad, not-bad. Movie on pause. Pause screen says, *Fifty Shades of Grey*. I shake my head. I don't know. Any man that agrees to watch this is…I shake my head again. Fuck it, let's see what the hype is about.

Damn, shortie staler than generic-brand white bread. Oh, she naked. They paused on a sex scene! My mother probably slapped John to the Paul Mitchell Academy or wherever he learned to do hair. There's never been a sex scene that she didn't squirm through. I glance outside through the blinds. Na, his car still outside. Unless he left running.

"Yerrrrrrr," I declare my presence again. I walk down the hallway to the kitchen. Smells like shrimp and…DICK. I cover my mouth in repulsion. I stumble backwards onto the fridge.

No, Mom. No.

It can't be.

You wouldn't.

I pick it up.

Na, it's torn open, teeth mark and everything. I crumble it in my hand.

I press over my strumming heart.

I chug the two glasses of unfinished red wine that remain on the kitchen island.

I stumble backwards again.

The whipped cream is out. I'mma be sick.

The floorboards above creak. And creak. And creak.

I storm to the front door and slam it as hard as I can. "I'm HOOOME." I yell up the stairs.

Immediately, feet stomp, scuffle, and jive.

They went from the kitchen, all the way to the bedroom upstairs? I repulsively lift my hands off the stair bannister. I'mma need this whole house disinfected.

"There's my baby," my mother, at the top of the stairs, says.

"Yeah-yeah-yeah, nice try. I need to talk to *friendly* John. Alone." I walk off towards the kitchen. "And tell him to take off my mothafuckin' slides."

In the kitchen, I practice my jabs and uppercuts until John enters.

"Danny, nice to see you."

Nice to see me, my ass. I look down.

He's barefoot. Hella comfy.

"What are we doing here, John? What's the endgame?"

"Endgame?" He looks into my eyes. "Oh, you mean," he points at himself, then away, "well, now that you ask. I've been meaning to talk to you. Give me one sec." He walks off to the front.

"Hurry up, I don't got all day."

He walks back into the kitchen with his hand under his shirt. He moves the whipped cream to the other side of the counter. "Here it is." He reveals a jewelry box. "I'm in love with your mother. The more I spend time with her, the more I confirm that she may be the one."

Yeah, aiiiggght. He probably just tasted the goods and decided he'd buy it after all.

"But seeing that you, her son, are likely the true love of her life, I wish to ask for your blessing."

No, no, and no.

His eyes do not waver. He really means it.

"John, you are a nice gay—guy. Some would even say *friendly*." I raise an eyebrow. "But what do I really know about you, besides the fact that you like to use my house sandals when I'm not here? What kind of man does that?"

"Your house sandals? I have no clue what you are talking about."

Hmm, he's good. I'm starting to think that the TV shows are wrong about the whole sweaty palm, avoiding eye-contact thing.

John smiles.

Word, John? That's how you gonna do me? With your *I just smashed your mom* grin. I clench my fists.

"What's this, John?" I toss the crumbled condom wrapper onto the counter.

"If you ask me, it looks like garbage."

Oh, he a funny guy too? I slam my fists on the counter. But what did I expect him to say? *I banged your mom. And it was awesome. You been locked in this house boo-whooing for the last few months. Never gave me the chance to lay the pipe down on your moms. Last night, though, you went out. And for added bonus, you stayed out late. Ha-ha. I already told everyone at the salon! Another notch on my belt.*

My mother rushes in. "What's going on here?"

John smoothly blocks the ring box with his elbow. "Just two men chatting it up."

There we go, John. Show your true lying-colors. Actually, that wasn't even a lie.

"What's this garbage?" My mother grabs the crumbled condom wrapper and unravels it.

Yikes. It's easy to confront John about what's been happening between the sheets in my home, but not my mother. To picture her, the lady that wiped my ass when I couldn't, doing what no mom should do, should be a sin on top of a sin.

"DANNY." My mother throws the wrapper at me.

I dodge it.

"John, I'm so embarrassed that you had to see my son's tiny condom wrapper."

WHAT!?

I look back at the condom wrapper on the floor. Then down at my crotch. My condoms definitely not small. If she thinks they are, then…my soul lifts off my body. What size condoms is she used to seeing!?

"Found it in the shorts from the barbecue. But we going to talk about that later." My mother nods. "Now apologize to John."

"No need for all that. We are all adults here, right?" He pulls my mother in by her hips.

She faintly slaps his hand down. "None of that in front of my son."

You tell him, Mom! But damn, that was my condom. The Gloria condom.

"Now, what were you two talking about again?"

"Nothing, Ma. Nothing." I mosey out the kitchen to my room. I'm going bonkers. I need to chill out.

CHAPTER TWENTY-FOUR

Tonight is our second meeting, and I'm excited to report absolutely nothing. Like, nothing-nothing.

"Daniel-son!" Rose moseys down the stairs. "You telling me you couldn't spruce up the basement before the meeting? It looks like the before-picture for a Mr. Clean ad." Rose runs her finger on the whiteboard. "Dead-ass? You could have at least cleaned this. You worse than that middle school janitor, Mr. Grange. Remember him? He spent more time soapboxing the hallways, talking 'bout, 'red meat contains the devil's blood,' than actually cleaning."

I watch Rose yammer on.

"He wasn't wrong, though. Too much red meat is bad for you. But lay off the soy. You've been hella soft lately," Rose says.

"You done? You clearly got lots to say tonight, and the meeting hasn't even started." I shake my head. "And for the record, I'm not on any type of diet. Them soy-jokes are played out."

Rose chuckles. "Why you mad, though? I'm just messing with you, cuzzo." She nudges me. "But you been acting different lately."

"Really? You don't know why?" I give her a death stare.

"I guess you got a few reasons. But Danny, my seed, my june-june, when have I ever let you go down without me throwing a punch at the opposition? Remember when those two girls slapped you at that seventh-grade dance?"

"Yeah." I chuckle. "You had that dance floor looking like a mosh pit."

Rose feints a few punches. "Tss-tss tss-tss-tss," she simulates how boxers breathe. "I get it, you was wild for sneaking a feel. But you my brother from another. If it was some other dude, I would have probably slapped him too, out of principle. But not you," Rose lightly backhands my chest, "for you, I shut that party down!" She starts shadowboxing in place. "Ooooh, don't get me started." She jumps in place. "Damn! You got me started!"

"Aight, aight. Let's do this." Not gonna lie, she got me a little hyped with that speech.

"When I catch that Gloria—wait—the day of the barbecue, did y'all—"

"No," I say before she can finish.

Rose ducks her lips. "Could have sworn you and Gloria had a little sumthin'-sumthin'—"

Shit, she knows?

"—but that bitch a liar. Lies more than a frat Brody at a high school party, leveraging his college status for some ass."

"Yerrr." Eldon swags down the stairs.

"Speaking of frat Brody types," Rose mutters.

Behind him, Broncaulio is eating up Esmeralda's ear. "So again, if you ever come to DR, I'll definitely make sure you have a good time. Simply put, for you, girl, I'd go to Cuba and shave off Fidel's beard."

"You know he's dead, right?" Esmeralda says.

What a clown. How many times is he going to recycle that line?

"Girl, you know what I mean. Dímelo, mi gente! I changed my flight for next weekend, so the clock is ticking."

"More like his cock is ticking," Rose whispers to me.

She not wrong. Broncaulio seems more intrigued about finding a room full of women than getting payback. (He's now got it in his head that the Daughters didn't say "chopping", they said "hopping—hopping dicks." Fucking idiot.) If it weren't for his cosplay orgy fantasy, I'm sure he'd be at a hookah lounge, deafening his ears with loud dembow and bachata.

"Alright, I don't got all night like last week. Everyone grab a chair and make a semi-circle around the whiteboard. I'll start with my update." I walk to the whiteboard, touch it, then sit back down. "Who's next?"

Everyone jabs glances at each other like pigeons.

"Come on, stop playing," Eldon says.

"Okay, okay, I went to the cops," I lie. Although me and Esmeralda did confront Detective Hanson, but all he did was flex the video at us. Reminded us what was at stake.

Esmeralda shakes her head.

Rubio stands. "We told you not to. We all agreed on that."

"I know, I know, but hear me out. This may sound racist, but I thought the reason the cops didn't believe Eldon was because he was Black. Eldon even said it."

"That didn't sound racist, it *was* racist. Let's not say that again," Eldon says. "It's one thing to know it. It's another to have it confirmed."

"You're Black too, dummy," Rose says to me.

"Yes, I'm Afro-Latino. I get it, Miss Identity-Crisis. Next time I'll say I'm not *as* Black as Eldon. Just to make you happy. Nonetheless, it doesn't matter what I identify as; it matters what the cops identify me as. And I think on warm days, I can pass for a tanned Italian. So I thought I had a better chance."

"You Black and Afro-Latino. Race and ethnicity, two different things." Esmeralda rolls her eyes.

Broncaulio chuckles. "You had a better chance at passing for burnt queso frito."

"Big facts." Eldon laughs. "If you tan well, then they know you definitely not in their family tree."

"Whatever y'all say. Anyways, I talked to my cop informant handler guy," I look at Esmeralda, "and he laughed me out of the precinct. Even worse, he blamed me for being a hornbag and told me to stop chasing skirts, so I wouldn't get caught up in some freaky role-play." I crack my knuckles. "That got me so tight, I'm ready to contribute for-real for-real this time." I continue the lie. Esmeralda suggested this was the best way to reassure the group that law enforcement is not an option. That way they can commit to doing it our way.

"*Right*. Like you said last time," Rose says. "But a friend of mine had a similar story."

"Really? What was her complaint?" I ask.

"Sexual assault."

The wood in the room constricts, crackles, and creaks.

Rose and Esmeralda shrug their shoulders.

"Happens all the time," Esmeralda says.

"I don't know how to follow that, but I'mma keep this rolling." Eldon walks to the whiteboard and tapes a printed map of North Jersey (everything north of New Brunswick and east of Paterson). "Yesterday night, I hit up my connects and visited every party in the area." Next to the map, he writes town names. "In North Bergen, there were two parties, but no sight of Gloria, Ida, and Jaslene." He draws a line through North Bergen. "In West New York, there was one party. Again, no sight of them." Another line. "Jersey City, three; Elizabeth, one; New Brunswick, six. Nothing. These girls popped smoke."

"Diablo! You hit up more spots than Alex Sensation does in a night," Broncaulio says.

"Ya-too-sa-bay," Eldon says in half-decent Spanish.

"That's unfortunate. I was certain them mark-ass-tricks would show up somewhere," Rose says.

"Do y'all have no vocabulary? That you must call them hoes, bitches, tricks, and skanks. It's degrading." I nod at Rubio.

"Na, I think we got it right the first time," Rubio says.

This motherfucker! Acting brand new again.

"Your brother has been acting so weird lately," Rose attempts to whisper to Esmeralda. But her loud mouth doesn't have that setting.

Eldon sits back down.

"I'm up," Rose says. "Unlike y'all two failures, I got it done."

Rose slaps a photo onto the whiteboard. "This right here is *the* bracelet."

"That looks like the cheap Santa Maria bracelets they sell on Bergenline," I say.

"Look closer, estúpit," Rose says. "It's a repeating sequence of an outline of a woman, a lit torch, and a man on a bended-knee. Look familiar? Everyone should say yes because this is their sisterhood bracelet."

"Wouldn't it be a Siren? You know, Daughters of Achelous. Plus, it was dark, and I definitely didn't see that on any—"

"Oh, shit," Broncaulio interrupts. "That does look familiar."

"Duh, I just said it would."

"No, no, no. I've seen it before the kidnapping. Una tipa at the chapi spot wears this exact one."

"What? Which one?" Rose shouts.

"I forget the name. Tío Martín told me to check it out during the family barbecue." Broncaulio takes out his phone. "But it's in my recents. Check it."

We all hover over Broncaulio's phone. It's the spot the high schoolers sometimes show up at to watch the chapis unload out of the vans.

"Let's go!" Rose says.

"Go where? We need a plan before we go anywhere," I say. "Are you sure you saw this bracelet at the spot Tío Martín told you about?"

"Without a doubt. Looking at wrists and bracelets is kinda my thing. You see, a wedding ring, engagement ring, promise ring, whatever ring doesn't tell you if a girl is about that cheating life. But a bracelet…tells you all you need to know. The cheaper the bracelet, the more meaningful the bracelet must be. Which translates to the more faithful the woman is likely to be. Peep." Broncaulio turns toward Esmeralda. "Would you dress up nice—not like you need to 'cause you already beautiful but play along. Would you dress up nice—heels, makeup, hair, nails, all that—and ruin all that prep with a cloth or coral bracelet?"

"No. Unless it…ahhh." Esmeralda embarrassingly chuckles. "That's funny. So you saying that if you see a woman at the club with a cheap-looking bracelet, she likely got it from someone important? A person so important that she doesn't care if the bracelet doesn't match her outfit?"

"*Exactly*," Broncaulio says, all cool. He gently lifts Esmeralda's hand by her fingertips. "I see you don't wear a—"

I swipe Broncaulio's hand down. Whoa! Don't know where that impulse came from, but I just didn't like him doing that.

"Thank you, Danny."

"Alright, enough of this." Rose gets us back on track. "It's simple. We find this girl with the bracelet. Then you guys be your typical fuck-boy selves. One of y'all is bound to catch her attention. We wait till she makes her move, then go from there," Rose says.

"That's not a very good plan. You dangling us as bait without an endgame," I say. "What if she was at the ceremony and recognizes us? Come on, Esmeralda, say something discouraging, please."

Esmeralda juts her palms out. "I'm here to make sure nobody

ends up in jail. Think of me as your chaperone or legal guardian angel. That's it. Nothing more."

"I got a better idea." Rubio smiles devilishly. "But the fellas are not going to like it."

. . .

"Say it. What the fuck?" This guy really trying to leave us in suspense.

"Daaaaamn, y'all don't trust me?" Rubio says.

"Not when you say, 'but the fellas are not going to like it'," I say.

Rubio chuckles. "Y'all dressing up as women."

CHAPTER TWENTY-FIVE

Tío-Primo Martín did not lie; not all bodies are made the same. Some natural, some fake. Some made in Colombia, some in DR with silicon manufactured in China. And I've never been Head Chief of Body Image. So tonight, I may revert to ol' Danny. Woof, woof.

Rose smacks the wig off my head. "Stop looking at the asses before you undo the duct tape. You're not bagging anything in that dress."

"This is so fucking dumb. If I get a rash on my balls, we fighting." I pull down my dress. "How do I keep this shit down? So annoying."

A cargo van with New York license plates double parks next to the nightclub entrance.

"Just deal with it. Now both of y'all, go! That's the van with the chapiadoras," Rose says.

Broncaulys and I, Danielle, step out of Rubio's car. This is the dumbest idea ever: we are to camouflage in, find the girl with the bracelet, make friends, and when we jot down our number in her phone, we'll activate location-sharing. This will lead us to Daughters' hideout.

"Wait, wait, wait. Before we enter. Me and Broncaulio just stand around, pretend to mingle until we spot the chapi-cult-bitch?" I know the plan, but I'm stalling because I just feel uncomfortable cross-dressed. Like this is *too* wrong. Like I'm literally giving up my manhood.

"Yes, Danielle. How many times you gonna ask?" Rose pokes me in the ribs. "You see Broncaulys over there." Across the street, in front of the club entrance, Broncaulio half-spins a chapiadora, squeezes her butt, and claps. The chapiadora gestures an *I-told-you-so* and hands him a business card. "Natural and poised."

"Yeah, but—"

"Yeah, but nothing. Go already," Rose orders.

"This some bullshit." I tug my dress down and wobble across the street. Wedge heels are easy to walk in, my ass.

"Diablo, mami chula. You got more tail than a lobster. Juicier than oxtail," Rubio hollers as he exits the driver's seat.

Pfft, he definitely gay with that wack ass line.

"Rubiooo. That was a good one," a schoolmate, who came to watch the chapiadoras arrive, says. Ah shit. I wobble even faster.

The bouncer pats me down. His fingers touch too much of my hips. I squirm. They never touch this much when I'm dressed normal. And why the fuck do dresses hug more than plastic wrap? It's one thing to shave my arms and legs bald. It's another to flatten oneself with a faja, then get squeezed again into a dress with less range of motion than a potato sack. PLEASE check my ID and turn me away.

The bouncer waves me into the bar.

What the fuck? These chumps didn't even ask for my ID. This. Shit. Is. ASS!

Focus…remember why we're here. The sooner we locate the bracelet, the sooner I get out of this human-sized finger trap.

A middle-aged man sits at the bar with a bottle of Buchanan's to himself. Poor guy, barely conscious. His head, leaning on the ice bucket, is likely the only thing keeping him awake. Shieeet, what am I talking 'bout? He doing better than me. A drink is what I need.

"Ew, you guys like these type of girls?" Rubio says as he looks onto the dance floor scattered with women. His fake ID was a success.

"Na, these my uncles' type. And they 'bout to be your type. Now, get away from me," I say.

Rubio continues to look around and gulps. "I'm nervous as shit, man."

"Nervous? All you gotta do is fake holler at these chapis until we spot the bracelet. You not dressed up like this." I pass my hands down my long-sleeve bandage dress. "They check your ID?"

"Of course. And by the way, I'mma say it again, and again, and again. I'mma say it tomorrow and I'mma still be saying it next week. You gotta give it to my designer friend, you look gorgeous." Rubio looks me up and down. "I know you a straight man and all, but this really is a waste of a fit. Could have competed at a show. And look at these thirsty dudes. What is up with them? They dripping over everything with long hair."

I take a long look around the room. Lots of men standing

around with their buddies facing the dance floor. Deliberating on which chapi they gonna spend their money on.

"They won't appreciate the effort it took to make you look like J-Lo in Vegas." Rubio shrugs. "Eh, but y'all can afford to be harassed. A little karma. Especially Broncaulio. Yeah, y'all good."

"No, we not good. Now go pretend, do me proud, and don't offer to take any drunk girls home. Trust me. They not drunk and it'll cost you more than your entire summer job." I nudge Rubio away.

He drags his feet to the closest vacant wall.

I can't believe this guy. Dragging his feet like he isn't already straight-passing. I glance at my firecracker-red nail polish. I won't lie, I do look fuego. I'd make a bad bitch. Bag all these clowns. But I don't wanna be a bad bitch! Fuck. I went to one event with Rubio, now he got drag friends that do makeup, that know how to tuck penises away. The worst part, this is my fault. If I didn't accept his challenge, he wouldn't have made new friends. And if he wouldn't have made new friends, he wouldn't have come up with this idea. I shake my head. Na, I love to see it. Him breaking out of his shell. I'm happy for him.

The DJ changes the music from bolero to dembow. The loud bass launches the middle-aged man off his bar stool. He fists the Buchanan's, and trips. A chapi with Lycra bottoms containing her fake butt catches him. Ha! Claimed! She gonna keep him just conscious enough to spend his money. Hilarious.

"Seat taken?" a man behind me whispers into my ear. He caresses the ends of my wig as his Curve cologne poisons the air. "Come on, baby-girl. One drink," he says with confidence. And

WOW, his breath is rocking like he Listerined with rum. The stench punched right through the cologne.

Dumbest plan…EVER! I clear my throat, fine-tuning it for my best Cardi B impression. I swipe the man's hand off me and turn around. "First things first, don't touch—"

"Come on, muñeca. You don't have to be so mean. I just wanna play." Tío-Primo Martín licks the tip of his beer bottle.

I immediately turn around and prayer-hand to the ceiling. "Why me, huh? Why?" I mutter to myself.

Across the room, Broncaulys is sandwiched between two chap-iadoras. He grinds his ass into one of them, making fair use of the booty-pop panties we borrowed from Rose (which definitely don't fit her anymore). Fucking guy is having the time of his life!

"Bebé, why you playing hard to get?" Tío-Primo Martín says. He places his wrinkled hand on my hip. Then trails his dusty finger down to my thigh.

Chills tingle through me like I found a limp dick crawling on me. I slap his hand off. Fuck this, I'm out of here. I hop off the stool and tug my dress down a bit.

"Don't you want to have fun with us?" a female voice says.

I turn around. The cult bracelet dangles on her wrist as she hugs Tío-Primo from behind, high across his collarbone.

Now ain't this some shit! Out of all the thirsties in the bar, she chose to milk Tío-Primo dry. And out of all the places Tío-Primo could be—like home with my aunt—he is here.

I inhale deeper than an Olympic diver at the springboard. Remember, she is why you are here. I exhale. "A double-shot of

Johnnie Blue and a Presidente Light. Okurrrrrrrrrrr?"

"That's all you had to say, beautiful." Tío-Primo Martín gently strokes my shaved chin. "The way you *roll* that tongue, you'd make a panadería go out of business."

I involuntarily squirm, but quickly regain control of myself.

The chapi-cult-hoe winks at me. Congratulating me on the expensive drink request. "Make that two Johnnie Blues."

Tío-Primo happily places the order. He seems confident of himself. Chest puffed. Chin high. Is this what old men do to clutch onto their last drips of manhood? This perfect medium between a brothel and dive bar, the last stop? The answer to *Do men cease to be men once their parts don't work*? They just end up in a place like this.

Tío-Primo hands me my drinks.

I've never drunk whiskey this expensive before. Not a bad deal if I was an alcoholic. I think I get commission off this too.

"Come on, let's dance," the chapi says.

Dance? *Yoooooooo*. It just gets worse and worse.

I pa'arriba-pa'abajo-pa'l-centro the shot and chug my beer as a chaser.

Tío-Primo hands us both twenty dollars; the cost for a dance.

She drags me and Tío-Primo onto the dance floor.

Dembow is still playing.

I two-step as much as the dress allows.

"Let's milk him dry," the chapi-sirena whispers into my ear.

Tío-Primo rocks his cranky hips towards me. He reaches for my hips with his hands.

I slap his hands down.

He performs a spin move and then another until he is behind me.

I do my own spin move to face him.

He extends his arms towards my hips again.

I slap his hand down.

The DJ switches the music to bachata.

Yes! Thank you, DJ.

Tío-Primo grabs both our hands and spins us. Again, again, and again.

My ankles bend, twist, and buckle. The only thing keeping me up is Tío-Primo's hands and the alcohol in my system. But coño, who popped the battery into this man?

I glance at Rubio, who is on the sidelines watching us dance. I gesture for him to peep the chapi's wrist.

Rubio's eyes open wide. He takes another sip of his drink.

Tío-Primo spins me.

Rubio walks away.

Tío-Primo spins me again.

Rubio walks back.

The room is blurrier than a rushed photograph. DJ, chill. You drowning me out here.

I rest my hands on my knees and catch my breath. Fucking DJ, did me no favors; a twenty-minute bachata-mix with zero breaks. Tío-Primo was relentless. No matter how many times I swatted his hands off my waist and butt, he never caught the hint. Like a baby, forcefully slapping his hand only made him understand half of the time.

But Rubio, what a little bitch. I signaled his dumbass to come split the trio up, but he just stood there trembling. While Tío-Primo smiled on, wearing me the hell out on that dance floor. I was a wobble away from breaking my ankle.

Still, it bothers me. Why does Tío-Primo willingly pay for our attention, with forty-dollar drinks and twenty-dollar dances? What makes this experience worth it? Is this more acceptable than strip clubs and prostitution? Does this coincide more with his values? And what about my aunt? I laughed when he told me the story about this place at the barbecue. There was a sense of normalcy to it, but this shit is unacceptable. My aunt is genuinely a nice person. The type of person that goes out of her way to brighten every room she enters.

"It was fun dancing, but I need to use the bathroom," I excuse myself. I wobble to the unisex bathroom. I enter a stall with cell phone numbers written all over the door and nest the faded-yellow toilet seat with toilet paper.

"Save me! Our uncle Martín up in here trying to bag me," I text Rose.

"GTFO. That is hilarious. And kinda incestuous. Some Shakespeare-type shit," she texts back.

"I said save me! This shit ain't funny."

Somebody enters the bathroom.

"Hey moron, what happened? That was the cult girl," I text Rubio.

"I know, I'm sorry. I tried, but I froze. It didn't feel right."

"You know what doesn't feel right? Having to protect my booty hole while my uncle-cousin spun me fifty times on the dance floor."

"My bad, it's just…I don't know."

The stall door rattles.

"Occupied," I say.

"Is that you, Danielle?" Tío-Primo Martín says.

What this guy want now? "Yes." I use my man-voice.

"Me gusta. I love it when a woman talks hard to me. With that extra oomph. That extra tambora." The stall door rattles again. "I locked the door, baby-girl. It's finally just us two, alone."

Us two? Locked door? "I'm taking a shit," I lie. "It's a floater."

The door rattles again. "If that's what your shit smells like, I can imagine what something else must smell like." His exhales become perceivable, loud and fast.

What!? Now that's a weird line.

BOOM. The stall door slams open. Tío-Primo Martín unbuckles his pants.

I stand from the toilet seat.

Tío-Primo pushes me back down and closes the stall door. He stuffs his hand into his boxer-briefs.

As he pulls his snake out, I punch him in the balls.

I lunge a desperate hand at the door handle. My mind can't process anything but RUN!

I pull the door half open.

Tío-Primo wedges his body between the wall and door.

I squeeze one step out of the stall.

He yanks me by my wrist. My shoulder goes numb.

I back-kick the door, slamming it on Tío-Primo. His slimy grip loosens enough for my fingers to pulp out. I run to the bathroom door.

I reach for the knob, but trip on my own feet.

Tío-Primo pins me against the wall. "You been playing hard to get all night. Those drinks don't come free." His breath dampens my neck.

I head-butt him square on his forehead.

He flails back.

I knee him. My dress rips at the bottom.

He lunges towards me with both arms extended out like a zombie.

I kick him away, out of arm's reach.

He falls backwards.

I stumble out of the bathroom. Blood dripping over my eyes. Spandex-briefs exposed.

I scan the club for Broncaulio and Rubio. "YO, we gotta go. NOW!"

"Chill, don't you see me with these mamis?" Broncaulio says.

"Don't you see the blood on my face?"

"Oh."

"What happened?" Rose says as I get into the backseat of the car. "You guys found her?" Rose looks back. Her jaw drops to the hand-rest. "What happened?"

"Imagine if I was a woman?" I utter.

"What are you talking 'bout? Why are you bleeding?"

"Would I have been able to fight him off?"

CHAPTER TWENTY-SIX

"Sounds like you got the full woman experience." Rose hesitantly strokes my back. "Can't tell you how many times men have thought my no meant yes."

"Really?" I say. "Am I like that?"

"You should know." Rose pauses. "Let's talk about it some other time." She stands and walks toward the whiteboard.

So, I am? Must not have wanted to hurt me with the truth. Ride or die. For all her jokes, she ignores my faults.

Do I ignore my uncles' faults too? What was wrong with Tío-Primo Martín? The lust in his breath, the entitlement in his wrinkled hands, and the lack of humanity in his eyes. He was a mindless zombie. A defected one at that. Couldn't even detect me—a shoe-size ten—for God's sake. My shoulders stand high. He got up from the floor, likely thinking I was Superwoman. Are men like that what my mother has endured?

Broncaulio writes *Justina* on the whiteboard and circles it. "That's the chapi cult member's name." Broncaulio says with a hint of arrogance.

"Who?" I say. Because if I heard him right…my blood begins to boil.

"La tipa with the bracelet." He smirks. "I know, I know, no need to thank me."

"What?" I grip my wig off the chair and stand. Na, na, na. I'm not hearing this right.

"Last time I went to that bar, I spent one-hundred and fifty dollars on drinks. This time, I spent nothing: drinks, dances, fake booty and teta-rubs came included with the wig and dress." He laughs.

"That's not funny," Rubio scoffs. "Some creeps cross-dress to gain sexual access to men and women. That was not how you were supposed to use the disguise."

Now Rubio wants to stand up for something? I grip the wig tighter.

"Whatever you say. Either way, I met her at the entrance of the club, after I palmed that ass, of course." Broncaulio tosses a business card toward Rose. "It's her surgeon. For if you ever need work done. I approve of the—oh shit! I forgot to get her number. You know, with all them booties, I was distracted and—"

THAT'S IT! I launch the wig at Broncaulio.

He dodges it by turning away.

I jump on Broncaulio's back, putting him into a rear-naked chokehold. "You fucking idiot." Broncaulio being Broncaulio. Tío-Primo being Tío-Primo. Men being men.

Broncaulio falls forward onto the floor.

I squeeze harder.

He reaches a hand out for help.

My mother rushes into the basement. "Danny!" She looks startled and worried.

I relinquish my chokehold.

"It's Martín."

How does she know? I hop off Broncaulio. "I know, Ma." I take a deep breath. "What was I supposed to—"

Her face changes from worried to angered. "Why didn't you tell me? Hurry up, let's go. Rose and Broncaulio too."

"Go where?"

"The hospital. He was attacked by a group of teenagers and hit his head pretty bad."

Rose's eyes open wide enough for them to plop out.

My heart skips a beat.

"After the beating, he dialed 9-1-1." My mother notices my injured face. "Mijo, what happened to your head?" She rushes to me. Kicks the wedge heels and waist trainers in her path to the side. Not questioning why they are there in the first place. Not questioning why makeup is smeared on my face. And why I was choking out Broncaulio.

Tío-Primo deserved every blow. The type of man the Daughters of Achelous are trying to rid humanity of. And if I'm as bad as Tío-Primo, then I deserve to be sacrificed. I look vacantly at my palms. But were my actions justified?

What kept me so blind? All his comments about women were just guy-talk. Stories to laugh about. What am I?

The doctors say Tío-Primo Martín may have suffered a concussion and is likely to make a full recovery. Wish someone could say the same about me.

My aunt hovers over him with rosary beads in hand, pouring tears onto his hospital gown. "Who would do this to him?" She folds her hands together and stares at the heart monitor display. "God, he is such a good man. Please."

It was ME, and I'd do it again. I place a hand on my aunt's back. But for her, I hope Tío-Primo comes out of the hospital gown sooner than later. The doctors now say they are keeping him overnight for observation: concussion protocol for a patient his age.

I stare at Tío-Primo's heart rate, wishing it would drop and not drop. Knowing I'm probably overreacting. Knowing I still love him because he is my uncle, but I'm angry. I ball my fists and squeeze tight, letting my nails sink into my palm. I just…I just… I move my blank stare towards Tío-Primo. He's dead to me! Along with the illusion that these men know what it is to be a man. I…I…

I rush out of the emergency room and burst into the first bathroom I find.

Breathe. Breathe.

I splash water onto my face and stare at myself in the mirror.

I imagine this is where bachateros write their lyrics. In front of a mirror after a few drinks and la traicionera is off somewhere ruining more male lives. But that's slander. Rarely do songs mention men cheating. Rarely do the songs allude to the fallacy of this type of manhood.

I need to do better.

CHAPTER TWENTY-SEVEN

I'm not one to go out on Sundays, but I need a social setting away from all this. Where no one knows what has been happening. Where I can act like nothing is happening. So I called up my barber, Michael. I figure if he asks all his customers, "What's the wave tonight?" or "Where the bitches at?", he was bound to have plans. And he did.

"Be open-minded. That's all I ask," Michael says as he unlocks the barber shop front door.

I grab him lightly by the arm. "I get how y'all work on the island, but if the girls are not eighteen and older, take me home now before I get caught up in some shit."

Michael chuckles. "Come on, do you think I'd ever do that?"

Hell yes, I do. I raise an eyebrow at Michael. The same guy that is waiting for that sixteen-year-old to turn eighteen.

"Whatever man, let's get to the back. We holding up the party," he says.

We walk past the barber chairs to the backroom, which is bigger than the shop itself. Back there, you can find racks of stolen clothes and electronics for sale and, like tonight, the occasional party: hookah, dominoes, and beers.

"Again, be open-minded."

"Bro, now you scaring me. Just go." I walk in behind him.

What the heck is this?

Chairs aligned in rows, a projector screen and a man ready to present in business attire.

I look at Michael. If only he knew what happened the last time I was in front of a projector screen.

He locks the door behind us. "Meeting can start now. This the special guest I was talking about."

Special guest? I point at myself. "Me?"

Michael nudges me towards a vacant chair. "Loco, it's all good. Trust me."

It's all good? This ain't no party. This looks like a pyramid scheme recruitment meeting. (When I turned eighteen, everyone invited me to these side-hustles. Fiending to trap me like they've been waiting for me to reach adult status.) But if he says it's all good, then I'll believe him this one time.

We squeeze past a few men to get to the last open seats in the back row.

If this is what it looks like, at least I wasn't the only one who got scammed or, at minimum, I wasn't lied to the most. One guy dressed like he going to a Halloween party. Another got on his best dancing shoes—black shoes with a silver-sequin skull at the toe box—and a matching black blazer with the skull on the back.

"You guys want to learn how to make money in your sleep?" the presenter says.

Oh hell naw! I stand up and glance at the exit.

Michael presses me down at the shoulders. "Open-minded, remember?"

Bitch, I didn't agree to anything.

"No, this ain't a travel membership nor a fake stock market scam," the presenter says. His words ease my initial thoughts. I sit back down.

"You don't have to recruit anyone, so everyone can drop their shoulders if my words alarmed you. What we teaching here is not complex, instead, simple observation. Look around the room. What do you see?"

Just a bunch of dudes looking side to side, avoiding long eye contact.

"Men. That's what you see." The presenter nods. "Now tell me what you don't see?"

"Women," I mumble. I really thought we were going to a party. One that I could let loose at and forget about the chaos for one night.

"I think I heard someone say it!" The presenter points a finger around the room. "Which one of y'all said it?"

Michael flings my arm up.

"Of course it would be you." The presenter smirks and nods at me. "My fellow men, did you also notice this?"

A few heads nod.

"Did y'all invite women?" I whisper to Michael.

"Na, this meeting is men only."

I shake my head.

"There are no women here because they're in office buildings, wearing blazer-skirt combos, or in college studying for better lives that don't include *low-skill* workers like us."

What? I chuckle. Of course there are no women here if you don't invite them. "Is he dead-ass?" I whisper to Michael, who is now on his phone barely paying attention to the presenter.

"No women to cook for us?" the presenter says. "Nobody to wash the dishes or do laundry."

Those are basic life skills, though. I look around the room. The other men are nodding in agreement.

"But that's not the real issue. The real issue is that none of them want men like us. Hard workers. We held women down for decades…"

Oof, bad word choice. Little does he know, I can get a whole cult in here that will say that men definitely oppressed them (held them *down*) for decades. *Down*, economically, emotionally, spiritually, and everything else.

"When we brought home the bacon, they wanted us: construction workers, bodegueros, warehouse workers, and so on. They. Wanted. Us! But now that they make their own money and go to college, they don't even give us a second look. Why? Because we don't have college degrees. Because we work for hourly wages with minimal health insurance benefits. I'm telling everyone here today, women have unionized!" The presenter pounds a fist into his flabby chest. "So we must unionize too!"

"Hell yeah," shouts an attendee.

"We spent way too much money on women, for women to not spend on us!" the presenter says. "If they are the new breadwinners, I want a piece of that bread too. With some butter on it.

Because when we were the breadwinners, we took care of them. We didn't abandon them."

I frantically look around at the idiots in the room who are sipping the Kool-Aid.

The audience looks ready to erupt with action.

"But tonight we will get answers. The cheat code from someone who knows a thing or two about getting college-educated women."

"He's talking about you, Danny. Kinda told him you was in college. You in college, right?" Michael whispers.

"Someone who has been in the frontlines, in the trenches for us. Danny." The presenter looks at me. "Come up here. Teach the audience how to make money in their sleep by sleeping next to a college-educated woman."

WHAT!? WHO? I look at Michael with my eyes opened wide. I don't care what he told them. "Nope, not me," I say. "Y'all got me confused for someone else." I stand and head to the exit.

"Look at him being so modest. That must be lesson number one," the presenter says.

The audience claps.

Fuck, this door requires a key to open. I glance at Michael.

Michael spins the keys around his index finger and signals with his eyes for me to walk to the front. The attendees start chanting, "Danny! Danny!" Pep-rallying me up to the front.

Oh, we breaking up after this. It's over. I drag my feet to the front.

I clear my throat, nervously looking at Michael for any clue about what I must say. Fuck that! Why am I even entertaining this?

Michael mouths, *pre-tend*. And rubs his fingers, gesturing there is money involved.

"I know him. I know him," says the boy from my last barbershop visit. His eyes are lit up with excitement as if I were a movie star.

"Our little prodigy already making the right connections, I see." The presenter chuckles.

I clear my throat again as I glance at the audience. I count at least eight attendees, but none more important than the boy. My eyes settle on him. What could I possibly say to these men that won't harm this boy?

"Speak your truth, king," says an attendee, who looks to be in his mid-thirties—too old to be calling me king. His beer belly adds extra base to his voice.

Mannnn. What have I been dragged into? All I wanted was a chill night out. But if there is money involved, which I desperately need in order to pull my weight around the house, then...

"Just go to college," I say. "Statistically speaking, women go to college at a higher rate than men. There are many reasons for this, and gender roles is one of them. Gender roles squeeze women into pursuing higher education. How many female construction workers, plumbers, garbagemen, and truck drivers have y'all worked with? The manual labor positions that men occupy are not accessible to most women. Hence, men don't go to college at a higher rate. Get what I mean?" Thank you, Feminist Studies. Don't know what I'd say if it weren't for that class.

The attendees look at me, confused. "So you want us to go to college to get women?"

"Fun fact, decades ago, women used to go to college to find husbands." I run the thought through my head. "Actually, women were sent off to college to find husbands. That is more accurate. So historically, attending college is a means to find your life-companion. And I don't see how that wouldn't apply today. Because if gender roles don't change, women will continue to not have access to a significant portion of the job market, and they will continue to go to college at higher rates in order to access the job markets available to them." Damn, look at me spitting facts. New Danny, who this?

"But why don't they want us? Why do I have to go to college because they decided to go to college?" the beer-bellied attendee says.

"Yeah," says another. "They can go to college and still want us."

I scratch my head. "Perhaps women want men that are as educated as them." I shrug. "An educated mind is typically a more progressive one. Seems natural that they'd end up with someone with a college degree. Also, when you spend four years around college-educated people, most of your friends end up being college-educated. Most of the women I know are college-educated." Most people I hang out with are in high school, don't see how it would be any different for college students.

"You are a genius," the presenter says. "My fellow men, by being ourselves, we can get college-educated women."

Huh?

"Let's just lie to them. Show up to campuses, campus bars,

parties, and other events. Like when Good Will Hunting found wifey at the ivy-league school's bar. He was a janitor!"

"No, that's not—"

Obnoxious claps mute me.

"You with the red plaid shirt! What do you do for work?" the presenter asks.

"I work in lumber."

"You are now a Forestry or Environmental Science major at every campus space you enter."

"Aye, I like that," replies the lumber worker.

Someone pats him on his back. "Good shit."

"You with the dancing shoes, what do you do?"

"I'm a cook at the Korean Fusion spot on the corner."

"You are now a Culinary Arts major." The presenter chuckles. "We all college-educated now." He massages my shoulders with his clammy hands. "Thanks to Danny here."

I politely wiggle away from him.

"And I'm a Cartoon major," the boy attendee says.

The room laughs.

Damn, not the little boy too.

Michael stands and begins a slow clap.

Everyone joins in on the clap.

"When is the next college party? We ready," Michael says.

I look at all the eager faces.

"The next party is…" I look around the room again. This is so wrong. These guys can't be serious. "I'll get back to y'all. College parties tend to pop up last minute." As if I would know.

"Word is bond, Danny. Word is bond. Now have a seat," the presenter says.

I sit down next to Michael.

"Give another round of applause for Danny," the presenter says. "He'll get back to us soon." He turns on the projector. "Danny brought up some great points. Here are the statistics."

"Statistics? This can't be real," I whisper to Michael. "I was talking out of my ass."

"They pay me three-hundred a night to host this event. Here is a hundred for speaking." Michael slides a hundred-dollar bill into my hand.

"A hundred for that?" I look into my hand. I do need the money. "When's the next meeting?"

Michael chuckles and lightly backhands my chest. "Let's be out. The boy gonna lock up the shop. I figure if I keep him close, I'll keep his sister closer." He winks at me as he unlocks the door.

The walk from the backroom of the barbershop to the exit felt like the lights were abruptly shut off on me. Like an anvil of darkness was dropped on my unsuspecting head. I felt darker than I've ever felt. Somehow worse than waking up in jail, hungover. I'm…gutted. How come I didn't say anything? Why did I take the front of the room and continue talking, even after I saw the boy? It was wrong. One sign of personal gain (the hundred dollars) and I performed like a court jester. I fit right into that room full of chauvinists, sexists, and misogynists. That room full of Tío-Primo Martíns. DISGUSTING!

The anger I felt fighting off Tío-Primo reemerges. Those fucking guys were gross and I…I just helped them. I WILL NOT PARTICIPATE IN THIS ANY LONGER.

The front door chimes behind us and suddenly, I feel as if I've been awakened from a lifelong hypnosis.

"Michael, I'm going home," I say.

Michael beeps his car open. "Whatchu talking 'bout? I got the shorties lined up at my boy's crib." He attempts to lay a peer-pressuring hand on my back, but I dodge it.

"I said, I'm going home. It's not a debate."

"So what am I supposed to say to the friend? She a cutie too, and word on the block is that she a virgin. So you better man up." He takes a step back and crosses his arms. "If you don't go, none of us getting punani."

"Okay."

"So you still in?" Michael's stern look bounces into a smile.

"No, bitch. No-no-no-no-no. No, no, no, no. NO. no. And *helllllllll* no," I declare. "Listen to yourself. A virgin? That's supposed to entice me?"

"Duh, bro. Nobody else has hit that yet. So you'd be doing us a service, naw mean? I wanna hear all about it."

I shake my head in disgust. I want to say more, but Michael is not worth it. And at the end of the day, anything else I say will just be used to call me *sus, gay, girlie, homo,* and everything that men who don't partake in womanizing are called.

I start to walk away, but I remember there *is* one thing left to say. "Michael, you are no longer my barber."

CHAPTER TWENTY-EIGHT

Another Monday, another Allies for All meeting. That's two extra points so far (because I skipped last week's). Rubio came along too. Vicky insisted he could come after explaining that he himself needs to learn how to support the non-straight-passing members of the LGBTQ+ community.

The guest speaker's topic, "Ego-Dystonic Sexual Orientation in Developing Countries," cropped up new thoughts. Do I act the way I do, with a heightened focus on sex, because I wish to showcase my sexual orientation to society? As if not showing off my straightness would bring on the same anxiety experienced during my first catcall. The same for my first kiss.

Looking back at it now, my father raised a hornbag. After the ass whooping for dressing like a housewife and the Sister Clarissa *cleansing*, he took it a few steps further by forbidding me from food until I kissed a girl. After one day, my hunger grabbed the first girl it saw by the merry-go-round. As she spun, I timed my peck. We both left with bloody noses, however I ended up with a full stomach. A Happy Meal at that.

Rubio was expressively into the guest speaker's talk. He rapid-fired so many questions that the guest speaker was forced to request that all attendees refrain from asking questions until the end.

I had plenty of questions, too: how to stop an anti-womanizer cult and a shady pro-house-husband militia. But Tijera's phone call was a pleasant surprise because although she covered for me the day of the kidnapping, she has been distant from me at work. She also never responded to my WhatsApp messages—last week, I had to walk into work to know if I was fired or not. But on the phone, she sounded like I was her Lord and Savior.

"You are," Tijera rolls up her sleeve just past her wristwatch, "five minutes late."

"Ask Miyamoto Musashi about the benefits of being late," I say with a huge smile, while jogging towards Tijera at our section of the conveyor belt.

"Who?"

"Some swordsman that arrived three hours late to a duel. Because he was late, he threw off his opponent's, Sasaki Kojiro, inner equilibrium. The Kojiro guy was so irritated that he rushed his first move, leading to a counter and lethal strike by Musashi."

Tijera whips my butt with her hairnet. "That's silly. Latinos are always late and I've yet to see the benefits of that. Now hurry up and help me."

"Yes, ma'am." I situate myself. "*So…*" I lean towards her. "My seduction of your daughter worked out after all, huh?"

"Seduction?" She looks towards the metal roof and crosses

herself. "What kind of sick mother do you think I am? I never wanted you to sex my daughter." Tijera cocks her hairnet back.

"Chill-chill-chill. That's not what I meant." I flinch away.

"You better have meant something different." Tijera pulls her hairnet back on and focuses on the chicken patties. "But like I said on the phone. My plan worked!" She smirks. "But first, let me apologize. I should have been more direct with you because when I said my husband was Mexican, it must have went over your head. You texted me at night! My husband did not like that. Questioned me for hours about who you were. One of his buddies works two conveyor belts down and it wasn't till he confirmed who you were and our age-gap that my husband stopped huffing and puffing around the house."

"Oh…I mean…" I don't know what to say. Sounds abusive. "Is everything okay?"

"Of course. He gets all jealous then when he sees that he is wrong, he apologies with grand gestures: flowers, gifts, chocolates. But forget about that fool. Let's talk about the sneaky boyfriend. Your date with my daughter didn't work *one-hundred percent*." She dances her eyebrows, begging me to ask for more details.

I inch closer. "What do you mean by *one-hundred percent*?"

"I'm very sneaky too." She shoulder-shimmies and winks at me.

Oof, this about to be juicy. Tijera never acts this happy. I wonder what she is going to say next.

Tijera swipes at my shoulder, but I dodge it. "So you not going to ask? You payaso."

I laugh. "Relax, Tijera, I thought you were going to tell me."

She waddles close to me, enough for her body-heat to be felt. "The problem with our plan was that it was outdated," Tijera whispers. "Don Quixote's Lotorio was a thing of the past. Men don't seduce women anymore. It's the women who hold that power now."

I nod. The taste of the Johnnie Walker Blue Label that Tío-Primo bought me fills my mouth. She's right.

"Come closer, pendejo. Don't want anyone hearing. Especially that idiot two conveyors down."

I crouch to her shoulder-level.

"I hung around that nearby college. Maybe it's the one you are thinking of going to. I waited for the prettiest white girl I could find. For whatever reason, you men like the gringas. And I paid her to *meet* the sneaky boyfriend outside of his T-Mobile job at the shopping mall. She was going to, you know, stand around till he built up the cojones to go talk to her. So by the time I dragged mi hija to the mall, he would be flirting with her."

"But I don't see how that works."

Tijera pinches me. "Let me finish."

What the heck? If I don't say something, she slaps me. If I say something, she pinches me.

"Turns out, my daughter is more the jealous type than him. She saw him talking to the gringa outside of his job. Had that look on his face when a man thinks he is Pedro Infante. He applied ChapStick over twenty times.

"Then my daughter called his phone.

"He muted her!" Tijera erupts into a laugh. "Men are so stupid!" And laughs again. Full laughs too. Not like the other week, when those laughs fell off more cliffs than Wiley Coyote.

I laugh with her.

She backhands my stomach. "What you laughing at? Don't you see all that work you made me do? You lucky it only cost me two tequila bottles to pay off that college girl." She plucks an odd-shaped patty off the conveyor belt. "My daughter broke it off with him, right then and there. She even got a slap in, too. Will Smith would've approved that slap." Tijera laughs. This time, more uncontrollably than before.

I want to laugh too but Tijera is becoming dangerous with her hairnet.

"Anyways, how it go with your thing that Friday? It better have been worth it."

"Remember how I said I had an ex-girlfriend? Well, what's the next level of relational distance after that?"

"Dead," Tijera says.

"Okay, maybe not that far. But somewhere in between ex-girlfriend and dead."

"Abused?" Tijera's face reddens. She bounces a deformed patty off me.

"No, no, never. I would never hit a woman."

Tijera throws another patty at me. "Abuse is not just physical, pendejo."

"Maybe I did torment her a little. But she is madder than I thought!" I say, while protecting myself from another patty. This time I catch it.

"How so? Don't tell me you are a little too Dominican too. I've heard about you guys. You guys are sneaky-sneaky."

"That's a myth. Have you heard bachata before? We are romantic men." I lick my lips and look out into the distance, while stroking my chin.

"Yeah, and I've heard Mexican boleros and baladas, too. Those singers leave behind enough kids to start their own fútbol leagues. Now tell me what happened before I throw another patty at you."

By the time I finished confiding in Tijera about the kidnapping, dozens of deformed patties went unchecked. The story injected youth into her. She was invested in my telenovela. "What happens next? What are *we* going to do about this? I know a lot of people who will do many little things for little cash. Have you called her since? Where does she live? I should have hired her."

"And then I dressed up as a woman and almost got raped by my uncle," slipped out of my mouth.

Tijera became more animated than a cartoon. Her hands flew everywhere like a rapper. "Did he notice you had a penis? You report him to your aunt? Men eat butt? You were never in real danger. Once he would have seen your chorizo, he would have stopped."

Would he have, though? Either way, it's the principle that matters. He saw a woman and was intent on sexually assaulting her; my clothes and appearance mattered more than mutual respect.

"Mijo, you need to send that story to Univision. Make a telenovela out of it. Or at least a book."

"I guess." I chuckle. "But let's change the subject."

"Yes, finally. Let's talk about the money."

"The money?"

"Yes, pendejo. I covered two shifts for you. I'm taking half of that check that is waiting for you in the office."

"*Wooooorrrd?*" My face cries the words, *how could you.*

"Just kidding." She laughs. "You're not the only one that can rile someone up. You're also lucky that story felt like payment enough. And I support you helping your mother out with the house payments. So what else you want to talk about?"

Wait a minute. A great idea starts to form in my head. "How did you get your daughter to break up with her sneaky boyfriend again? This time, I want full details."

Tijera places a hand on my shoulder. "So I went to that school," she looks around to see if anyone is eavesdropping, "found a gringa I thought he would like…"

CHAPTER TWENTY-NINE

There she is, stepping out of the School District IT office. Walking like life is normal.

I creep lower in the car seat. Rubio does the same.

"Stop being sketch." I tap Rubio's elbow up.

Because Broncaulio was focused on other *things* at the chapi spot to ask Justina for her number and secretly activate location-sharing, we have resorted to this, a stakeout mission.

"She doesn't know you. Even if she did, you're not like me. You're decent. And I'm more like my dirty uncle." I observe Jaslene. "They wouldn't dare harm someone as decent as you."

Silence succumbs the car until Rubio sniffles.

"You a'ight? What happened to your eyes? You're tearing."

"You've never said something like that to me before."

"What? What I say?"

"You just complimented me. First time it didn't come in the form of a diss."

"What are you talking about, bro? Focus."

Jaslene stops at the edge of the sidewalk to pick up a phone call.

A passerby walking past her breaks his neck to check her out.

Oh boy, don't do it, brother. Don't do it.

He walks past her.

"Good job," I say to myself.

He performs a double-take.

Come on, man, keep it moving. Don't overthink it.

He approaches Jaslene with a slick grin. Noooooo. Don't fall victim.

Jaslene points at her phone with an attitude.

Word, homie extra rude.

He swipes the air in a dismissive manner. Likely saying, *you ain't shit anyway*. Which is facts. He, along with her, ain't shit too.

Jaslene waves her hand in our direction.

I duck.

"You're safe. She's not waving at us," Rubio says.

The same Astrovan from Wawa double-parks in front of her. She hastily hops in.

"Aight, let's see if you redeem yourself for the other night. No freezing, no chickening out. Just follow them." I squeeze past the middle-console to the back row.

"So it seems like the next stop is the club from the drag show. Must be here to pick up Gloria," Rubio says. "I still can't believe she is involved in this."

I glance at Rubio. Should I tell him? "Rubio…what makes you feel like a man? Most men would consider you to be…a sissy man or a woman."

"And who are most men?"

"Most men are most men. Whatchu mean?"

"What I mean is, most men you know are from the party crowd. The sex-driven ones. Or the ones that love sports. The competition-driven ones. How many men do you know or have met outside of parties and sports?"

I pucker my lips in thought.

"Your crowd is not most men. They are simply your type of men. The artists, the gamers, the intellectuals are invisible to you. Same way you ignore any girl that you don't find attractive."

"If you know me as such a man, then why do you chill with me?"

"Because you're actually a decent person when you are not drooling over women. Like when you was with Ida. With her by your side, you were decent. And part of me believes that is the real Danny. The Danny that came to this same exact spot with me and let loose after a while. When you take off that veil of macho man, you are my best friend." Rubio playfully tosses a balled-up receipt at me. "But to answer your question, I am a man because I feel and understand myself to be a man. Same way you innately believe you are a man. There is no long explanation for it. I am a man because that is what I know myself to be."

Something inside me pushes out the truth. "I had sex with Gloria," I abruptly say.

"Damn, kid. How was that?" He tilts his head, pleasantly surprised.

How was it? Bomb. It was a home run that might have sailed to the foul-side of the pole. So now it's under review.

"Don't give me that I-don't-kiss-and-tell silence. I'll tell you this,

I'd go straight for her."

"It was cool, I guess. Post-sex, though, had me thinking about myself. If I was a man or not."

"Of course you are. Oh shit! There she is."

Gloria struts out of the club, looking as juicy as…I glance away. Unsure of myself.

Rubio gasps. "Ahhh, it's the trans thing that got you confused. That's why you been acting weird. I know what you are thinking, and I'm here to say, she is a woman. Nothing more, nothing less… oh, they're moving again!"

We put the convo on hold. Rubio focused on trailing the van. While I had his words on repeat. She is a woman.

One hour of sunset and wilderness roads later, we seem to be near our destination.

"The good news: this is starting to look familiar. The mix of trees and rocky hills. Without a doubt, we are heading towards where we picked you guys up from. The bad: it's getting darker by the minute. These trees don't help either."

He's not exaggerating. Under this gigantic umbrella of green, orange, yellow leaves, it's a miracle that several rays of sunlight still manage to reach the ground.

"It's all good. We just need to know where their lair, dungeon barn is. And how many entrances and exits. As well as escape routes."

"The last one is easy. One road in and out."

"How you know?"

"While you were looking at the trees, they pulled up to the barn."

"So why the fuck we still on the move!" I smack Rubio's backrest. "Never mind." It's not like we could have tailgated them into their spot.

Rubio parks the car on the side of the road. "You ready?"

I scoot up closer to the mid-console. "Where's the ski mask?"

"About that…"

No way. This clown forgot the mask.

"The only thing I could find was a Ghostface mask." He hands me it. "Should work the same, right? They won't see your face."

"Ghostface!? What the fuck? This isn't *Scream*." Shit, what I wanna do *is* scream but there is no time for that. Daylight is dying and soon I won't be able to see anything. I slide it on and make my way towards the barn.

I bear crawl up a steep, dirt hill, using exposed tree roots as grip. Alas, there it is. The van parked in front of massive double-doors (that's one entrance so far), which are closed for the moment. Man, how simple this could've been if the cops would open their imagination to this whole cult scenario (and if they weren't racist) or if Detective Hanson even showed an actual interest in helping us. Oh, how I wish I could just jot down the license plate and report it to the cops. Let them take over, but I gotta do what I gotta do.

Nobody in sight, but from a single window above the double-doors, I see a white light flickering off every few seconds in random intervals. I can only assume that the projector is on.

I ninja it, tiptoeing tree to tree, avoiding leaves until I reach the side of the chapel-shaped, red barn. I crouch to the nearest window, which is half covered by leaves piled on the sill.

This is it. I press my back flat on the wall and peek a glance into the window.

Women scramble to form a circle. The commotion scares me into pressing harder against the wall. Once the movement from inside settles, I give another peek. Through a door, three girls in all black, hoodie drawn tight, form a line in the middle of the circle. They face the far wall, where I believe I see another door. Outside-light forms a thin bar on the floor (exit #2). I calculate fifty yards or so between the front and back doors.

The white bedsheet blinks bright. The girls who must be Ida, Jaslene, and Gloria drop to push-up positions and giraffe their necks high to look at the sheet.

AGENDA: FINANCIAL INDEPENDENCE 201
1. Negotiating like a White Man
2. The Time Value of Money and Inflation

Next slide, a question: True or False—Do employees, whether aware or not, pay a rent to work for their employers?

That's easy. True. The owner of the capital charges you to use his office building, technology, and/or equipment. That's how the owner makes money. Sorta like how the other barbers pay Michael a rent for a chair at his shop.

One of them extends an arm straight out, while maintaining a three-point push-up stance. She answers the question.

This is what the cult does when they're not out kidnapping sucios? They teach life skills. That's not all too bad. What kind of evil, not evil, cult is this?

The presentation continues and I'm just more and more confused. Each slide—although not going into depth on the topics—confirms that they are indeed presenting on life skills that women have historically been deprived of: stock market, mortgage rates, taxes. As well as lessons my immigrant aunts and uncles can't teach. Are these women the bad guys?

Am I the bad guy? Am I saving Ida, or am I saving myself? Am I saving future Tío-Primo Martíns from kidnappings, or am I destroying an organization that may actually be doing good? Because I'm settled on the idea that most men, especially those I've been learning from, ain't shit.

Slide after slide, push-up stance to squat stance, I observed them through the window. The physical element is odd. But doesn't look demeaning. I guess they're just holding laborious stances. I mean, surely they can up and leave whenever they want. They did drive themselves here. I mark the location of the barn on my phone's map.

My phone vibrates.

"GET THE FUCK OUT!!!" Rubio texts. Along with a photo from inside the barn: me peeking into it.

Without thought, I launch into a sprint, hightailing through the dark blue wood line, which appears to be expelling the last of the day's light. *They not catching me again. They not catching me again.* I recite between strides.

They not catching me—who is that? I hide behind the closest tree. I peek. Yeah, that's someone, and it's not Rubio. Hoodie. Feminine in stride. A Daughter of Achelous?

"Estúpido. Captain Run-Towards-the-Danger-Instead-of-

Away," the person says discreetly, making sure their words don't travel too far.

Shit, she saw me running. But…I peek again. By her movements, I can tell she doesn't know where I presently am.

I scan the floor for a weapon. A branch. A rock. Anything. Oof! I spot what looks like a small sack. I peer out to see if she is facing my way. She's not. GO! I sneak tree to tree until reaching the sack. Shit, it's half disintegrated into the earth. At least her back is to me now. Just beyond her, I can see the drop-off that I climbed earlier.

"I'm not playing hide-n-seek with you. It's getting too dark for that," she says. "I'm not here to harm you, Danny. Oops. I mean, Ghostface." She chuckles.

We'll see about that. I bum rush her from behind, and bear hug her around her arms.

"Whoa-whoa-whoa. I'm on your side," she says. She isn't putting up much of a fight, so I want to believe her, but I'm taking zero chances. Ida and the van was the last time I'd fall for any of these bitches' words. I lift the cult member onto my shoulder.

"Danny, you're ridiculous. I'm like fully complying."

Okaaay? She's not lying. She is almost gifting herself to me. I put her down and start to release her. Na-na-na. She hitting me with that reverse psychology. I force my mask onto her, but backwards, so the black part of the mask covers her eyes. I lift her onto my shoulder and trek to Rubio's car.

Definitely not part of the plan, but I need answers. No more Mr. Palomo.

CHAPTER THIRTY

"So what's the endgame, huh?" I splash water onto her veiled face.

Part of me feels guilty watching her flail in fear. Squirming for a millisecond of breath. But I've read that simulating the drowning sensation is an effective form of interrogation, which lands in the gray area between it and torture. So, I'm not the bad guy here.

"Little R, take off her hood," I say to Rubio.

Rubio prayer hands to the ceiling and exhales. He was not pro this plan, and neither am I, but we can't play nice anymore. Sometimes the ends justify the means.

"DANNY," my mother yells from the first floor. "What's all that noise? You better not be wrestling with Rubio again. I still haven't recovered from the last time he sent you to the hospital." The floorboards above the basement creak as they approach the basement door.

"Uuhhh-uh, we are working out, Ma," I shout back.

"Really?" The doorknob turns. "I need to start working out too. Mama's got her groove back."

I'm sure she does. And because of that, John is next on this chair.

The door swings open. "So what the workout plan look like down there?"

"CLOSE THE DOOR." I freeze in fear. "I mean," I clear my throat, "sorry about that, didn't mean to yell."

"Better not have."

"We need to keep the trapped heat in here to get the best workout. That's all."

"Ew, y'all stinky then. Never mind." She closes the door.

I press my hand over my heart, gripping hard to control its beat.

The door opens again. "And we're gonna have a nice chat about that yelling later." She slams the door.

Me and Rubio listen as the floorboards and staircase creak further away.

"Aight, let's make her talk."

As Rubio removes the Ghostface mask from the cult member's face, I position myself behind her, while beginning my interrogation intimidation speech.

"Y'all bitches think y'all slick. That y'all can mess with Danny Estrella. That I'm some little dumb-dumb that wouldn't fight back. Y'all must have forgotten, but I found y'all. Y'all didn't find me." I pause to think. "Kinda, sorta. But who cares? Tell us what we need to know, and we may let you walk before—you do know there is a minimum 24-hour time period before a missing person is reported?" I pull her head back by her ponytail and look into her eyes. "That's lots of time."

Is she laughing at me?

I smush smoked salmon onto her mouth, and watch it disintegrate into mush.

She spits it out.

"What's so funny?"

She continues to laugh. "Oh, boy," she catches her breath. "Y'all so paranoid that you're doing the most. I told y'all I'm on your side," she says. "Now un-rope me before I get food poisoning or something."

"Why should we do that?"

She glances at Rubio and laughs again. Suddenly, she looks more familiar.

"Justina? From the chapi bar?"

"What!? How you know that?" she replies.

"Okaaayyy, what's going on here?" Rubio says.

"Like I said, I'm on your side. I've been the one saving you degenerates from the start. The text Rose received, the person who escorted you to the woods, the text I sent Rubio. It's all been me."

"In the woods, you told them our position, though," I say.

"It was the only way to preserve my identity."

"Then why are you helping us?"

"Because while I may be one of them…I'm also one of you."

"I'm confused. I don't even know you," I say. The only things I know about Justina is that she works at Tío-Primo's favorite bar, and that she's a member of the cult.

"Of course you don't, so what? You thought you were the only one? I'm your older sister."

"Older who!?"

"S-I-S-T-E-R."

"I cannot confirm it, neither deny it." Esmeralda examines Justina. "Off the bat, she looks, at minimum, like a cousin." Esmeralda grabs hold of my shoulders and leads me next to Justina. "Squat a little." She exhales emphatically. "Listen. I'm no Jerry Springer and I'm no Maury, but if there was a posthumous episode…"

"Aight-aight, your turn," I say.

Me and Esmeralda exchange places.

"Same curly black hair, full yet not too full lips. Tilt y'all heads to the side." Hmm. "I'm not gonna front…" I nod repeatedly in confirmation. "Y'all both ugly as shit!" I kinda believe her now. The resemblance is there. And if she's been the one helping us out, blood is good reason to.

"DANNY." Esmeralda pops up from her squat-position.

"Rubia, untie her please."

Rubio glares at me in annoyance. He hates his new nickname, but now that he out-out to me, I can't help but use it.

"Wait-wait-wait. Before we untie her, we need to ask more. Anybody could look alike," Esmeralda talks some sense into me.

Justina huffs in annoyance. "Y'all gotta chill. It's not that deep. To be Dominican is to have at least one half-sibling or cousin that you find out about by chance."

"Very true. Should be a Dominican proverb," Esmeralda says. "Still. How do you know Danny is your brother, and in turn, I'm your sister?"

"I've never met our father and in my search for him, I found out he recently passed away. Then comes Ida, who suggests to tribute Danny. We all deliberate and approve because, as far as Ida knew, you are a second-generation womanizer. Plus, we all saw the video of Danny eye-fucking his coworker's ass. I researched you more. Bam! Our fathers died on the same day, same last name."

"Yeah, he was kinda good at that; giving people his last name," Esmeralda says.

"So I confronted my mother, who had kept my father's identity secret since forever. Turns out Danny was my younger brother. Also turns out that I had an older sister, but I could never locate her."

"If you were looking under Esmeralda Estrella, you wouldn't have found me. I changed my last name to my mother's maiden name when I was eighteen. It's Bonifacio now," Esmeralda says.

"Pleasure meeting you, big sis." Justina sizes Esmeralda up. "You seem badass. Not like these fuckers."

They smile at each other.

"Y'all wanna hear something more fucked up?" Justina asks rhetorically. "China's previous One-Child Policy was wild because it was codified law. What parents would do is have a child. If it was a girl, they were allowed to birth another under the policy's exception. So they had two chances at having a boy before they start paying hefty penalty fees.

"These fuckers wouldn't register the second girl with their province. Think birth certificate. Then they'd abandon the second girl or sell her to a village that needed more girls, in order to get a third chance at having a boy! *WILD*. Even wilder than that is that in Latino culture, it's just culture. What I discovered was, our sperm donor didn't want me because he wanted a boy! He refused to be financially responsible for me. That's all he saw me as. An eighteen-yearlong recurring payment."

"No fucking way," Esmeralda blurts out. Might be the first time I've heard her curse in a long time.

"Cold world, right?" Justina looks at both of us, skipping Rubio. "But something inside me told me that I couldn't abandon my blood. I really should hate y'all for our father's sin, but if I left Danny there at the initiation, I'd be no different from my absent father.

"So now I'm in a dilemma. I can't abandon Danny, yet I can't abandon the sisterhood. They've been nothing but good to me."

"How you even get mixed in all this?" I ask.

"I showed up to some sorority event two years ago at Rutgers University called Misogyny in Anime. Because I was a senior in high school trying to do college shit. The event was about female characters drawn with gigantic breasts. And the pervy, old man that serves as comic relief."

"That is so random," I say.

"We do all types of misogyny events like reggaeton, healthcare—nurse fetishes—and other topics. Think of anything and there is misogyny or sexism at play. But more importantly, it's how we recruit a diverse group of women. But for me specifically, it was anime. I love it, I binge it. So like I said, I was at the event, skip to the end, I was answering and asking hella questions. Then soon after the event, while I was working at my uncle's bodega, making sandwiches—"

"Hold up." She looks even more familiar now. "On 45th and Park Avenue?"

"Yep, that's the one."

The shorty with the fatty from the bodega that makes a bomb ham and cheese is my sister!? I'mma be sick.

"*Ayo.*" Rubio's mouth balloons with laughter. "Ain't that the girl you said—"

I elbow Rubio in his ribs.

"Said what?" Justina says.

"Nothing!"

Rubio chuckles and taps his finger by his temple. "Ah-hah, you see. Told you you think too much with your…" He allows his facial expression to finish his sentence.

"Can I continue?" Justina raises an eyebrow. "That's what I thought."

Damn, she's definitely Esmeralda's sister.

"So, I'm making a ham and cheese for a customer, when I get a text from an unknown number saying, *we saw you at the event and we'd like to extend you an invite to a meet and greet with like-minded women.* So I was like, sure why not. I pulled up, yada-yada. They asked if I'd like to join their sisterhood and also informed me about their younger high school side of the sisterhood. So I joined."

"That's it?" I ask.

"It couldn't have been that simple," Esmeralda says.

"Nope. It was. After the rigorous initiation process, I was in."

"Can we get more detail?" Esmeralda asks.

"Negative. I may be helping out, but I swore to never reveal the secrets of the sisterhood. But if you word the questions right,

I may be able to give more insight." She dances her eyebrows. "Y'all smart, right?"

Esmeralda and I glance at each other.

"Okay, since you're bound by loyalty, we won't jeopardize that," I say. "Question one: why did you join?"

"Do I really need a reason to join a group of women that seek to equal the playing field? Some people want to see progress for the future generations. We want to see it now, in our lifetime. What ought to be should not be left as a challenge. I don't seek to spend my whole life convincing thieves—men—to give me back what is mine."

"Hmm." Esmeralda mums. "That's kind of gangsta. Where do I sign up?"

I nudge Esmeralda. She isn't wrong, though.

"My turn. Is Danny's life in danger?" Esmeralda asks.

"No. But his manhood is."

"What!?" I say.

"Shut up, Danny. I'm asking the questions now." Esmeralda gives me the death glare she is insanely good at.

I'mma be quiet, but *yooo*…she just said some wild shit that pertains to me.

"Why?" Esmeralda continues asking questions.

"If you've spent more time with him than I have," she chuckles, "you know why."

Esmeralda pauses to think. "Yeah, he would be the type of guy you'd have to get rid of in order to see progress."

"Exactly."

"Yo! I'm right here," I say. They plan to diss me all night?

Everyone ignores me.

"How can we save Danny?"

"Beats me. Every time I get him out of trouble, he drags himself back into it."

"Aight. My bad if I've chosen not to live the rest of my life questioning every girl I meet."

Everyone continues to ignore me.

Anda el diablo! They really gonna silence me into the invisible man.

"Let's get this straight. I've decided to be loyal to both the sisterhood and my blood. Think of a Venn diagram. I'm staying in the overlapping middle, instead of picking a definitive side. Because again, I won't abandon people like my father did."

"Is it safe to assume that you won't expose Danny?"

"Nobody knows I'm your half-sister. I'm keeping it that way. I'm also gonna have to come up with a hell of a story for how I miraculously ended up an hour away from the barn. But I'll think of something."

I turn to Rubio. His eyes and mouth are wide open in awe. His head ping-ponging between Esmeralda and Justina's paddle of questions and rebuttals.

"Am I still a tribute?" I say.

"Yes."

Finally, I exist again.

"Can I be replaced?"

"Can't say."

"Can there be another tribute?"

"Yes. Oops. Y'all got me. That was a secret." Justina winks.

"And that's why if you keep showing up, there may not be another tribute."

So I can be replaced? "Equal or greater value?"

"Now you're thinking."

Bet. One more question. "Is a single-mother allowed to date and have sex?"

"Yes. Wait, what? Definitely yes."

Esmeralda backhands my shoulders. "Yes, dumbass. If a married man can date and have sex, you best believe your mother can when she is single."

"Jeez-la-fucking-weez. It was just a question."

"A dumb question." Esmeralda shakes her head. "How many members are there?"

"Can't say."

"Am I safe?"

"Nobody knows who you are. We only care about the tributes."

"So Rubio is safe too?"

"Yes."

"There you go, Danny. I'm popping smoke." Esmeralda strides towards the stairs.

I latch onto her wrist. "No, you not."

Esmeralda breaks character and laughs. "I thought you were Danny the *Man*. El matatan. El duro."

"I'm no longer that type of man."

"Hmm. I hate to say it, but perhaps this is the best thing to happen to you. Who knew a group of misandrist women could turn you against your scumbag ways?"

"Skkrrr. We are not misandrists. Yes, we do a little capture and release—"

"Wait, so I'd be released?"

"Most of you would be." Justina grimaces.

"What the fuck does that mean?" I frantically look at Rubio and Esmeralda, then back at Justina. *The chopping, his manhood, most of you would be.* Everything points to my dick being chopped off.

"Y'all chopping off my dick?"

"Anywho. I think Danny can confirm that we are an empowerment group. He saw what was being taught. Since I've joined, I've—"

"Yerrrrrr. I asked a question. What about my dick?"

"—invested in the stock market with confidence. I've built my credit score. I've learned salary negotiation tactics, how to read a mortgage, the time value of education. You see, it's not just still-money that depreciates over time, it's also education. And that's what most men lack. By the age of sixteen, they think they understand the world. Typically generalizing life in one statement: it's a man's world. By twenty-five, their frontal lobes are fully developed and there is no helping them change after that. All while women have to keep educating themselves in order to adapt and progress, men just stay the same because *I'm a man.* So again, we are not misandrists. We are just not comfortable with *what is.*"

"What does misand…whatever even mean? And let's not forget about that *most-of-you* comment," I say.

"It's the counterpart to misogyny. It's a prejudice or hatred towards men," Esmeralda says.

"Exactly," Justina says. "But we don't *hate* men. We just loathe sexist, straight cis-gender men."

"So y'all hate the old Danny. Not this one in front of you." I nod. "I'm brand-new Danny. Straight out of the box. I love women."

Rubio smacks his lips. "You don't love women, you love pussy," he interjects.

"Hello there. Whose side are you on?"

"Oops, my bad. Forgot what we were doing here."

"If you think one course on feminism, a few allyship meetings, and one drag show makes you a new man, you, my estranged brother, are the equivalent of a white person with one Black friend."

"Oof! She got you there." Esmeralda's face lights up in amusement.

"But it's a good start," Justina concedes.

"Justina, enlighten me. Where do we go from here?"

"How do you know I've been to Allies for All meetings?" I interject.

"We know everything. And as for where we go from here, we go our separate ways until…I don't even know. This family reunion is nice, but I can't be seen with y'all.

"And remember, we don't know each other, and I can't help. It's the same deal the sisterhood is getting. Hopefully, all goes well and we meet up after this is all settled. Oh, and by the way, why the smoked salmon? That wasn't cool. I could've been allergic."

"You put a dildo in my mouth, so I found the closest thing to a yeast infection."

"You're wild." Justina heads up the stairs. "But you might need to think of something wilder." She exits the basement.

"So what do we do now?" I say.

Both Esmeralda and Rubio are stuck in thought.

Part of me wants Rubio to drive me straight to the Dominican consulate to get my cedula. But I'd be leaving behind all my problems to everyone I care about. My mother with the house. Rubio without a friend. Esmeralda with Detective Hanson. Broncaulio, who would personally Uber himself to the initiation if left without guidance. One day, Rose will corner Gloria in an alley, and I'll need to be there to save her from going to jail herself. And then there is Ida. I think Esmeralda was right when she told me that everyone is worth saving. Especially Ida. I can't abandon her. I also don't wanna abandon Justina, even though we've just met. I run my hand through my hair.

"She did say there can be other tributes," Rubio says. "Let's get them other tributes."

"Would that work?" I say. That idea sounds easy enough. And after my talk with Tijera, the idea crossed my mind. Dangle someone in front of the Daughters, so enticing that they'd forget about me. There are plenty of guys that can replace me but that would be putting another person in harm's way. And Broncaulio needs replacement too. Because I don't think he's leaving until he accomplishes his ridiculous goal of bagging one gringa.

"You got a dumber, less illegal idea?" Esmeralda says.

"Actually, I think I do." Tijera got her daughter to break up with her boyfriend. I think I can make the Daughters break up with me and the others. "But don't tell the others about Justina."

Next weekend, we taking the cult down at a party. Where it all started.

CHAPTER THIRTY-ONE

Eldon vetted the perfect party for us to trap the cult: the first costume party of the Halloween season (all of October). Where we can disguise ourselves without cross-dressing. Where we know how to identify them (their bracelets). Where we will finally have the upper hand. But first, I need a costume.

"I'm going to stick out like a pig roast at a vegan function. Why you even have this costume?" I say.

"I'm Jamaican, Danny-boy. I hustle everything, everywhere, anytime. Now stop being a long bitch, and let's find you a bun tonight. Get it?" Eldon laughs.

"First of all, this is a wiener, not a hot dog. Second of all, I knew I shouldn't have trusted you." The same guy that claimed his Spanish was too weak to cross-dress. I reach around the back of my neck for the zipper. "Get me a cardboard box and a marker. I'll be a nudist-on-strike instead."

"Stop gwan like a fassy. All this bitch-boy crying. Here are some sunglasses." Eldon slides Ray-Bans onto my face (the only part of the body that isn't enclosed by the costume). "Ay, now you look like that meme. Nobody can tell it's you under there, Long Bitch Danny."

"A'ight. Chill out with the bitch jokes." I readjust the Ray-Bans. Only my cousins can diss me for free. "What's your costume?"

"Give me a sec," Eldon says. He rummages through his closet. "There it is. Hand me the beanie hanging on the door."

I look behind his room door and find a Jamaican-flag knitted-beanie. "This?" I spin the beanie around my finger.

Eldon steps out of his closet wearing a tie-dye shirt.

"Bro, no you not." I cock my head back. "Dead-ass?" I hand Eldon the beanie.

"Whatchu *meeean*?" He puts the beanie over his 'locks.

I chuckle. "You want me to guess what you are?"

"It's easy. I'm a Black guy dressed as a Rastafarian," Eldon says. "At least that's what every other person in the party is going to think."

I smack my lips. "You wild for this."

"You hating. It's not my fault that people think dressing like a Jamaican Rastafarian is a costume. I might as well use this fit once a year and save my money." He tucks at the edges of the beanie, making sure it lays perfect. "Everyone is gonna be so impressed with my accent too." He chuckles. "Wagwan, bitches."

I lean against Eldon's dresser and grip the edges. "You sure we should go through with this? We can pretend it never happened and keep our penises from their grasps," I say. "Rose is a woman, so naturally, she is safe. Broncaulio boards his flight to DR tomorrow. We the ones truly risking something." I look at my reflection in the dresser mirror.

This has gone way beyond anything imaginable. Way above anything Detective Hanson and Esmeralda could have foreseen. My options, absurd. Pursue these psychos, save myself from expulsion and jail; don't pursue these psychos, keep my penis. Fail, lose my pee-pee; succeed, I'm a free man. And what about Justina and Ida? My penis is worth way more than expulsion and jail. There is no doubt in my mind about that. But that's only its worth to me. What's the greater good here?

And Yo! Why has the detective been so hands-off? I get that Esmeralda is doing a great job of keeping him at bay, but Esmeralda may be right about him. He shady as fuck.

"You know, I've had a similar thought myself. But I was humiliated. Felt weak tied onto that chair. They took my balls and shoved rubber ones into my mouth." Eldon makes a squeezing motion with his hands. "I want my balls back."

"You see, bro, you think too much like a man. Don't you see that's how they got us in the first place? If we didn't roam around like we owned the world, we would have never been in this mess."

"No, what happened was, you squealed my name to Gloria, Ida, or Jaslene. You know all three of them. I'm here because of you," Eldon says. "I've been throwing parties for years. Why now? It's you. You pissed them off."

"Errrr, wrong. What you meant to say was, I would not be here if I didn't spend so much time getting girls drunk and manipulating my way into their panties. That video Gloria played for us was gross. You can't treat women like a game," I say. I push off the dresser and stand tall.

"Well, isn't that cute? Danny, the pretty boy that girls throw themselves on, is calling me gross." Eldon steps closer. "I have to work for my poom-poom. I have to be aggressive in order to touch some oxtail. If not, the women just gravitate to guys like you." Eldon presses his finger into my chest.

So he believes he out here merely surviving because sex doesn't jump onto his bed on a whim? If women don't throw themselves at him, he sets traps, lowers inhibitions, and talks a slick game of false promises and lies? He believes not being handsome is unfair. But women are real. Unlike our made-up belt-notch competitions. "You right. You are ugly." I chuckle.

"And you look like a pee-pee." Eldon laughs.

I can't change his mind today, but one day I may. As soon as I figure out what's the difference between being horny and being a man. Too many questions remain.

I look at my wristwatch. "The others should be on their way to my crib. Let's bounce."

"Damn, Danny, what are you supposed to be, Oscar Mayer or a pink, white penis?" Rose says. "If it's the latter, I expected the costume to be a little skinnier." She laughs onto Rubio's shoulder.

I look at Eldon. "Told you it's a wiener."

Rose circles Eldon, checking out his outfit. "I dig it, mon. Cultural appropriation for Halloween." Rose extends a high-five.

"Wait, no diss for me? I'm offended." Eldon unenthusiastically high-fives Rose.

"Na, I save the disses for Danny. He thinks he is cute and funny.

The worst combination for any man. You, on the other hand, are just funny…looking." Rose laughs onto Rubio's shoulder again.

Eldon looks at me. "Told you I'm too ugly to be acting cute."

I backhand Eldon on his chest. "My turn. And let me guess. You are a piece of unflushed caca disguised as Ash Ketchum," I say.

Rose squints and shakes her head. "You always saying some wack shit. I'm Dustin from *Stranger Things*, estúpit."

"You surely are a stranger…*ting*," Eldon says.

Eldon and I high-five each other.

"Enough of this. Let's go over the plan," Rubio says.

"And what are you supposed to be?" I chuckle.

"Grow up, Danny." Rubio crosses his arms or wings. He is feathered from knee to shoulder in bright colors. I don't even want to guess.

"Time for Plan Tijera!" he says, changing the topic. He starts scribbling and drawing away at the whiteboard.

I snatch the marker off his hands. "Na, you not planning anything this time. It's my plan."

"I got the best handwriting though," Rubio says.

True. I sit back down. "Aight, but no add-ons or extra shit. If a light bulb goes off in your head, turn it right off."

"Fine. It was only a drag show and a little cross-dressing," he mumbles under his breath.

So here's the plan. I pull up to the party first in incognito mode. I scope the party out and find Daughters of Achelous bracelets (a job better suited for Broncaulio since he apparently got a keen eye for bracelets, but we don't trust that he won't use the bracelet intel work for his sexual gain). Second, Eldon comes with his obvious disguise. We dangle his ass as bait, hoping a Daughter bites and looks to snatch him. Once we confirm a Daughter has seen him, I'll approach Eldon, adding suspicion to me. I'll even take off the Ray-Bans. That's when both of us will walk outside to let Michael and his boy—who are also dressed in a wiener and Rastafarian costume—inside. They won't know what's going on. As far as Michael knows, I was sorry for the other night and I'm making it up to him. But the girls will snatch them, thinking it's us. Broncaulio and Rubio are in charge of getting Michael and his boy to the party. (After their performances at the chapi spot, we are keeping both of them out of sight as much as possible. Broncaulio catches his flight tomorrow, so his getaway is less than twenty-four hours away. Rubio is better suited as a wheelman.)

I prayer-hand. May Broncaulio not get enticed by the blessed booties that will be at this party. May Rubio only drop off Michael and his boy, and not let Broncaulio enter.

CHAPTER THIRTY-TWO

As if I manifested it with my doubts, Broncaulio never brought Michael to the party (at least not on time). Didn't even send a text saying he was incoming. Nada. Hung us out to dry.

Ooof, when I catch him, I'mma smack him down harder than a capicúa on a dominoes table. Because here we are again with the bullshit. The flames, the darkness, the barn. Only differences are they didn't bother tying us up on chairs or dildo-gagging us. No need for it. They tranquilized the shit out of us and sprawled us out on the floor. Oh, and there is some random guy in a sunflower costume that is too tall to be Broncaulio on the floor too.

The Halloween costumes are a nice touch, though (if there is a silver-lining to getting captured again by the Daughters of Achelous). Like when TV shows aired Halloween specials. Never truly part of the plot, but fun to see things shaken up a bit. But this Halloween special is very much part of the plot. The sexy doctors, princesses, and super heroines skipped the formalities and went straight to resolving unfinished business: the chopping the girls talked about when me and Broncaulio were high up in that tree. How do I know? Well...

Ropes are tossed over a wood beam, confirming what I already suspect.

My heart rate kicks up a tick. The idea of death floods my mind. I billow out a hard exhale.

Someone once said, "Give a man enough rope, and he will hang himself." Don't know who; my brain hoarded it along with everything else. But who gave me all this rope? Was it patriarchy, Dominican culture, my father, my uncles, my mom, my aunts? Is liking women my life's demise? Is it something to die over?

I've thought up millions of ways to die before. Never intentionally. My brain sort of wandered there from time to time.

Rescuing my mother from a burning house. Bad sushi. Snake bite during a hike. Hiroshima. Instant combustion at the spark of the stovetop. 9/11. School shooter. Suicide by drowning. By jumping off the Empire State Building. GW Bridge. My brain has plopped me into many scenarios, yet they all seemed more plausible than this.

Sailor Moon smiles as she anchors one end of the rope.

How could I ever have predicted this?

...my penis at the other end.

(EARLIER)

"I'm here," I mumbled to myself as the Uber driver stopped outside of the party. How it all started. A fucking basement party. But this one was vetted by Eldon, who knew the host. The plan was air tight. For added insurance that the Daughters would show up, Broncaulio texted Jaslene asking for a going-away *gift*; one last memory of the States. A text he would have sent, regardless of the situation. Making it less suspicious than rain falling from dark clouds.

As per the plan, I arrived first. Nervous again, but this time with good reason. I've been to dozens of parties, but never on a mission. Well, never on this type of mission. Because finding a shortie to holla at was always a mission.

First, I'd gather the essential equipment and tools: fresh clothes, sexy date-night type of cologne, haircut or shape-up, ChapStick, and gum. Then I'd check social media to see who planned on showing up. Hit up a few friends to see if I'm rocking solo or walking in with reinforcements. To see what the liquor situation was, enough heads meant more bang for my buck with the handle instead of the 750 milliliter. At arrival, I would say what's up to a few acquaintances and people I secretly didn't fuck with. The more greetings, the more attention women gave me. And then I'd scope out the lineup. Filling slots in my I-would-hit list. Could either strike up a conversation, introduce myself during a game of flip-cup, or wait for the right type of music because the real dancing doesn't start until the lights are off. That's the type of stuff I missed while booed up with Ida. That process. The hunt. But that is precisely the thing I need to stop. Couldn't even enjoy half of those parties because there was always a countdown ticking in my head—had to bag something before the night was over. Whenever I struck out, the night felt like a waste. That's Eldon-level pathetic.

At this party, though, I wouldn't have blamed Eldon. It was a perv buffet. Butt cheeks leaking out of fairy and pirate costumes, nipples one fast movement away from slipping out. I bit my hand in restraint so many times that I left molar imprints in them.

The point is not to be asexual. The point is to stop treating women as a competitive penis sport—words Vicky from Allies for All texted me after I asked her, what about men hollering at women is so wrong.

To start, I scouted the party. The back entrance led to the kitchen where a portable cooler filled with jungle juice was, and tossed next to it, empty Everclear bottles; signs of weekly allowances tapped out. Yet no signs of GI Jas; our new codename for Gloria, Ida, and Jaslene.

"Hey, are you…like…a…giant Slim Jim?" asked a borrach Minnie Mouse, jungle juice in hand, spilling with her various hand gestures. Cleavage looked juicy enough to dip my finger in.

I grabbed her cup and placed it on the kitchen counter. "I think that's enough for you, teta mouse." I walked towards the basement entrance just past the kitchen.

"Hey, you not…that was not nice." Her heels clacked in a wobble. Little did she know, that was the nicest thing someone could've done for her before an Eldon or a Broncaulio utilized her drunken state as a cheat code.

At the top of the steps, I stared and stared at the strobing lights illuminating the basement blue every second or two. Should we really be doing this? Esmeralda said she informed Detective Hanson about the plan, but he provided no feedback. Thinking about it now, I never signed any papers. And Esmeralda's Rohypnol-centered defense? It's been at least two weeks since she last updated me. I turned back into the kitchen and chugged a cup of jungle juice. My idea of washing away my anxieties. Being a little tipsy would help, I thought.

"Oh my God! You are like a…beer bratwu-rst."

I snatched her drink and chugged it too. Wiped the red off my lips and strode down them steps.

At the bottom, nobody greeted me. Not one single head nod. Nobody pushed me to a table with hella liq. One Bad Bunny did ask me for just the tip because he thought I was a penis. I warned him to be careful. Some girls kidnap for comments like that. Could be any of these girls.

Once posted up on the far wall, where the party was widely visible, we deployed Eldon and his obvious disguise.

Eldon walked into the basement, lugging the jungle juice cooler from upstairs. A few mamis and unwelcomed bozos crowded around him. His arrival ruffled the tall grass. That's when I spotted the first possible Daughter of Achelous. She wasn't dressed up as Wonder Woman, but her hands-on-hips stance had energy to it. One of malice. And then I felt nice. Tipsy. Drunk. Borrach Obama, the 44th president of high school inebriation. Vision blurred, words slurred.

"I know who you are and what you're here to do," I whispered into the girl's ear.

"Oh yeah? And what's that?" She took a step to the side.

"Pe-NIS," I said. The weight of the jungle juiced smacked down. Soon the entire party was yelling the word penis, one by one, in an ascending volume. That's right. I'm a hot dog, and I came here for some buns.

She playfully slapped my arm. The universal sign for flirting. "Dang! Wish I had my phone out to record that."

I applied ChapStick, accidentally passing some on my nose. "How 'bout you still whip it out, and I put my phone number in it?" I lean against the air, tripping a few inches. "Watch where you going," I said to the nearest moving object. "Sorry about that. Where were we?" I gently lifted her princess hand. "I love your nails, by the way." I twirled her. Watched her Cinderella dress flail open at the bottom. "And everything else."

She laughed. "Are all wieners this steamy?"

Ding! Ding! Ding! She understood the difference between a wiener and a hot dog. She saw me for who I was. Next thing I knew, me and…I never caught her name, bumped and grinded while the room spun and spun around us like a perico ripiao.

Cinderella backing it up on a wiener. The stuff of fairytales. I looked around the dance floor to see if anyone else had peeped me baggin'. Eldon. Where he go?

Eleven missed calls, twenty new messages. The concentrated blood flow at my penis hopped to my heart. I closed one eye to make the room stop spinning.

"We need to switch now! If Danny doesn't respond within five mins, I'm fucked," Eldon's last text message, six minutes prior. Scrolling down, Eldon had been led to a private room on the second floor.

"Everything okay?" Cinderella said. She contorted her neck to look back at me, maintaining her crouched twerk stance. She bussed it low then rose up my pole.

Eldon or booty? Eldon or booty? "Yeah, everything is great.

I'll be right back." I grabbed Cinderella by the waist and pressed my penis harder onto her butt for one last wine.

When I peeked into the room Eldon was in, he was backed up against a wall with his hands raised. A Daughter, dressed as Cardi B, appeared to hold pepper spray. Someone (too tall to be Broncaulio or Michael) in a sunflower costume was handcuffed to the queen-sized bed. His feet (I assume it's a he) dangled off it.

"Hurry up! Now," I texted Broncaulio before busting into the room.

"Cut the shit, Cardi B. We know who you are," I said.

Boom! The door shut behind me. Boom! The bathroom door crashed against the wall next to Eldon. Boom! How quickly things change. I gotta give a round of applause to these bitches. I've hot-boxed plenty of bathrooms before, but GOD DAMN. How they squeeze twenty girls into a closet? They unloaded out that joint locked and loaded, lighting us up with tranquilizer darts. Before I knew it, I was dumb bobo crashing on top of the sunflower costume-wearer. Meanwhile, Broncaulio probably at the party—if he ever arrived—getting some cheeks grinded into his likely boner. Along with Michael's thirsty ass.

And now, here I am, at this stupid barn again. Penis tied up. Numb. Lying on the floor. Blinking and breathing, my last remaining functions. I wish they had put us to sleep instead. Or at least faced me away. I rather not see what happens next.

CHAPTER THIRTY-THREE

Harley Quinn lightly pulls the rope attached to Eldon's...

Tomb Raider walks across the barn, unfastening the big pocket on her cargo shorts.

Eldon curses everyone but his grandma out. He shakes, trembles, cries.

Tomb Raider takes out a pair of gardening shears. And in one swift motion, SNIP!

Eldon's *flagpole* tumbles. The rope is tossed to the floor.

My eyes launch out of their sockets. My balls tuck in, rushing to take my eyeballs' place. My penis is next.

I never apologized to Ida. Never told my mother how much I love her. Never told Esmeralda that I admire her. And I'll never get the chance to tell my father that he was wrong: there is more to being a man than spiking our penises anywhere it can clamp into. It is not a man's world.

But that's life. You learn the hard lessons too late—the word, hard, short for hardwired. A few drinks and I was back to toxic ol' Danny. Mujeriego Extraordinaire, my factory setting. A Basement Bellaco. Ten bodies. That's my life's legacy. Sex. What the heck have I been doing all these years? And what am I going to do now after I'm castrated like Eldon just was?

Chung-Li bandages Eldon, who has added more red to his tie-dye shirt.

I play sports to get girls. I hit the gym to get girls. I get good grades in an attempt to one day secure a high-paying job, to then get girls…I…enter social settings to get girls. I dress the way I do to get girls. I learned to dance to get girls. I compete against other men to get girls. I do everything for pussy. I'm a fucking slave.

"Danny! We are talking to you." Sailor Moon tugs on my rope. My body tenses up. Goosebumps porcupine out of every pore. It sucks even more that I can't move my head enough off this floor to see my penis. To give it one last goodbye.

A cult member adjusts my head's position so that I can focus on the now illuminated screen.

On the screen, a poor-lit video of me at my first party since the breakup. I'm highly visible in that dark basement because I thought I was gonna kill it in that all white outfit. I wore that bucket hat to get girls too.

"Do you recognize that cup?" Sailor Moon says.

My tongue goes flaccid. "That's, that's-that's my cup. When I-I…a marker, I draw a crown on it."

"Then explain this."

A white substance is dropped into my cup.

"Y'all drugged me at that party?"

"Nice try. Those hands are veiny like a man's."

Clear nail polish reflecting a glint of light. Usually I wouldn't, but that night I did. Ida loved clean fingernails. Yet, there appears to be a subtle difference between my hand holding the cup and the hand dropping the drug, but hard to tell with the party being so dark.

"So who did?" Eldon? A way to take me out of the hunt.

I can barely see Eldon in my peripheral anymore, but I assume he's lying unconscious on the floor.

Tomb Raider walks across me towards him. Bending down to check his pulse. She gives a thumbs up.

Cardi B hands Tomb Raider an icepack. I see Eldon's limp hands being crossed near his crotch. She bags something into a Ziplock full of ice then walks across me again. Begging me to look at what's inside: his manhood.

"No, keep watching."

After my drink was spiked, I approached Ida. I'm all in her ear while her cousin, Primo, stands with his hands in his palomo pockets. Ida and I enter a private room together. The end.

"You roofied me, Danny." Sailor Moon's (Ida) voice crackles.

"No, Ida, I would never. I love you too much." Oh wow, that came out quick.

Ida jerks her head to the side to recollect her composure.

"My Ida Frida. Remember Autumn and Daniel Jr? The names of our future children." I gulp. "I can't help but think I aborted them. I know. I know. It sounds silly, but that's how much I loved you. To the point where our future was real to me. I threw it all away for some dusty vagina that I don't even remember. You can exact whatever revenge it is you seek, but not these other women." My glance oscillates around the room (as much as physically possible). "Y'all don't know me." Tears cascade down my ears, then onto the ground. "I don't even know myself. I've been conforming to my idea of normal. Doing what other men around me did and trying to be the best at it. But I'm trying." I grunt. "I'm learning. I'm awakening."

I look at Harley Quinn. She is motionless. Still holding on to her end of the rope that is attached to the giant sunflower's… stem. "Gloria, if that's you, I'm sorry too. I didn't know what to think of our encounter. But now I know I envy you. You have a gift of self-expression and self-awareness that I don't have. You know who you are. Meanwhile, I'm at ground-zero because I've lived never questioning my identity. Who is Danny?" I shrug internally. "I've lived as a default template. Emulating others.

"Rose. I don't know where you are, but I appreciate you. You ride-or-die. De lo mío. We clown each other heavy-heavy…heavier than you." I force a chuckle through the tears. "Outsiders think we hate each other. But your loyalty is guaranteed till the end. But you needed to hold me accountable, instead of beating up all those girls that I kinda assaulted. Family is not an excuse to tolerate ignorance and unacceptable behaviors.

"Rubio! You wild for taking me to that drag show." I laugh at the ceiling. Already accepting reality. Might as well laugh before it's over, right? "Thanks for challenging me to something real. This might be the end of the rope for me." I chuckle. "Get it? Rope. You taught me the difference between adult and man. I understand now. A little too late, but I understand. Gender roles limit a man to being half an adult. Even more obvious, masculinity and sexual orientation are not the same. Perhaps if I would have embraced masculinity and femininity as equals, I would have learned to express my emotions and thoughts. Esmeralda did say I was a good communicator. I just chose to never communicate certain things because they weren't masculine enough." Boogers flow into my mouth.

"*MAMAAA, just killed a man. Hung a rope against his penis, pulled it now he's dead.*" I laugh hysterically and fizzle out into a sigh. "My Superwoman. An amazing teacher with an idiot student. I should have watched you closely. You were the real blueprint. A woman who did both roles. An adult. Te amo." I exhale. "Don't get mad about the dirty plate I left in the sink. I promise, this time will be the last time I do that."

I look at Ida, who has fallen to her knees beside me. Her grip on the rope, loose.

"Do what you must," I say.

My tears flow faster. I stare at the blurred ceiling.

My body tingles.

The cold floor.

The dry prickly rope.

I can feel again. I smile.

…

A slow clap commences. "Wow, that was a first," someone says.

"We should get him to guest speak at next year's initiation," another says.

"Only if he is willing. We still neutering him. Ida, it's time."

I tense up, while Ida hesitantly stands and grabs the rope. Rolling it over her wrist for added strength.

CHAPTER THIRTY-FOUR

A human-sized plátano smashes through the barn window and parkour-rolls into the room. "Which one of you mamis trying to be my queso frito?"

Ha. This clown said we would know it's him when he shows up. Too bad he showed up at the wrong party. With Eldon down, there is an extra rope with his name on it.

The Daughters of Achelous take a step backward. "And who are you?" a sister says.

"Plátano Power, baby. Last time I wasn't ready. Today I am." He partly unzips his costume and unloads Gatorade bottles, Five-Hour Energies, and a long string of condoms.

"What is this?" a sister says. She shakes her head as she scatters the beverages with her feet. She picks up the five-foot tall thread of condoms and tosses them back to the ground. "Who are you again?"

Broncaulio winks at me, before replying, "Who you think, muñeca? I'm the one that's gonna leave you like mangú. Mashed."

No way this idiot came here alone with an orgy on his mind.

I concentrate on the window he smashed through, hoping some type of reinforcement jumps through it, until I notice Ida in my peripherals.

With everyone distracted, Ida sprints to the sunflower costume-wearer and unties him.

The man in the sunflower costume emerges out of it. "Everybody back the hell up!" He waves a gun, keeping everyone away. "Ida, take off my mask." He stumbles a bit, still feeling the effects of the tranquilizers.

I hold my breath in anticipation.

"I'm Detective Hanson with Hawk Union Police. You are all under—" He collapses to the ground. His gun slides next to me.

Without hesitation, I reach for it, but the tranquilizer's effect inhibits my movement. I walk my fingertips to the gun. I. Need. To. Grab. It. I nip it by the handle.

Tomb Raider rushes to snatch the gun.

I. Need. To. Grab. I—

Someone else plucks the gun off the floor.

"I'll be taking this. Matches my outfit," Justina says with a devilish tone. Her rent-a-cop outfit graduates to beat-cop.

"Dang! Beat me to it," Tomb Raider says. "Whatever." She walks toward Detective Hanson. "Well, if it isn't Boobie Hanson." She tilts his head. "Tonight is a special night indeed."

"*The* Boobie Hanson? The one that got away?" Justina says.

"Technically, everyone here got away at one point. But now that won't be the case."

Broncaulio is tossed onto the ground.

"So, where were we?" Tomb Raider says.

Justina points the gun at Tomb Raider.

"What are you doing, Justina?"

Justina's trigger finger quivers as she visibly weighs out her options. "Danny! Please tell me there is a plan."

"Uhh, I mean..." If I tell her there *was* a plan, I'm sure she'd side with the Daughters. The winning side. Or maybe she is still on their side and is trying to trick me into revealing whatever plan we do have. I can bluff this! "It's over, ladies," I say confidently.

A polite door-knock silences the room, catching everyone off-guard, especially me.

The Daughters frantically look at each other. I glance at Broncaulio, in search of a hint of hope. He mouths to himself, eyes closed, "Yo puedo con to'a. Yo puedo con to'a." Fuck!

"Everyone, shut the hell up!" Justina shouts. She inches towards the barn's large double-door.

Giggles and chatter of excitement can be heard outside.

"Someone go check that out," Justina orders.

The door creaks slightly open. "Excuse me. How can I help you guys?" Tomb Raider says.

An inflow of men in Halloween costumes stampedes through the door, knocking a Daughter to the floor. They scatter across the room like roaches in the light. None hesitate to beat the other to a Daughter's ear.

"Hi, I'm a Cosmetology major. How about you?" Michael says. He glances at me. "Damnnnnn, Daniel, you was starting the party without us?"

~

The men were relentless. Which bought us enough time for the police to arrive. And when they did, there were only so many we could tackle and pin down. Luckily, we had all that rope. I cut Broncaulio and Rubio some slack for arriving late. I guess it was my fault. Just like the family barbecue, to be late is to be early—I mistakenly gave them the punctual time. Still perfect timing, especially for Eldon, who Rubio was about to rush to the hospital until we realized it was a fake penis that was chopped off. But then we noticed that Eldon was still in such a state of shock that we ended up taking him anyway.

We were all so numb that we couldn't see or feel our penises. I mean, I saw something that looked like a penis attached to a rope by my crotch. What else was I supposed to think? We believed it. So much that I word-vomited my last words. Let out all that emotion. But it's over.

Watching it all unfold, it's quite a shame that only the women were cuffed. The men had technically not done anything illegal. Trespassing did not hold up. And nothing sexual happened—which I'm grateful for—but I wish something would have stuck. At least get them on the sex-offender watchlist or something.

"What should we do with Gloria and Jaslene? Technically, they are not official members yet," Detective Hanson says. "I'll leave it up to you two, my informants."

Informants? Plural? Ida and I look at each other. I'm surprised. She isn't.

Gloria and Jaslene sit tied-up on the grass. Eyes seared open from the possibility of jail.

"I think they were misguided and deserve a second chance," I say. "What do you think?" I study Ida. Still wrapping my head around the idea that Ida and I were on the same team.

Ida mulls it over in her head. "Yeah, why not?" She nods. "I've witnessed people change after seeing reality for what it is." She smiles. "They both didn't know it would go this far. This wasn't advertised at any point. From the outside looking in, it seemed like a female empowerment organization. Well, it was for the most part."

"Alrighty then." Detective Hanson walks towards Gloria and Jaslene.

"So, did you mean everything you said?" Ida says. She interlaces her hands and wiggles her fingers.

I exhale deeply. "Yeah. They didn't know what they were doing."

Ida backhands my shoulder. "You know what I meant. Don't play me." She side-eyes me and smirks.

I separate Ida's interlaced hands and rest them on top of mine. I look her in the eye. My trembling body squeezes out the last remaining tears. "I'm sorry."

Ida pulls away.

Did I say it wrong? Were my words too tense? Forced?

"Now this." She points at me in a circular motion. "This is it. The Danny I always envisioned." She grins. "Danny with emotion. Danny the human."

I smear the tears off my face.

I spread my arms wide for a hug.

Ida hesitates, then tilts her head in a why-not fashion. She hugs me tightly.

A weight lifts off my shoulders. Her squeeze affirms an apology accepted.

"Well, well, well. If it isn't Marc Antony and J-Lo. Pimpinela. Jesse y Joy. Con quién se queda el perro?"

Ida and I bust out in laughter.

"Come here, you get a hug too." I embrace Rose.

"You know I'm going to take your words to heart. I'm going to start holding you accountable. And you may not like it," Rose says into my ear. She pokes my ribs. "Now get off me." She readjusts her costume. "Wrinkling my outfit with all them tears."

"Broncaulio!" I scan around the yard.

From behind a tree, Broncaulio sticks his head out. "I'm busy, bro."

Busy? I walk around the tree to get a better angle.

Staggered stance, hand on hip, and a forearm braced high on a tree. "For you, girl, I'd scratch and sniff the scalp under Trump's toupée." Below him is Justina, tied-up.

"That's my sister, man. Release her."

"Well damn, nobody told you to have two Miss Universes for sisters."

What a clown. I laugh.

"Danny, can we talk for a bit?" Detective Hanson says. "Sorry for all the secrecy, but I needed someone to look out for my little cousin. And she said you were the man for the job."

"Cousin?"

"Yes," Ida interjects. "The detective here is my half, second, third, maybe fifth-cousin—I don't know. It's complicated. All I know is that he's at all of my mother's family's functions." She sticks her tongue out and jokingly puts a finger in her mouth. "Every once in a while he'd recount this story about a group of girls that kidnapped him when he was in high school. My uncles eat that story up every time. He'd say it was a true story, but nobody ever believed him. It's my Italian side, so the stories always include a bunch of jokes. So we just thought it was an elaborate joke. A great one at that. But he continued tracking them for years. He never found proof, so nobody believed him. So, he became a cop. Still, nobody believed him. Then I was recruited by these girls and realized there was truth behind the once-hilarious tale." She jumps up with energy. "But we did it!"

"Wait-wait-wait, so is that why you roofied me at the party? To get me in trouble so your brother can use me?" I chuckle.

"Nobody roofied you." Ida looks around in confusion. "Wait, that was really your cup? You don't remember what we talked about at the party?"

I purse my lips.

"You're kidding me, right?" Ida says. She looks at Detective Hanson.

He tosses his hands up. "My job was to make sure Danny would get to this point unobstructed. I admit, the pissing on the school door and Esmeralda showing up was an unexpected curveball, but I figured Danny was handling Esmeralda by how non-pressing she was. Everything looked as planned as could be. Especially after I kept Danny free from Esmeralda on Fridays. Also, Danny never requested any real help from me, so I figured we were good to go."

I can't even process that right now. Something 'bout the meetings between Detective Hanson and Esmeralda were set up for Fridays so that I could be free for the initiation events? And I was actually *in* on this plan from the start before Esmeralda got me out of jail?

"But you at least got the letters I sent you? I mailed them to your address," Ida says. "Gave you updated details every week like I told you I would." She notices that I still have no clue what she is talking about. "Because the Daughters constantly check our phones...is any of this ringing a bell?"

"Yikes. We moved since our breakup. I live on the other side of Hawk Union now."

"Oh, shit." Ida covers her mouth. "At the party, I told you about the plan, and how I was going to choose you as the—are you okay?"

My head whooshes in a circle. Light-headed. "But if you didn't roofie me, who did?"

CHAPTER THIRTY-FIVE

Detective Hanson exits the diner after pretending to smash up a USB with the high school surveillance footage from that night; a piece of evidence that he destroyed as soon as he caught wind of it. The performance was his favor to me as I got to the bottom of the Rohypnol case. Now it's just me and the last person I need to apologize to.

I stand and walk toward her side of the booth. My fingers shake. Knees feel bouncy. I sit back down on my side of the booth.

"What was that about?" Esmeralda questions my awkward movements.

"I wasn't going to say anything, but I know what you did." I stare into my empty coffee mug and fidget my index finger in and out of the handle.

Esmeralda crosses her arms and looks left at the morning commuters, who are muted by the glass window. She glances at me and sighs. "I don't know what you're talking about."

I chuckle. "You almost had me, but then I saw a video of some strong-looking hands. And they reminded me of the interrogation room. I remember thinking, *Wow, Esmeralda surely hit her New Year's Resolution hard this year.*" I lift her hand.

She pulls back.

"Look how jacked they are. Those are some CrossFit hands. But that's not all. Jaslene mentioned she saw me leave in a hooptie that night. Later, Rubio confirmed seeing you driving that hooptie (half the truth because he was wishy-washy with confirming if it was Esmeralda or not). And of course, you have a hooptie. Which explains how I got to Hawk Union High that night. Also explains your quick arrival at the police station."

Esmeralda re-tucks her curls behind her ear. Gathering herself. "So that's how you figured it out?" She nods. "Believe me, it was never supposed to go this far. I was supposed to roofie you a little, get you arrested, then claim you were a victim of a crime. That's all. Just like I got that other guy acquitted for the DUI charge. It was my way of getting back at...dad's spirit." She grimaces at her last words, probably realizing how silly they sound out loud. "But when Detective Hanson came out of nowhere with that deal, it got complicated. My original plan didn't account for him." Her face wrinkles and reddens in shame. "I just—"

"Hush. Zip. Nada," I mimic her words from the interrogation room. "Just answer me this. If you had the chance, would you do it again?" I ask.

"Of course not!" She grabs my hands and softly squeezes them. "You must believe me."

I purse my lips and turn away towards the bar stools.

"Danny, listen to me. This was all to get back at our father." The strength of her grip dissipates. "Who am I kidding? This was to get back at you, too. I was everything Dad wished you would become. Educated, professional, independent. I'm basically the perfect son! But all I received was neglect. So why wouldn't I resent you? But, as we kept complying with Detective Hanson, I realized I was wrong about you. But it was too late." Esmeralda flings her back onto the booth's backrest. "I understand if you never want to speak to me again. I deserve it. But just know, I never had any intentions of leaving you in jail. I was always going to get you out."

I nod. "You're right. I should never want to speak to you again." I stand and walk just past her side of the booth.

She stares outside the window, refusing to look at me.

The shame, the remorse, the guilt. She deserves it all. If I didn't know any better, I'd think she was a member of the sisterhood. Not just a regular member, more like a member of their executive board. Corporal Punishment Chair sounds about right. But I know better.

I lunge into the booth and hug Esmeralda. My big sister. My companion in the hardship called growing up with a mujeriego father. "I love you, I forgive you, and I apologize." I quickly release her. "Interesting. No matter how much huggin' I've done lately, it still feels weird. Like it's wrong."

"Yeah, let's not do that again."

We chuckle.

"How does it feel to get tricked into admitting something? I wasn't certain it was you. I was ninety percent sure, though."

Esmeralda flings a sugar packet at me. "You fucker!"

I laugh. "But in all honesty, thank you. This..." I can't even describe what I've gone through. "...wild, tv-worthy experience—although not your intent—has opened my eyes to many things, especially my flaws. You are one hell of a lawyer. And one hell of a woman. I'm proud of you and low key…I look up to you. You may not be the perfect son, but you are the perfect big sister."

Esmeralda's eyes well up. "Really?"

"Eh, to be honest, you overdid it. We were lucky they weren't cutting off real dicks. But no harm, no foul. I even think me and Ida are friends now. So, yes. Really."

We hug again. This time tighter. With no emotion but love.

"And sis, you don't need anyone's approval. Let alone a man's."

"I think you're right." She nods. "So where do we go from here? Should I start acting like I actually like you?" She smiles.

"Where do we go from here?" It's a question I've thought hard on. "When I graduate, let's all take a trip to DR to see Pop's property *we* inherited. Me, you, and Justina."

Esmeralda's smile widens. "Let's do it. I'm down."

"Now, about acting like you like me, that's a tough one. Because as your little brother, I'm here to annoy you. So just make yourself available. Because to annoy is to love, right? And I got a lot of annoying to catch up on."

(One Hour Later at the Diner)

"Wait-wait-wait-wait. So Detective Hanson isn't gay? He turned down my advances because he was focused on distracting me? So that you can be available for those cult kidnappings? Meanwhile, I was here trying to keep him off your back!?" Esmeralda says.

"Wild, right?"

"Why didn't they just fill me in on the plan? Or just retell you it?"

"Ida couldn't use her phone and was sending me letters to my old address. And Detective Hanson assumed I was handling you. Also, I mean, look at you."

Esmeralda squints at me, confused. Ha ha. The response I was instigating for. "Look at *me*?"

"Yeah. Look at you. You look like you wipe your culo back-to-front. That dirty coochie."

"DANNY!"

CHAPTER THIRTY-SIX

"Daniel Estrella, it's your turn to present," Mr. Greene says.

The only thing between me and Salutatorian is this Feminist Studies final. I take a deep breath and exhale. Let's get it.

I stride to the front of the classroom. Composed and focused. What's a presentation compared to what I've been through last fall? Nothing to be scared of. Nothing I can't overcome.

I clear my throat.

I glance at all the eyes in the room. Some on their laptops, others half asleep, but most locked in. This is my free-throw shot to win the game.

I take another deep breath.

"My mother is not Superwoman…by choice.

"She raised me as a single mother, even when my recently deceased father was alive and well.

"She worked two jobs and only recently began dating again.

"Resilient is the word…but it shouldn't be.

"She is Superwoman…but she shouldn't have to be.

"Like many superheroes, she was the result of a failed experiment.

"An experiment called patriarchy…

"Although not the best comparison, hear me out. Complimenting women on their resiliency is like complimenting slaves on their work ethic. Don't get me wrong, their unbreakable spirits are worth every praise, but nobody should have to be that resilient and that hardworking.

"And what about the ones who were rejected by the experiment and turned deviant? Those that couldn't attain the heroic level of resiliency to overcome the odds. Those that we label, crazy, because they wish to express themselves. Or the ones we label, bitch, because they called a spade a spade without pulling their punch.

"For every Superwoman, for every CEO, for every woman you label as successful, there are many more that broke, bent, and collapsed striving to overcome society's barriers.

"So dear men, the normal our ancestors established and the one we maintain is not right. And it's no coincidence that other men are our main competition for jobs, promotions, awards, and more. The system is rigged that way. It happened when we split the word human into man and woman. When we split man and gay, woman and transgender woman. Every time further forgetting that human is the most important label you can attribute to someone.

"Human…that's what we are. And when we place more importance on gender, sexuality, race, religion, age and more, it means we are looking for an excuse to not treat someone as human. An excuse to make life unsafe for some. And one cannot be human unless they are safe.

"So I plead, let's go back to being plain ol' humans. So my mother no longer has to be super, in order to barely survive."

THE LAST BODEGA IN JERSEY, VOL. I

(COMING MAY 2023)

GENRE: Age 16+, Composition Novel

SYNOPSIS

Jersey City, once a vibrant immigrant community before gentrification uprooted most of the vecindario, has one bodega standing. But that may not be the case after today, as Stroberi, the young bodeguero, has a decision to make: sell the store or continue serving the remaining community.

TURN TO READ
FIRST CHAPTER

STROBERI'S INTRO

La Bodega. The last corner of the block that is still ours. El barrio relegated to seven-hundred square-feet. All of which will be gutted and turned into a gourmet bagel shop after today. We fought hard to keep the store alive, but like grandma says, "The Devil only offers what you can't refuse." Like a quarter-million dollars for a grocery store that has bled red since the Walmart opened.

When I lock up tonight, it will be the last time. The end of an era. No more quarter-juicies, which are now fifty cents. No more arguments with the customers over the price of plátanos. Now the verdes turn into maduros; and the maduros into fly traps. It's just not the same anymore. But the remaining vecinos still come in for their EBT and WIC needs. And of course, for their loosies, lottery tickets, and deli sandwiches.

I fling the storefront gate upwards. It rattles like a train on tracks until hitting the top. I take one look left and right. The block is calm. Occupied by the tumble and crinkle of litter and the buzz of the streetlights. Nobody in sight. More importantly, no stick-up boy catching the early worm (me). This really is the last day. I take a deep breath. The last bodega in Jersey City. Wow. Just thinking it sounds wild. Like the start of a dystopian world.

I sigh.

Maaaaaan, what am I talkin' 'bout? Fuck this bodega! Never wanted to be here in the first place. I inherited it from my Pops last year. His dying wish was that I continue serving the community. Well, the community never served me. They've only given me a jail sentence. Because that's what owning a bodega is, a jail sentence. Clock in at 6AM; clock out at 10PM. Listening to the same bachata, salsa, and balada mixtapes over and over. Dealing with the same clowns every day.

You know how many tecatos I've kicked out of this store? Too many. Every day at least one. And if I was unlucky enough, I'd kick out the same one five times in one day. Do you know how hard it is to reason with someone whose eyes are looking one way, lips babeando the other way, while their mind is orbiting the planets? Yo, like I mean, what the fuck!? I rather play La Gallina Ciega with a used diaper as my blindfold.

I'm too young for this. I should be in college. Studying some smart shit. Whispering Romeo Santos lyrics into the ears of educated women. Not these raised by wolves, Cardi B wannabe's that come in here saying, "what up, son?" or, "good looks, my nigga." I cringe every time.

That's why tonight, at 7PM, when the Jew comes with the papers, I'm signing the deal. Sorry, Pops. The community ain't worth more than a quarter mill'.

I flick on the lights. I close my eyes waiting for G-Hombre, the bodega cat. Yep, that's his name. G like the letter G, and Hombre like the Spanish word for man. His real name is Giambi, named after Jason Giambi from the A's and Yankees. But the way my dad would say it, the cat responds to nothing but G-Hombre. "G-Hombre, what you got for me today?" I call out.

It's our morning ritual. I walk in, and he gifts me the trophies from his night's hunt. Tom and Jerry shit. A mouse or two that crawled its way down from the apartments upstairs. Only caveat is I gotta keep my eyes closed until he's done. And from the sound of it, he put in work last night. I hear him bouncing wall to wall, brushing past the chips.

He goes silent. Must be everything. I open my eyes.

WHAT. THE. FUCK.

This the shit I'm talkin' 'bout. Fuck this place! Like, really? I cross my arms. I should have never let those teenagers use the bathroom. Kids can't smash at home, so they think they can smash here. A used condom next to a baby mouse.

"Last day," I mutter to myself.

I stretch on latex gloves, scoop the *trophies* and dump it in the trash outside because one thing about customers, they nosey. Before they even step a toe in here, they appraise the place. Ready to complain about anything and everything that has nothing to do with them.

Second thing about customers, they could all be fiction writers if they turned their exaggerations and mouths into pens. See a mouse in the trash and they'll assume Fievel and his whole American Tail live here. See the used condom and they'll think I'm smashing the whole vecindario. *I heard it was Juanita. Nah, I heard it was Juanita's mom. Nah, it was Juanita's cousin that came from New York last week. The one with the fatty.* The rumor when I took over the bodega was, *He is going to turn it into a hookah lounge.* All because I put on un dembow: music my dad never allowed. But you also have to laugh at the nonsense and admire it at the same time. These customers can turn one fleeting glance from a stranger into a tale about a stalker. Probably the only thing I'll miss about this place. The stories.

The door chimes open.

"Yo, we're closed for another fifteen minutes," I say.

"Oh, my bad. I saw the lights," a man with heavy bags under his eyes, pushing a baby stroller, says. His baby asleep. "Stroberi, is that you?" He smiles wholeheartedly.

Damn, he said my birth name (My dad's attempt at naming me after Darryl Strawberry).

"Look at how you've grown. It's been years since I've been on the ol' block. Thought about your Pops and felt like I had to come visit."

At the crack of dawn? I look at him and his baby.

The man catches the judgement in my eyes. "Don't worry about the baby. She's nocturnal. My baby-moms hit the clubs during her pregnancy, so she only falls asleep if she out en la calle." He adjusts the baby's blanket, then looks around in nostalgia…or in judgement, tit for tat. Although today, I wouldn't be offended. It's the last day, and I took the liberty of being extra lazy with restocking.

"Wow, even though it's been a minute, this place doesn't change. Where's the old Caco Pelao?"

"Dead."

"Oh. What? When?"

"About a year ago. The doctors said it was kidney failure. I think it was the sixteen-hour-a-day bachata-balada diet he was on. All that amargue."

He rubs the nape of his neck in embarrassment, then chuckles. "I guess that's a way to go out. But my bad. Didn't know." He purses his lips, wrestling with what to say next. "By the way, I'm Yoskar. Your Pops did me a huge favor back in the day. 'Bout ten years ago, when you was what? Ten? Nine?" He lets out a hearty exhale. Pushes the stroller directly across from me at the register.

I can tell my Pops meant something to him. Especially with how chill he's leaning on the ice cream fridge. Like he owns the place. Like he spent many hours talking to my Pops in this same exact position.

"Damn, I missed his funeral." He shakes his head.

"Don't worry, you can still pay your respects. His body is buried at Bay View, but his spirit remains here. Your pick." It's not a lie. Sometimes I sense my Pops in here. His devotion sprinkled all over the fridges, shelves, and crates like ashes. Especially behind the counter. I call it the viewpoint of his life. "If you don't mind me asking, what my Pops do for you?"

"What do you mean?" He quickly takes out his phone and starts texting away. Once he notices my pause, he says, "My bad. Just needed to send an urgent text."

"You said he did you a favor."

"Pshh," he swipes the air with his phone, "saved my life."

My dad saved this man's life? *Yeah aight.* I can sense exaggeration from a mile away, but that doesn't make me any less intrigued. "Well, as you can see, the bodega is empty and the crackheads haven't resurrected yet," I say, inviting him to tell the story.

He chuckles. "I see you a funny guy, just like your dad."

"Ehh. I'm just more of an asshole." We exchange nods of amusement.

"Where do I start? I was eighteen and thought I could finesse anything. It had always been that way. Always managed to get out of situations. But this situation, let's just say it went downhill once I showed up at my ex's baby shower."

"You showed up to your ex's baby shower?" I laugh.

"Peep it." His hands move in a rhythmic manner: the sign of a good storyteller. "I showed up, right. Pshh. Pa qué fue eso."

ABEL VELOZ is that one primo that you don't quite know how you're related to. A First-Gen Dominican-American hailing from Hudson County, NJ. When he writes, he wants you to feel like you're at a summer barbeque, family reunion, or chismeando with fulano at the bodega. Same Spanglish, same people, nothing white-washed.

He previously worked in Military Intelligence (Army Veteran), holds a MS in Global Affairs from Rutgers University, and speaks Mandarin.

Oh, and he lovvvvvvves a good chisme.

ACKNOWLEDGMENTS

Alexis, my wife, best friend, and ride-or-die, thanks for making my dream of publishing a fiction novel one of yours. Couldn't have done it without your love & support. My success will forever be yours.

Mami, thanks for always reminding me that no amount of money, degrees, or possessions is worth more than family and happiness.

Pa, thanks for teaching me to do good by everyone (even those that do you wrong), and to never let others change the good in you. May you rest in peace.

Kiko Panch & Manny, thanks for believing in me and for softening mom up. Y'all made life as the baby of the fam' easy.

Edward, thanks for grinding this process out with me and for the kick-ass cover. I appreciate you, your efforts, and your immense talent.

Primos & Primas (all 809 of you), thanks for all the honest feedback and constant critiques. Especially, Luz, Rosemary, and Alma.

Willy A. Rivas, thanks for being there for EVERYONE. Your legacy is one we shall never forget. Que descanse en paz, LUPS.

Please leave an honest review on your preferred platform. It'll go a long way in supporting the author, both financially and in his craft.

abelveloz.com

A Little About the Journey

I committed to writing when I picked up an Elizabeth Acevedo novel (*With the Fire on High*) that was lying around my (now) wife's dungeon apartment in Bayonne. She had read it for her short-lived bookclub (y'all know who you are) and I flipped to a random page. After reading one page I had the audacity to say out loud, "Mannn, I can write this!" Then I did the same exact thing to Junot's *This Is How You Lose Her*. No disrespect to them, but what I really meant was that I had what the literary world calls "voice". Basically, without ever hearing Acevedo or Junot speak, I was able to hear their voices in my head. It reminded me of people from the block telling a story. And simply put, I knew I had "voice". From high school to grad school to the drag show article I wrote in the NJ Star Ledger, people often told me that I write how I speak, and when they read my works, they read it in my voice. So I, with no real knowledge of what went into writing a book, started writing. I wrote and wrote and wrote until one day I wrote something worth reading. That's the moment I scrapped my first manuscript and started writing this story from scratch.

That was half the battle...

The other half was fighting self-doubt and imposter syndrome, which constantly pleaded for me to stop writing. Luckily, my family and friends kept me going with their unwavering belief in me. Today I can say, "I grew up not knowing any authors, but the children of my family and friends won't have to say the same." Representation Matters.

This book is for us.

www.ingramcontent.com/pod-product-compliance
Lightning Source LLC
Chambersburg PA
CBHW021220310726
48971CB00006B/1626